Praise for The

Perfect for fans of The Hunger Games, readers will fall in love with this creative, vibrant, and compelling masterpiece. The mystery and romance are perfectly balanced throughout this fantastical read. The Whisperer's Wish keeps you guessing until the end. I highly recommend this book for anyone looking for a thrilling escape into the realm of magic.

— Tamara Grantham, bestselling fantasy author

Cheryl,
Thanks for reading!
♡ Janilise Lloyd

THE WHISPERER'S
WISH

A CROWN. A CONSPIRATOR.
A RACE FOR THE CURE.

JANILISE LLOYD

Expanse
Books

Published by Expanse Books, an imprint of
Scrivenings Press LLC
15 Lucky Lane
Morrilton, Arkansas 72110
www.ScriveningsPress.com

Printed in the United States of America

Paperback ISBN 978-1-64917-278-5

eBook ISBN 978-1-64917-279-2

Editors: Erin R. Howard and K. Banks

Laurelin with Pygsmy Illustration by Chicken Doodle.

Map Illustration by Eric Dotseth.

Cover by Linda Fulkerson, bookmarketinggraphics.com

To my brothers, Spencer and McKay.
Thanks for all you have taught me.

Livon

Amare

Hillsborough

Dade

Sedona

Meadow

Galena

The

Evera

Pygsmy Pine Lake

The M

Lingua

Aremia

The Shifting Tre

Creo

Albia

Mystic Lake

Livon

Fortis

Steel Harbour

Mirangian Desert

Skara

Scentia

Ocean

Chapter One

As I crept down the pitch-black hallway, my toe caught on the uneven carpet in front of the bathroom door. I stumbled forward, bracing against the doorframe to stay upright. A hundred bleary-eyed, midnight trips to the toilet wasted in an instant. I'd been so confident I could walk this route in my sleep.

I crossed the short distance to Pippin's bedroom door and peered through the inch-wide crack. A sliver of moonlight fell over his sleeping body. The knot in my chest loosened a notch as I saw his green quilt rise and fall with each breath. I shouldn't have been surprised he slept through the noise. Lately, Pippin was nearly impossible to wake.

The doctor said that was to be expected as he neared the end.

The knot tightened once more.

Tonight, I'd cross a line that could not be redrawn, and it was all for Pippin. His freckled face and green eyes filled my mind, though it was the younger version, before cancer sucked him dry. I kissed my four fingers and pressed them to his door. "Love you, little brother," I whispered.

I tip-toed down the stairs, hoping not to wake Mom and

Dad. As I rounded the corner, my jacket caught on a chisel Dad had left on the kitchen table. It clattered against the checker-tiled floor. I flinched but scampered forward anyway, breathing a sigh of relief when I reached the back door.

Exiting the house felt like stepping out of my own body. The carefully crafted shell of Laurelin Moore, a typical Linguan girl, crumpled behind me. I knew that the next time I came home, I'd be someone else. Life would never be quiet again.

The iron gate at the front of our yard creaked as it closed behind me. "Lock," I commanded. The metal glowed a faint purple, a signal that my family's home was protected. I zipped my black jacket up to my neck and scanned the dark street, checking for prying eyes. Lingua buzzed with news of another pygsmy whisperer—the first in ninety years—and everyone was trying to catch a glimpse of who it might be. By morning, the rumors would be confirmed. The entire province would know the whisperer was me.

I shoved my hands in my pockets, making sure I had the glass jar, an extra vial of elixir, and the hastily scribbled note that contained my confession. With my hood covering my long hair, I ran down the sidewalk toward the nearest rail station. My feet splashed in puddles left by the midnight rain, soaking my jeans as I went. Underneath the station's white canopy, a bean-shaped railcar waited. "Galena," I said as I hopped inside. The white car shot forward, taking me to the upper-class district of Lingua for the fifth night in a row. Tonight, I'd hit my biggest target yet: Silas Evermore, the Duke of Lingua.

Though the bright car was empty, I was too anxious to sit on one of the scuffed-up plastic benches. I clung to a black handle that hung from the ceiling and watched the twisting buildings of Lingua flash by my window. The patter of rain tapered off as we passed through the heart of the province. There, a statue of Mira towered over the city. As we flew by, I offered a silent prayer that she'd help me get through this night.

2

The face of my watch peeked out under the sleeve of my jacket. There were two hours left until sunrise.

Only two hours.

I took a deep breath. I wanted to be Lingua's Rook in the Pentax, and the only way to impress Duke Evermore enough to be chosen was to reveal my magic.

Since Queen Isadora's death ten days ago, the streets had filled with gifted teens showing off their magic, hoping to be chosen to compete for the crown. Our next ruler could be Tom-the-neighborhood-drunk for all I cared. The fact that the winner of the Pentax would become king or queen was nothing more than an unfortunate side-effect in my eyes. I was in it for the wish that was given to the victor—a wish that would be granted by the Matrons, the most powerful beings in Ausland. It was my last shot to save Pippin.

The railcar slid to a stop in front of a wrought-iron gate set in a stone wall that kept the nobody's like me out of Galena. I pressed my palm against the door. It slid open obediently, releasing me. The black sky glistened with purple mist, a remnant of the magic used by Lingua's people day-in and day-out. I checked over my shoulder. The street appeared deserted, but I knew that this area was on high alert and I did not want to get caught. It would ruin my audition.

The muscles in my legs were tight with tension as I sprinted around the perimeter of the stone wall. The duke's white mansion was on the northeast corner of the extravagant subdivision. I ducked behind a bakery's dumpsters to avoid one police officer and crouched by a bench to dodge another.

Finally, I reached the back of Evermore's mansion. Beyond it was a forest of lyre trees, covered in berries: a pygsmy's primary source of food. Finding one here should be easy.

Lyrun rach min baum, I called through my thoughts, searching for the nearest pygsmy. I felt a prickle of consciousness from the closest one and latched onto it, pulling the mystic into me as I repeated the ancient pygsmish phrase that meant *help me serve and protect*. I smiled as the tiny creature hovered in front of my face. Her green eyes matched the color of my own. She cooed as she bobbed up and down in front of me, her body shimmering in its translucent state.

I pulled a few lyre berries out of the jar and placed them on my palm. The pygsmy brushed her flowing, green tendrils across my skin, tasting to make sure I was safe. At last, she decided to trust me and landed in my hand. Her translucent color solidified as she did. Her long, needlelike nose pierced the first berry and the creature began to sip, twitching her wings with satisfaction. Vibrant, golden track marks swirled around her purple body, a sign that this pygsmy had plenty of elixir to share.

Harvesting elixir wasn't my goal tonight, but I found myself unable to resist a pygsmy full of the invaluable liquid. The elixir that ran through a pygsmy's wings could heal any broken bone, infection, or punctured organ. It could enhance a gifted person's powers or even temporarily give them a new one. Elixir had its limitations though. For someone whose condition was a part of their biology—like Pippin's cancer—elixir could only extend their time rather than heal. Still, pygsmy elixir was the most desirable commodity in Ausland, and people would go to extraordinary lengths to get their hands on some. The trouble was, pygsmies were almost impossible to catch—except for someone who could control them.

Someone like me.

While the pygsmy drank, I stroked the hard, thin edge of her wing, like running my finger across the string of a violin. The pygsmy watched with apprehension. Her mind was wary, and her legs tensed to fly.

Quickly, I began to sing.

Lyrun rach min baum
Tre alis vera trinidad

4

The pygsmy stopped, finding comfort in the words of the lullaby.

Siv faer trialus mun
Plevun ris mylor vineer

The creature's wing glowed. Excitedly, I tugged on the string of the vial of elixir I always kept around my neck and flipped open the top. From the bottom tip of the pygsmy's wing, a drop of golden liquid waited to be collected. It splashed into my vial, mixing with the elixir already inside, swirling in milky-gold spirals. Five more drops followed after it.

I snapped the vial shut with satisfaction. *Sempr nots*, I thanked her.

As the pygsmy finished eating, I spoke to her in her language. *I'm going to ask you to do something for me tonight. Well, more than you already have, I guess.* I bit my lip. *It's going to be uncomfortable, but I promise you'll be safe.*

What more could a human want than my elixir? the pygsmy questioned.

All you have to do is stay in this jar. I held up the glass for her to see the fat berries littering the bottom. *There will be plenty to eat, and I'll stay nearby. I only need a man to see you. Once he does, I'll let you go. I promise.*

The pygsmy withdrew her nose from the berry and turned toward me. *I do not want to, but I can feel that I have no choice, whisperer.*

I pushed away the guilt that flooded me. I rarely used the full sway of my powers on a pygsmy. I didn't like forcing them to do anything. Instead, I tried to persuade but ultimately let the creature decide. Tonight was different—I couldn't afford a mistake.

Fly with me, I said.

With an edge of bitterness in her mind, the pygsmy wrapped her elastic tendrils under my armpits. As she lifted me into the sky, my body became weightless, allowing the tiny creature to carry me. We flew toward the duke's window, but I wasn't worried about being seen. As long as I was attached to the pygsmy, my body was translucent, like her own when she was in flight.

Sempr nots, I said as we landed on the balcony outside the duke's window.

The pygsmy did not respond.

I peered into the bedroom, feeling uneasy. The duke's wife snored loudly as she slept next to him.

Over the past four nights, I'd been to the homes of four prominent members of the nobility, leaving a pygsmy in different locations throughout the homes for the people to find. A pygsmy under that degree of control could only be compelled by a whisperer. I'd hoped to pique their interest and let the rumor mill do its thing, spreading excitement about a new whisperer in the province. My plan had worked. Tonight, the mystery would end. I would finally own up to my abilities.

I took a deep breath. I could do this for Pippin. Besides, if —*when*—I was selected as Rook, I'd face much more difficult tasks during the Pentax.

Be brave, I told the pygsmy as I slipped her into the jar.

My courage is not in question, she bristled.

I gave her back a reassuring stroke and then placed my hand on the window pane. "Open," I whispered. The window glowed purple. The lock unlatched and then the glass slid to the side. The frame screeched, and I cringed, expecting the duke to wake. I breathed a sigh of relief when he did not.

I pulled myself through the window. The planks of the wooden floor creaked as I tip-toed to the duke's bedside. The ten feet from the window to his nightstand felt like one hundred.

I felt the duke's breath on my hand as I placed the jar beside him, the pygsmy still inside despite the open top and her natural inclination to flee.

Leqin. I told her to stay.

I left the spare vial of elixir that contained only three drops on top of my handwritten note that identified me as the whisperer. I hesitated. For sixteen years, I'd kept this secret, enjoying a relatively normal life. Once it was known I could whisper, nothing would be the same. The demands for elixir would be relentless; I could be in danger. I nearly decided to snatch the note and leave before I could be found out. Instead, I took a deep breath and reminded myself that Pippin was worth it.

Before I could change my mind, I crossed the length of the room and slipped back out the window, leaving it open so the pygsmy could escape in the morning.

I climbed over the side of the balcony railing and dropped into the flowerbeds below. Checking over my shoulder, I dashed across the carefully manicured lawn to a tall tree with a good vantage point of the duke's room and prepared to wait.

When the sun began to rise, the duke and his wife stirred. I chuckled as Evermore's eyes popped open. He clearly did not expect to be face-to-face with a pygsmy. Most people never see one in their lifetime. He gasped and grabbed the jar.

Despite the brave face the pygsmy had put on earlier, I heard panic in her thoughts. *Please don't hurt me,* she said.

I shoved away the fresh wave of guilt that brought. I knew she was safe. *You're going to be fine. I'll make sure of it,* I said.

I allowed the duke to look for another moment. Then I said, *Flevair,* and released the pygsmy.

She darted out the open window, her mind elated with freedom.

My eyes returned to the duke, who grabbed the vial of elixir. Technically, harvesting elixir was illegal, so my stunt would either land me in the Pentax or in prison. But the law had always made an exception for whisperers. It existed because of poachers who hurt pygsmies to get the elixir from them. I didn't know of any exceptions to the law against breaking and entering though.

At last, the duke picked up the note. I saw him mouth my name, *Laurelin Moore,* as he read my confession. There was no going back now.

One more time, I silently called for a pygsmy, then I coughed loudly from my spot in the tree. The duke's eyes snapped up to where I was perched. I waved to him and his eyes grew wide.

"You know where to find me," I shouted as the pygsmy lifted me into the air.

Duke Evermore ran to the edge of the balcony, the note and vial of elixir still clutched in his hands. His mouth hung open as he watched me disappear into the morning sky.

Chapter Two

The wooden chair creaked beneath me as I shifted my weight. Pippin lay unmoving in his bed as some color returned to his pallid face. Mom had given him tea with the elixir I had collected in Galena. I was glad to see it still had some effect on his health, but we'd been running on borrowed time since he was diagnosed with liver cancer at ten years old. In the four years since then, Pippin had gone from needing the elixir every other month to once a day. At some point, it would stop working. I couldn't think about what would happen then.

The noise from the crowd that had begun to gather outside my house drifted up through the window. I expected them to come, but that didn't lessen my annoyance with the mob. News about my powers traveled even faster than I expected, and I could no longer keep the truth from Mom and Dad. They knew I'd outed myself. They'd been huddled in the kitchen, trying to decide what this meant for our family ever since.

Whispering was a gift my parents decided to keep secret when I was a child, and I'd chosen the same when I was old enough to understand. Nearly a century ago, the last whisperer, Eva, had been kidnapped for her power. Though in the eyes of the law, it didn't count since it was the king who ripped the five-year-old girl from her parents' arms in order to exploit her power. At least she'd been well-fed and reasonably cared for during her time as an elixir-producing slave. In all, she had it better than many whisperers before her. Countless others had been captured by hawks on the black market and kept alive only if they continued to hand over elixir that made the thieves fat with riches. Or some other villain would hold a whisperer's loved one hostage for elixir. Few people who had my gift had stories with happy endings.

Mom and Dad were less than thrilled I'd exposed myself to such danger. Still, I'd seen the hope flash through Mom's eyes. She knew if I was chosen to compete in the Pentax, it could be our chance to save Pippin. Dad would come around, too.

Finally, Pippin's green eyes fluttered. I grabbed his hand expectantly. We shared a lot of characteristics, but hair color was not one of them. His was like a flame; the burst of wild red curls demanded attention. Mine, on the other hand, was vanilla ice cream—pale, flat, and forgettable. I studied the freckles dotting his cheeks. His were darker and more abundant than mine. Most teenage girls couldn't stand their little brothers, but the feeling that Pippin could slip away in an instant somehow erased any of his flaws. He was perfect.

"Hey, Laura." Pippin's voice quivered, his eyes open now. "You a Rook yet?"

I laughed. "Not yet, but I gave it my best shot a couple hours ago."

Pippin smiled weakly. "You'll make it. The duke won't be able to pass up a whisperer, even if she's not nobility."

I prayed to the Matrons that he was right. I ruffled his hair. "It's nothing for you to worry about either way. You just work on getting better."

"I'm not getting better, Laura. We both know that."

I hated the way he said that with such finality. I rearranged the green quilt that lay over his shrunken body. "Hang in there a little longer—just until I get my wish from the Matrons. Their magic is so much stronger than a pygsmy's. It can heal you. Promise me you'll hang on."

There should be a law of the universe that little brothers couldn't die.

Pippin gave a feeble laugh. "I promise." He turned his head to the window. "What's all the noise out there?"

I was careful not to let any of my annoyance with the growing mob show on my face. "It's nothing. Don't worry about it."

Pippin pulled himself into a sitting position, his face scrunching with the effort. He straightened his back, trying to see what was going on.

I sighed. "Stop. You're going to hurt yourself. It's just some people who want me to get them elixir. Ignore them."

Pippin removed the quilt from his lap and threw his bony legs over the side of his bed. He wobbled as he stood, and I rose to catch him.

"You need to lie down." Panic fluttered in my chest.

"Take me to the window," Pippin said.

Reluctantly, I helped him over to the pane and averted my eyes. I hated the way the crowd made me feel selfish with their cries for help. I'd done my best for years, secretly leaving elixir at the homes of people I knew were in need—neighbors with sickness or injuries and poor people who could sell it for profit. But lately, Pippin had needed so much that I rarely had any to spare. Only six drops of elixir could be taken from a pygsmy without killing it, and it took a full year to regenerate one drop.

"Who's that?" Pippin asked.

I followed his eyes and my heart stopped. Silas Evermore was pushing through the throng. He paused at the gate and rang the bell. Dad appeared on the porch in his wheelchair.

"That's the duke," I answered Pippin robotically.

"Well, there's only one reason he would come here." Pippin bounced on his toes. "He's chosen you to be the Rook! You did it!"

"I can think of two reasons, actually. But let's hope you're right and he's not here to arrest me."

After years of hoping for a break that never came, I was used to being disappointed. But as I watched the duke follow Dad down the path to our front door, I wondered if this might be the day that changed everything for Pippin.

"C'mon. Let's go see what's up." I scooped Pippin into my arms, which was far too easy to do. He had to weigh less than sixty pounds.

We jogged down the stairs. Mom stood in the living room looking out the front window, her fingertips at her mouth. Her eyebrows hadn't relaxed in four years, but the line between them now was especially deep. She wore her silver-streaked, brown hair in a messy bun, a floral-print apron tied around her waist.

The front door opened, and Dad came in with Silas Evermore following behind. His jet-black hair matched the dark pants of his official Linguan uniform—dress slacks, a button-up shirt, and a purple suit jacket with winding, golden embroidery meant to mimic the markings of a pygsmy. When his brown eyes connected with mine, he straightened his jacket lapel, as if searching for an excuse to look away.

"Welcome to our home, Your Grace." My mother tucked a loose strand of hair behind her ear as she offered her hand.

"Nora Moore, it's a pleasure to meet you. Thank you for allowing me to come in. You have quite the gathering out front."

Mom's smile wavered. "Yes, we were rather hoping to avoid that. But I suppose it was inevitable with Laurelin's decision." Her eyes flashed to me before she focused on the duke again. "Please, have a seat." She gestured toward our brown leather armchair, the nicest piece of furniture we had, even with its long tear in the front.

Carefully, I placed Pippin on the lumpy, green couch next to me. Mom sat on his other side, and Dad placed his wheelchair between us and the duke.

As usual, a pile of wood shavings from Dad's latest project

had collected in the corners of his wheelchair, but his face lacked his genial smile. "We don't want any trouble. We know that we should have registered Laurelin's gift with the province as soon as we discovered it, but you have to understand. You see the crowd that has gathered outside our house. You know the stories of the mistreatment of past whisperers. We don't know why the Matrons decided to give Laurelin the power to whisper, but we just wanted her—"

The duke raised his hand. "Alexander, please stop. I am not here to punish you or your daughter. If you recall, my great-grandmother was Eva Evermore, the last known whisperer. Eva kept a journal that detailed many of the struggles she faced because of her gift. I understand why you would be reluctant to acknowledge Laurelin's power openly."

The duke looked at me now. "That said, I hope you realize that your gift can do a lot of good. Today, each province must decide which young person will represent them in the Pentax, which will determine Ausland's next ruler. As you have chosen this specific time to reveal your magic, I can only assume you're hoping to be chosen as the Rook from Lingua. There are many talented young people in our province, and plenty of those talents exist among the children of the nobility. It would be typical for me to select one of them to be our Rook. So, Laurelin, I must ask. Why do you believe I should choose you?"

I felt like an inchworm crawled around the pit of my stomach. My eyes bounced around the room as I tried to think of what to say. Dad's nails dug into the pads on the arms of his chair. Mom twisted the tie of her apron between her fingers. Pippin slumped against the back of the couch, staring at me without a trace of worry in his face.

I couldn't acknowledge the real reason I wanted to compete. As understandable as it may be that I hoped to save my brother, it wouldn't be a good enough reason for Duke Evermore.

I cleared my throat and put together a half-truth. "I'm tired of being seen as weak, and I think Lingua is too. As the province of Language, our gifts for storytelling, songwriting, persuasion, and orating are overlooked by the other provinces. Imagine—Lingua, the capital of Ausland. The wealth and the opportunity that would come to us would be unlike anything we've seen for centuries. I can make that happen. I'm different than the others. I want this more than all of them combined."

Silas watched me carefully as I spoke, but his eyes slipped to Pippin for a moment. "It does appear that you have great reason to fight." He paused. "I'm pleased to hear your conviction. As the great-grandson of the fearless Eva, I think I have more confidence in whisperers than most. The other members of the nobility will despise my decision, but I am willing to take that risk for the good of the province. I believe you have what Lingua needs to win. I'm extending the offer to you, Laurelin. Will you be Lingua's Rook?"

Mom let out a little squeak and squeezed my knee. Her eyes watered, but a smile stretched her lips. This was the chance she didn't know she'd been waiting for.

"You don't have to agree, Laurelin. Think this through," Dad urged. "How much time does she have to decide?"

"None, I'm afraid. Ausland's tradition dictates that the first competition of the Pentax happens fifteen days after the death of the previous monarch. There are three days required for training and pre-competition events. That means we leave for Creo in two days. I must insist Laurelin decides now. If she declines, I need time to make other arrangements."

Knowing Dad's opposition made this harder, but I couldn't pass up the chance to save Pippin. This was our only option. Still, I intended to squeeze everything I could out of the deal.

I cleared my throat. "I would be honored to represent Lingua, but I do have a few conditions that would need to be met, of course."

The duke blinked and sat back in his chair. "I see. An opportunist. Very well, what do you have in mind?"

"Those of us who are born into nothing have to take

14

advantage of the chances that come our way, Duke Evermore. I wouldn't expect you to understand."

He gave no response aside from a half-smile.

"Laurelin, manners," Mom whispered.

I ignored her and pressed on. "My first condition is that I choose my trainer for the Pentax. I know the requirements. The trainer must be at least eighteen years old, gifted, and from the province of the Rook. I know just the person for the job. You can choose my handler, though. All that fashion and interview nonsense isn't important to me anyway."

Silas thought for a long moment. "Very well." He managed to force a smile. "You may choose your trainer."

"My second condition is that my family will receive 150 darics for each round of elimination I survive."

Beneath his blonde hair, Dad's face was beet red, but I didn't care about his embarrassment. I cared that my family would be well off while I was gone. Dad worked hard, but he didn't make nearly enough from his carpentry. The accident that left him wheelchair-bound happened before I was born, and it made finding regular work a challenge. Mom had left her job at the hospital when Pippin got sick. They spent all the money they received from the sale of Grandma and Grandpa's farm in the first year of Pippin's treatments. For a while, things were okay because I was able to sell elixir on the black market, but I hadn't been able to spare any for that in several months.

"That's a lot of money," Silas grumbled.

"I'm aware, but it will be easily made up to you when I win. I also want a pair of police officers assigned to my house at all hours. The family members of whisperers are always in danger, and I'm not willing to take chances while I'm away. Those are my conditions."

Evermore let out a long breath, and drummed his fingers on his knee. After a pause, he said, "I must be crazy, but you shall have what you demand. I need to know who your trainer is no later than tomorrow evening. The announcement of my decision will be in tomorrow's papers. I suggest you stay low."

I snorted. "You don't need to worry about that. We're already hostages in our own home." I motioned to the mob outside the gate.

Silas smirked. "I will meet you at the rail station in two days. A police escort will arrive that morning to get you there safely. Expect to receive more instruction from me then. Oh, and pack light. Your handler will take care of your wardrobe."

Silas pulled a pair of sunglasses from his pocket and put them on. "Best of luck to you, Laurelin." He extended his hand to me and then my parents.

I didn't like the way he ignored Pippin.

As Dad showed the duke to the door, Pippin threw his arms around my neck. "Thank you, Laura."

I laughed and hugged him back. For the first time in a long time, I felt hope. Now I just had to deliver on my promises.

Chapter Three

When I stepped into the night air, the cool mist that brushed my face was a welcome relief. The atmosphere in the house had been smothering since the duke left. Mom alternated between tears of joy at the possibility of saving Pippin and tears of sadness that I was going to face the dangerous tasks of the Pentax. I tried to remind her that it was only a couple short weeks, but that only seemed to bring on a new round of crying. Dad, on the other hand, rolled around in his wheelchair, brooding.

And then there was the growing crowd outside our house. Though the announcement about my selection wasn't news-official yet, the word still traveled fast. The shock of someone outside the nobility being chosen as Rook seemed to have pleased at least a few, as some in the crowd held up signs of support. I probably should have tried to talk to them, but I was no good with speeches—just another reason I didn't want to be queen. If I didn't have to save Pippin, I'd probably use the wish given for winning the Pentax to get out of being queen instead.

I snuck around to the side of the house and watched the few stubborn stragglers who remained, despite the chilly weather and dark night. They slumped against the front gate or sprawled out on the ground, sleeping. I didn't know why they thought I'd choose to give them elixir at midnight as opposed to mid-afternoon, but I had to give them credit for their determination. I'd have to use other means of transportation tonight.

With my eyes squeezed shut, I searched the skies for a pygsmy. When I felt one, I chanted the familiar phrase, *Lyrun rach min baum.* Compelled by my call, the pygsmy began to fly to me.

One of the beautiful creatures appeared, his markings dull. At some point, I must have taken this pygsmy's spare elixir. *Will you fly with me?* I asked in pygsmish, feeling guilty. I didn't like using pygsmies as my personal taxi system. They were magical, glorious beings—the offspring of the Matrons. They deserved more respect than carrying my butt across the province.

You're not after elixir tonight? the pygsmy asked. *I don't have more to give.*

No, not tonight. But thank you for sharing with me in the past. You helped my brother survive.

He's better now?

I swallowed loudly. *No, he's not. But I hope to change that for good, and I need your help to do it. I have to talk to a friend in Meadow. Will you take me to the Careen?*

The pygsmy hummed in front of me, considering. His green tendrils flowed like jellyfish tentacles around him. *You're kinder than the others who seek our elixir. I will help you tonight.*

I exhaled. *Thank you very much,* I said as he wrapped his tendrils around me and lifted me off the ground.

Guilt washed over me as we soared over the desperate people in my front yard. If only the supply of elixir was really as endless as they all thought, I might be able to help them.

The weightlessness that came with flying filled my heart, and I concentrated on the beauty of Lingua at night, with its swirls of magic hanging in the air. The glittering mist was a welcome sign that our gifts remained in the province tonight. The Matrons were generous to share their magic at all, but they were also eager to remind that it could be taken at any time. A few times a month, our magical gifts would disappear for a day or two, and there was no way to predict when. It hinged on the whims of the Matrons. Their magic was projected through crystals worn around their necks, so maybe it was when they took off their necklaces? Those days weren't all bad, though. Because so much of the province relied on magic to function, most businesses shut down and people stayed home with their families.

I pulled a scarf over my mouth to keep from inhaling the glittering streams of magic as we darted through the sky. Below, the land was full of oddly shaped buildings that bent and curved in ways that defied laws of physics. Our buildings stayed in place because high-level orators commanded them to. Dad said the know-it-alls from Scentia hated coming here because it bothered them so much to see their perfect logic tossed out the window. That was okay. I doubted I'd like the buttoned-up, futuristic province of Scentia very much either. I supposed I would find out soon enough. I'd compete in almost every province during the Pentax.

In the distance, the Careen rose above the many skyscrapers in Meadow. There was far more concrete than grass everywhere I looked, but our city wasn't named for the landscape. It was named after the meadows, home of the Matrons and hundreds of other mythical creatures.

We began to lose altitude as the pygsmy swooped down behind the Careen, the center of Lingua's cultural life. The pygsmy left me right where I asked. *Sempr nots,* I said to him. The gentle creature brushed my neck with his wings before he flew off.

I did a quick sweep of the area. On a bench between the building and the rail tracks, a man sang and played his guitar with no audience. That was typical of Meadow—I'd never walked more than a block without hearing someone perform, no matter the time of day.

A hand reached out and grabbed my arm. Startled, I whirled and took in the face of a middle-aged woman, wrapped in a wool shawl to keep out the night's chill. Her brown eyes were wide and manic. "Laurelin Moore, the whisperer in the flesh. I knew Julian's curse would have to end. The Matrons would send us another whisperer. We shouldn't be punished for one man's greed. And here you are." Her chin quivered as her sharp nails dug into my bicep.

I tried to yank my arm free and take a step back, but the woman pulled me closer, pressing her face nearer to mine. The wrinkles around her eyes lessened as, impossibly, she pushed them even wider.

"I have a daughter," the woman continued, her breath hot on my skin. "Only three years old. She has the Cripps. It's only a matter of days until it's too late. Please, just a few drops of elixir would save her life." A tear streaked her cheek. "Can't you spare any?"

The vial of elixir I'd brought for a very specific purpose burned in my pocket. I couldn't shake the image of a sweet child, lying in bed, her body speckled with oozing, black sores and a raging fever.

"Fine," I grumbled, reaching into my jeans.

The woman's expression melted with relief. "Thank you! Oh, thank you!"

I pressed the vial into her hand. "Don't tell anyone I did this for you."

She nodded, sending her brown curls bouncing. "You have my word. Praise the Matrons!" she shouted as she rushed off down the street.

I continued toward the tracks. Such silly superstitions. I hadn't heard Julian's curse mentioned since I left public school to be taught at home with Pippin. Kids used to say the kingdom was cursed because Julian, a whisperer who lived at the same time as Eva, tried to steal the Matron's crystals for himself. Eva stopped him, but some said the Matrons had decided humanity wasn't worthy of whisperers anymore.

Before then, Ausland had always had at least one whisperer and sometimes a few at a time. Of course, I always knew there was no curse. I was proof against it. But I did wonder why there had been such a long gap. Previous whisperers were able to train each other and pass down knowledge. I had to figure out what I knew all on my own. I was sure there were parts of my powers I was missing because I'd never been properly taught.

As I ran toward the tracks, I patted my chest to make sure I still had the vial of elixir on my necklace. It pained me to know I'd have to give it up. It was habit to keep the extra vial on me for emergencies, but the woman had taken the elixir I planned to use tonight, and I needed a good trainer to win. The right trainer.

I looked across the street at the woman's retreating figure, hoping she'd get good use out of the elixir. I was filled with rage when I saw the woman stop in front of the guitarist on the bench. I heard the clang of coins as she passed him the vial.

The woman had no sick daughter. Like so many others, she only wanted the elixir for profit.

I ground my teeth together. She had no clue how valuable that was to me.

Forcing myself to let it go, I squeezed into the narrow space between the tracks and the sidewalk. It had been a while since I last came here, and the cramped space always sent my heart racing. I tried not to panic and forced myself beneath the rails. The rush of a railcar roared overhead and blew my hair over my face. That was a close call—I hadn't seen a car coming.

In the darkness, the only company was the noise of scampering rats. Tiny paws ran over my shoes as I placed my hand along the cement wall and felt my way forward. After about twenty feet, I found the divot in the cement I was searching for. My fingers brushed against a metal handle and I pulled, hearing a faint ring of a bell that was inaudible when I visited during the day.

A sleepy, male voice came through a crackling speaker. "I'm closed. Come back tomorrow," he grumbled.

I pulled the handle again, holding it down so the bell continued to ring.

"For the love of the Matrons!" the voice said, angry now. "Go away!"

I sighed. Aaron's door was well protected. A low-level, magical command wouldn't work on it, even for a great orator. The door required a password. Fortunately, I knew what it was since I was the one who placed the enchantment. I put my palm against the door and whispered, "Pygsmy brew." The disguised door glowed around the edges and then slid to the side.

"Hey!" Aaron shouted. "Who are you? I'm armed! Don't go any farther."

I stopped, raising my hands in the air. "Relax. It's me, Laurelin."

The dingy light in the cement hall flipped on and Aaron stood at the end of it, a metal baseball bat in his hands.

"A bat? In your line of work, you don't have a better weapon?"

Aaron frowned. The bat glowed purple and changed into a six-inch dagger.

"Yeah, that will do it." I laughed nervously.

The knife glowed once more and shifted back to a bat.

I blushed as I realized Aaron wore only boxers and a white T-shirt. He shied away from the light in the hall and rubbed his blue eyes with his free hand. "What are you doing here in the middle of the night, El? You better tell me Rosita's having a midnight sale on her flatbread, or I'm going back to bed."

"Sorry I woke you. I came with a peace offering. It's not flatbread, but I think you'll like it anyway." I held out the vial of elixir, feeling another twinge of regret. Every drop mattered.

Some of the annoyance left Aaron's face. He crossed the

distance between us and reached for the elixir, but I closed my palm and shoved my hand in my pocket. "First, we need to talk."

"Of course, it's not that easy," Aaron sighed. He stalked off down the hall, leaning into his bedroom to slip on a pair of pajama pants. Then he gestured for me to follow him to his living room that was more cluttered than a sixty-year-old cat lady's. Where most people had pianos, coffee tables, and couches, Aaron's shelves were crammed with boxes of random knick-knacks. For someone who could turn a rusty spoon into a shiny bracelet, nothing was considered garbage.

Aaron plopped down on a torn bean bag. Packing pieces puffed into the air, then dusted his hair white. He gestured for me to take the three-legged stool across from him.

"So what's up?" he asked as he rubbed the sandpaper stubble on his chin.

I blurted out, "I want you to be my trainer in the Pentax," but a railcar rumbled above us and my voice was lost.

"What?" Aaron shouted over the roar.

I waited for quiet. "I said, I want you to be my trainer in the Pentax."

Aaron's eyes looked like they'd pop out of his head. "The Pentax? Whoa, wait, back up. You're a Rook?"

I blushed. "Um, yeah. I thought everyone knew by now."

"I only got back from a trip to Amare a few hours ago. I went straight to sleep when I got home."

"Well, surprise! I guess you're the last in Lingua to know I'm a pygsmy whisperer. And yes, I've been chosen as the Rook. Watch for it in the papers tomorrow if you don't believe me."

Aaron scoffed. "I'd say I was the first to know you're a pygsmy whisperer, but you're right about the other half. Total shock. What do you want be a Rook for anyway?"

"You knew about my gift?" I asked, ignoring his question.

He laughed. "El, you regularly supplied me with elixir for three years before you suddenly stopped coming around these last few months. Even the best poachers can't do that. Yes, I knew. Never thought you were the power-hungry type though. You seriously want to be queen?"

I picked at a fuzzy on my gray jacket. "This isn't about power."

Aaron looked at me, puzzled. "Then why would you—" Comprehension dawned on his face. "You want the wish! Can't see why though. Anything you want, I can get for you."

"Not anything I want." My stomach squeezed at the thought of Pippin. "Anyway, this conversation isn't about my reasons. I need to know. Are you in? Will you be my trainer?"

"Why would you want me? I don't know anything. I'm just a black market hawk—the lowest of the lows. I don't think they'd let me be your trainer even if I agreed."

"I've already taken care of that, so yes, they will. And your black market skills are exactly why I need you. You've been to every province a zillion times. Nobody knows them like you do. You can help me figure out everything I need to know. I can win this thing with your help." I didn't care that I sounded desperate. Aaron was the closest thing I had to a friend. He saved my life when my first attempt at selling elixir on the black market went terribly wrong. His arrogance could be grating, but I needed him now.

Aaron shifted uncomfortably. "You need someone who can help you learn to fight and strategize. If you need something stolen, I'm your guy, but I don't think that's the goal of the Pentax. Find someone better, El." Aaron stood and headed for the door, making it clear he was done talking.

I jumped in front of him and placed my hands on his chest, refusing to be distracted by the surprising firmness of it. "I'll give you whatever you want. A lifetime supply of elixir. All the money in the world—after I win, of course. Anything. Please, just help me."

His eyes dropped, looking at my hands on his chest. "I don't play the government's stupid games. I can't be your trainer." His tan face was exhausted. For a moment, he looked thirty rather than eighteen.

"I don't either. Don't you see? This is our chance to prove ourselves. I'm not some upper-class snob. I'm just a poor girl from Lingua, the province everyone thinks is weak. Wouldn't it be great to come out of this thing on top? We could change the rules. We could change everything. And the future queen of Ausland would owe you a major favor. Besides, think of the possibilities. You'd travel around the country on the government's dime. You can do all the trading you want in every province we visit."

I could see it in his face. He was considering it.

"A lifetime supply of elixir?" Aaron repeated.

For a moment, I paused. Selling Aaron elixir had always bothered me. Though he was far better than most hawks on the market, I still hated the thought of how it was used by the people he did business with. I wanted to use elixir to help people who really needed it. But Pippin's life was at stake. Nothing was too costly.

"Whatever you want. Just help me win."

Aaron covered my hands with his. For a moment, I thought he was making a move. My breath caught in my chest. Then he pushed my hands away, and gave a half smile.

"Okay. Count me in. But remember—you owe me big time. And I expect flatbread. Lots of flatbread."

I rolled my eyes. "I have a feeling you'll never let me forget."

It was a big price to pay, but with Aaron on my team, I actually stood a chance.

Chapter Four

As I stood by the front door and embraced Pippin, I was filled with deep, bone-crushing loss. I had no guarantee he would live through this competition. For two days, I'd done my best to think of anything other than saying goodbye, but here we were, staring it in the face.

"I love you, Pip," I whispered, with his curly hair pressed against my cheek. Under my hands, I could feel his shoulder blades and spine. His scrawny arms were wrapped around my waist, gluing himself to me with surprising strength.

"I love you too, Laura. Don't worry about me, okay? I'll be all right."

I let out a soft chuckle. I'd worry about him every minute I was away, but there was no need to burden him with that thought. "I'm going to do my very best for you," I said. "A few weeks from now, you're going to be the healthiest kid in Lingua."

Pippin lifted his cheek off my chest to look me in the eye. "I can't wait to beat you at chess again."

I ruffled his hair. "Being healthy won't make you a genius, kiddo. But hey, keep dreaming. It'll give you something to live for." I winked, knowing full well he could beat me anytime, anywhere. Then I let him go, doing my best to hide how much it hurt.

Dad rolled his chair forward. His brown eyes were full of the softness he usually reserved for his proudest carpentry projects. "I want to say I'm sorry for being so moody lately. I hate to think you're putting yourself in danger to do something I wish I could do myself. Your intentions are good, Laurelin, but I hope you know it's not up to you to save your brother." He cleared his throat. "Anyway, your Mom and I wanted to give you something to remind you of home and to show how proud we are of you." He held out a purple velvet box that fit in the palm of his hand.

I opened it and gasped. Inside was a silver ring with a square, black onyx. The bottom, right-hand corner of the stone was a vibrant red that pulsed ever so slightly. "A lifestone?" I asked. "Aren't these expensive?"

Dad shrugged. "I called in a favor from an old friend. It's connected to Pippin, so you'll never have to wonder if he's all right. Obviously, we wish the whole thing was red, but as long as there's some color ..."

"Thank you. It's just what I needed." I bent over and gave Dad a hug, then Mom after.

I took a deep breath and picked up my duffle bag and suitcase. "Two weeks will pass in the blink of an eye and this nightmare will be behind us. I love you all."

Mom's eyes watered, and Dad couldn't quite look up at me. "We love you, Laurelin. Sure wish we could be there to watch you win," Dad said.

"Be safe, sweetheart," Mom added.

I felt naked as I stepped out the door, headed for the competition without my powers. They'd been gone since yesterday. Usually when the province's magic would disappear, it was only for a day or two. I tried not to see it as a sign that the Matrons were unhappy with Silas's choice for Lingua's Rook. I could only hope they'd return my magic before I made a fool of myself at the Pentax.

Like the duke had promised, a couple of officers had been sent to escort me to the rail station, which turned out to be a necessity I hadn't expected. The roads were lined with people who shouted at me. Some of them yelled encouragement and praise, holding signs that read, *Finally, a Rook for the commoners*, or *We want to see Laurelin as Queen.* Others hurled hurtful labels like selfish, greedy, and monster. Their signs read, *Elixir for the people. Why can't you share?* and *No to a queen who's full of greed.*

I hoped the scene would be calmer once we reached the station, but it was teeming with angry people as well. Barricades and officers kept them from me, but they couldn't block the hateful words from reaching my ears.

"Boy, El. You know how to bring out the crowds." Aaron's familiar face was a lighthouse in the storm. He was surrounded by four giant suitcases, and I knew they weren't full of clothing. Aaron's wardrobe consisted of the same five colored T-shirts and a couple of pairs of tattered jeans.

"Do you think you brought enough stuff to trade?" I whispered.

"You know my motto: be prepared." He winked. "So this is what it's like to be a whisperer. I can see why you kept it secret for so long."

I squinted out at the mix of supporters and haters. "You know, I can't even blame them. If I were in their shoes, I'd do the same." I almost slipped and said something about Pippin.

"I don't know why they have to be so mean though. You don't owe anybody anything." Aaron's lips were tight as he looked over the crowd.

The shrieking mob quieted some as Duke Evermore approached with his own entourage. He wore a gray suit, purple tie, and sunglasses. "Good morning, Laurelin." He looked over his glasses at Aaron, taking in his worn clothing and sunburned skin. "You must be Aaron Gray. I've heard a great deal about you, including your peculiar occupation."

"We come on equal footing, then. I've heard plenty about you as well."

"I would consider us far from equal," the duke mumbled as he turned away from Aaron's extended hand.

Aaron opened his mouth, but I grabbed his arm before he could say anything. "Can we get going?" I asked, my eyes wide.

"Duke Evermore, wait!"

Lord Hilton, a portly man with a blustery face, jogged toward us from the other end of the platform. Behind him, I recognized his son, Evan. His magic was impressive and unique. He could write any word on paper or elsewhere and the object would appear.

Lord Hilton reached us, breathing heavily. "You can't send Laurelin. You're making a huge mistake! My son deserves to be Rook. He's the most talented of the nobility's teens, you know that's true."

The duke put his arm on Lord Hilton's shoulder. "Darrin, your son is very talented. It was a difficult choice, but it has been made. Laurelin is Rook, and I won't change my mind."

Lord Hilton's face grew red. He lunged at the duke, but a pair of officers interceded.

"You'll see! She'll make a fool of Lingua!" The officers dragged him away as Evan shot a resentful glance at me. "Mark my words, Silas. You will regret this!"

All the blood seemed to have drained from my face. I stood, holding my breath. I knew the nobility wouldn't be happy with Duke Evermore's choice, I just hoped I wouldn't have to face them myself.

The duke wrapped an arm around my shoulder. "Pay him no attention. I have every confidence in you. Now, we'd better be on our way."

Trying to shake the image of the fuming man, I bent to pick up my bags, but Evermore stopped me. "Let the servants load. It's time you start acting like you want to be queen."

"Er, right. Sorry, Duke Evermore."

"We're going to be spending a great deal of time together over the next few weeks. You may as well start calling me Silas," he said as he ducked into the railcar, not bothering to give instructions for his own bags.

It was strange to think of addressing him so casually, and even stranger to allow others to wait on me. "Sorry," I whispered to the dark-haired boy who picked up my luggage. Then I followed Silas onto the first of the two railcars. Aaron walked behind me.

From the outside, the railcar hadn't appeared much different than the usual white ones that dotted the landscape, but inside was a different story. Instead of hard, plastic benches, the car was lined with cushioned, velvet bucket seats with armrests and cup holders between them. The flooring was plush carpet instead of the yellowing linoleum of the public railcars. A thin, attractive woman sat next to Silas with an open notebook in her lap. Her cheekbones were so sharp they could cut flesh.

"To Creo," Silas directed the car.

As we pulled out of the station, I looked past the angry mob toward home. I longed to be on the couch, snuggled next to Pippin, with mom humming from the armchair and dad whittling away at some new trinket. In my daydream, Pippin was the healthy boy I hadn't known for years. My heart ached for him to be that way again.

"You okay?" Aaron asked out of the side of his mouth.

I smiled and dropped my gaze to my lap. "I'm fine."

Silas interrupted then. "Laurelin, this is Tess. You may not be familiar with her from your circle, but she's the most well-known designer in Lingua. She'll be your handler, which means she'll style you for all events. She'll also manage your schedule and any media inquiries."

Tess smiled. Her brown, tight curls were pulled into a high ponytail. She wore a white pantsuit with a low-cut black shirt underneath, and sparkly black heels. "I look forward to dressing you." She scanned my faded jeans, worn sneakers, and purple long-sleeve shirt. "I see fabulous potential."

That was the nice way of saying I had a long way to go.

"Mr. Gray," Silas pulled a thick book out of the briefcase at his feet, "you need to begin studying this. Immediately. It gives a history of past Pentax competitions, comprehensive information about the other provinces, and a profile of all the Rooks. Your job is to pass on any relevant information to Laurelin."

Aaron took it, his eyes wide. "You want me to read all of this? By when?"

"Tonight."

"Oh, well why didn't you say I'd have so much time? I thought you were going to say, like, noon or something." Aaron gave a breathy laugh, then gawked at me.

I snorted and whispered, "Sorry."

Silas removed his sunglasses. "As for you, Laurelin, the first task is the Presentation of Powers, which will be held tonight. It's an opportunity for each of the Rooks to display their gifts in front of an audience and the judges. Some might say it's not an important part of the Pentax because it isn't scored, but you can do a lot to impress the other judges with how you choose to show your talent. First impressions matter."

"The presentation is tonight?" I squeaked. "I don't even have my magic today. What am I supposed to do?"

"That's not a concern. The Matrons respect our human tradition of the Pentax. They have long agreed to leave all powers alone during the competition. Once the Pentax officially begins, your powers will be restored."

I nodded, feeling only slightly calmer. The thought of displaying my magic in front of a room full of people made my head spin.

Silas continued. "I'll be the judge representing Lingua. The others will be the highest-ranking nobility of their provinces as well, so there will be five of us in total."

31

Without looking up from the open book in his lap, Aaron muttered, "Always the nobility."

I tried not to let hopelessness fill me. A bunch of nobles weren't going to like a commoner Rook. "That doesn't seem like a fair way to judge the contest. Every one of you is going to be extremely biased toward the Rook from your own province," I said.

Silas smoothed his purple tie. "No one said the Pentax is a fair competition, Laurelin. It's far from it. Already, you come in at a great disadvantage because you're from Lingua." His sharp eyes met mine. "The fact that Ausland has had only four Linguan rulers in its history has more to do with the biases of the judges than it does with a lack of magical talent in our province. You'll have to work twice as hard as the others to establish yourself as a legitimate contender."

Aaron stopped reading. "She's a whisperer though. Doesn't that give her an edge?" he asked.

Silas shrugged. "Whispering will be an intriguing gift to the judges and other contestants. Ausland values finding a young person to fill the throne. It helps us avoid frequent turnover, so it's been rare that a whisperer falls in the fourteen to twenty-one age requirement for the Pentax. Only three others have ever competed. Still, whispering doesn't hold the same fascination for the other provinces as it does in Lingua. The others don't care about pygsmies like we do. They want elixir, of course, but in their eyes, there are many more desirable gifts compared to whispering."

"What happened to the three whisperers who competed?" I asked.

Silas looked at me unflinchingly. "One of them won, one was eliminated in the first round, and the other was killed."

Sure he must be joking, I searched his face for a trace of humor. I found none.

"Um, did you say killed?" Aaron asked the question that burned in my mind.

"That's right. The Pentax isn't supposed to be wildly dangerous, but it has to serve its purpose. The goal is to test the Rooks, to discover which one can strategize, think on their feet, and make good judgments. The consequences of failure can be severe, there's no denying that. Laurelin knows what's at stake."

I didn't know much about the logistics of the competition, but he was right—I did know what was at stake. The competition was a matter of life or death for Pippin. If I failed, did it really matter if I lived? I couldn't face a future without Pippin anyway. "You don't need to worry about me. I can handle it," I said.

"I'm counting on that." Silas gave a rare smile.

"As for the rest of your schedule," he continued. "Tomorrow, you'll have most of the day to train, with a required social event in the evening. Tess will fill you in on the details."

Tess gave three small claps. "I can't wait! It's going to be a party."

"Day three will start with a training session, then conclude with a media interview," Silas said.

"Media interview?" I groaned. "Is that mandatory?"

"Oh, you have nothing to worry about, girl," Tess said. "We'll have lots of time to prepare. Plus, you'll look fabulous, and that's what really counts."

I kept my disagreement to myself.

"May I continue?" Silas asked, annoyed.

"You may," I said. Out of the corner of my eye, I saw Aaron's grip tighten around his book. Keeping him from killing Silas might end up being my biggest challenge.

"Day four will be the first round of competition, which will happen in Creo. It's tradition to begin in the province of the past ruler. Because one Rook is eliminated at the end of each round, there are four rounds total."

All I had to do was survive four crazy tasks. I could do that for Pippin.

"That means one of the five provinces misses out on hosting

a round. After Creo, the locations for the other three rounds will be decided by random drawing later today. The best-case scenario would be to have Lingua host the second round, but it's good news as long as we're somewhere in the order. If we're the province that's skipped, you've got even tougher odds to overcome because you'll always be competing in unknown places."

Suddenly, I wished Mom had spent a lot more time teaching me about the other provinces during our history lessons. I took a deep breath. That's why I had Aaron. He could tell me anything I needed to know.

"Now, I'm going to guess you didn't sleep very well last night. We've got a few hours until we reach Creo. My advice would be that you try to get some sleep. We want you in your best form tonight for the presentation." Silas reached into the bag at his feet and tossed me a small blanket. "Rest. That's an order."

I pulled the gray blanket over myself and settled into the cushioned seat. My mind was running wild with thoughts about the Pentax, so it took a while for the soft lull of the moving car to put me to sleep. When it did, I dreamt I was standing on a black stage surrounded by sneering faces, my magic still gone. The judges disqualified me before the competition even began. Mom, Dad, and Pippin sat in the front row. My stomach felt hollow as I looked into Pippin's eyes, which were full of disappointment. I'd failed him, and I'd never forgive myself for it.

Chapter Five

S ilas's loud voice jarred me from sleep. "We'd better hurry. The rain will begin in thirty minutes, and we won't want to get caught in it." He left the railcar without further explanation.

Tess hurried after him, her brow furrowed. I figured she was worried about what a rainstorm might do to her hair and make-up.

Somehow, my head had found something soft to lay on. Heat flooded my cheeks when I realized it was Aaron's shoulder.

"Er, sorry," I said, standing quickly. I busied myself with zipping my jacket to avoid Aaron's eyes.

He followed Silas and Tess onto the platform. "No apology needed. Now I get to add *human pillow* to my list."

"Your list?"

"Sure. I'm keeping track of all the roles I fill so I know how much to bill you when this is over. So far, I have *trainer, reader-of-book larger than Aunt Sally's backside, buffer between you and the hot-shot duke,* and now, *human pillow*." Aaron ticked off the titles on his fingers.

"Even as queen, I don't think I'm going to have enough money to satisfy you," I mumbled.

There was a heavy floral scent that hung in the air, and I was instantly transported to Grammy's garden. She had a gift of willing her dreams into reality, and it worked on any living thing—even plants. A flower wouldn't dare do anything but flourish in her presence. Her magic might have changed the course of Pippin's cancer, but she died a year before his diagnosis.

In front of us, a vast, green wall made of interwoven vines and flowers towered fifty feet in the air. The platform stretched out toward a tunnel that burrowed through the wall. We had reached the edge of Lingua. I'd never been this far from home in my life.

"How does Silas know it's going to rain?" I asked Aaron. Above us, the sky was blue and cloudless.

He laughed. "Creo is the province of creation. They make their own weather. The rain comes in the afternoon every third day to keep the vegetation watered. You're about to enter a whole new world, El. Try to keep up."

The three servants who had traveled with the duke were busy unloading our luggage from the rear car. I snickered as a petite brunette woman staggered under the weight of one of Aaron's cases.

"We better rescue her from your monstrous luggage," I said, pointing at the girl.

His face turned red and he hurried over. "Sorry about that," he grumbled. "Got to be well dressed at the Pentax." He gave a nervous laugh.

The girl eyed Aaron's ratty outfit in disbelief.

I rolled my eyes and grabbed my own luggage. They had plenty to manage between Tess and the duke.

As I headed into the tunnel, the pavement ended, and all that was left was a long dirt path. Above us, flowers larger than my face glowed in soft shades of yellow, orange, and pink that slowly faded then intensified in their brightness.

The thin wheels of my luggage didn't navigate the loose dirt well. A few feet in, I snapped down the pull bar and grabbed the handle.

The light from the sun grew stronger as we neared the end of the tunnel. It was a strange color though—not the muted, whitish-blue hue of Lingua. The yellow light was vibrant, almost green in its excitement.

I gasped as we emerged from the tunnel. The wooden platform towered over an intricate dome of green vines that was replicated a hundred times, creating a sea of giant mounds in every direction. With equal parts horror and fascination, I watched as loose, thick vines snatched people off the top of a neighboring platform, flung them into the air, then whisked them away to unseen destinations below.

Silas and Tess stepped up to the edge of our platform.

"We'll see you at the bottom," Silas said.

A slithering vine wrapped around their waists, then tossed them upward before they vanished under the web of green. The three servants were next, each clinging to several bags of luggage with all their might as they were thrown through the air.

"Please tell me there's some other way to get where we're going." I became lightheaded as I looked over the edge of the platform. It was a very long way down.

Aaron laughed. "They're very eco-friendly in Creo. They didn't want rail systems because of pollution, so the vines take you where you need to go."

"How do they know where that is?"

He shrugged. "It's the magic of Everly, Matron of Creation. They'll take you to the place you think about."

He took the bags from my hand and left them in a pile with his own. A vine snatched up the luggage, and I hoped we'd see it again.

"Come on, El!" Aaron called as he waited on the edge of the platform. "The less you think about it, the easier it is to go."

Apparently, the vine had run out of patience. Without warning, it wrapped around my waist and dragged me forward, snagging Aaron as it passed. Our bodies were smooshed together, which might have been awkward if I wasn't occupied with other concerns. I wanted to scream as the vine whipped us into the air, but it felt like my stomach was in my throat, smothering the noise before it could get out. Then the vine plummeted toward the ground and tossed us onto the dirt.

"That was awful!" I spit mouthfuls of muddy saliva as I dusted off my clothes.

"Welcome to Creo!" Aaron chuckled as he brushed off his jeans and blue T-shirt. Somehow, he had managed to keep his face out of the dirt.

A trickle of sweat dripped down my back. I pulled off my gray jacket, suddenly feeling like I was being suffocated. The woven vines above us seemed to function as a greenhouse, keeping the air hot and humid.

Our luggage lay in a scattered heap on the ground a few yards off. My smaller bag was crushed beneath one of Aaron's monstrosities. He scurried over to it, pulling a face as he handed me my squished case.

"Sorry about that," he said as he passed it over.

"Deduct it from my bill and I'll call us even."

The other part of our group was way down the dirt road, with Tess in the lead. They walked toward a daunting but crumbling castle made of gray stone. Like everything else, it was mostly covered in green vines. In the opposite direction were quaint homes and sprawling fields. Beyond that, only the edges of the large, green dome were visible.

"Is that Queen Isadora's castle?" I asked as we walked toward the palace, luggage in hand.

"Yes, ma'am. Not what you expected?" Aaron asked.

"Why is it falling apart?"

The eastern and western flanks of the castle lay in piles of ruin, and the vine in those parts was brown with crispy leaves. Even toward the center of the castle, where the vine was still lush, large chunks of gray stone were missing.

"It's dying," Aaron explained. "The queen was the castle's creator. Now that she's gone, her castle is decaying."

"In only twelve days?"

Aaron shrugged. "Happens fast."

"Then why are Silas and Tess going inside?"

They had reached the palace's cherry wood double entrance, where a group of servants showed them inside.

"We are too. The handbook says this is where we'll be staying for the next four nights."

I balked. "Will it still be standing by then?"

"Sure, sure. The place is enormous. It's got at least two weeks left before it collapses completely."

"How comforting," I sighed. Between the stress of the Pentax and worrying about the ceiling falling on me in my sleep, I doubted I'd get much rest here.

Chapter Six

It turned out I didn't need to worry about the ceiling since there wasn't one—at least not a real one. It was made of vine, with large spaces that let in plenty of sunshine.

I would need to invest in a bottle of sunscreen.

Silas, Tess, and the servants waited for us in an open stone lobby.

A middle-aged gentleman with dark hair greeted us. "Welcome to Aremia, home of the Great Isadora. My name is Julio, butler of Aremia."

This surprised me. He wasn't dressed as I expected a butler to be. Instead of a tuxedo or crisp uniform, he wore tan cotton pants and a green tunic with a vine design that followed the plunging neckline. His feet were bare on the bamboo floor.

"Each of you has been assigned a lady's maid or valet who will escort you to your rooms. I suggest you hurry if you'd like to avoid the rain."

A small woman with short brown hair and kind eyes approached me. "Hello, my name is Sofia. I'll be your maid during your stay. May I show you to your room?"

"Yes, thank you," I responded.

Sofia reached for my bag, but I grabbed the handle before

she could take it. Silas gave me a stern look before he followed his own escort around a stone staircase to a corridor on the right. Still, I kept my bag, feeling too silly allowing Sofia to carry it when I'd be empty-handed.

"Did you have a good trip?" Sofia asked as we wound through several non-descript hallways.

It was as if I'd been plunged into a maze. The walls were either stone or vine, and no art adorned them to distinguish one from the other. If I had to go anywhere on my own, I'd get lost after the first turn.

"It was all right. Your transportation system is going to take some getting used to, though."

Sofia laughed. "Yes, I hear that from almost every visitor. Honestly, it doesn't get much better with time."

I blanched. Hopefully, I wouldn't have to use it often.

Sofia led me to a room, which had one wall made of stone, but only because it was at the back of the palace. The rest were composed of tight, twisting vines, with plenty of gaps between them.

The floor was dirt, and a strange lean-to had been erected over my bed. I understood why a few minutes later, as rain came pouring down through the makeshift ceiling.

"Agh! It's not supposed to rain inside," I said as the drops touched my skin.

Sofia squealed. "Hurry to the closet. It has a permanent ceiling to keep clothing dry."

I followed her to a small inlet at the left of the room.

"You'll want to keep anything that can't get wet under your bed or in the closet," she said.

When the rain stopped, Sofia whisked me away to an elaborate dressing room where Tess waited for me, her hands on her hips.

"Time to get to work," she said. The blaze in her brown eyes made me uncomfortable.

Tess dragged me over to a warm tub and intrusively began stripping me down.

"I can do this myself, thank you," I said, my cheeks warm.

"Fine, just hurry."

I peeled off my clothes and slipped into the warm water, appreciating the lavender scent coming off the bubbles.

After the bath, Tess spent hours putting goop in my hair, filing and polishing my nails, and removing body hair in places I didn't know I had any. I bit my tongue as she ripped a strip of wax off my cheek. Was peach fuzz really so offensive?

A petite kitchen maid dashed in at one point and left a tray of food, which I inhaled as I sat in a swivel chair in front of a mirror. Behind me, Tess played with my hair, which she'd just colored white. It wasn't far off from my natural blond, but it added a layer of silver that shimmered when it caught the light.

Tess settled on a half-up, half-down hairstyle that left elegant curls to frame my face and drip down my back. She swatted a chocolate chip cookie from my hand as she lifted me out of the chair and dragged me across the room.

"Hey, I was eating that!" I protested, but she was unconcerned with my appetite.

"Stand here." She indicated a raised pedestal in the middle of the room, surrounded by full-length mirrors.

At this point, it was silly to feel self-conscious in front of Tess. She'd seen every inch of me. But still, as she examined me from the side wearing nothing but my underwear, my skin prickled with embarrassment. To distract myself, I watched the glowing flowers above. They were shades of yellow and orange, bringing a soft, restful glow into the room that contrasted with my anxious mood.

My leg bounced as one minute turned into five. Tess held her chin in her manicured hand as she scrutinized my body.

"Er, is there something I can—"

"Shhh," Tess hissed.

I shut up, studying my unrecognizable face in the mirror.

My family never had money to spend on things like make-up. My normally-flat green eyes glistened under all of the eye shadow and mascara, and my pale complexion glowed with pink blush.

"I've got it!" Tess clapped her hands together, her curly hair bobbing with the motion.

I let out a sigh of relief as she finally tore her eyes from my body.

She tilted her head upward and closed her eyes, extending her hands in front of her. Silas had been right—our powers were back, and Tess's amazed me.

She spoke in a low chant, "Pygsmy-purple satin, lavender chiffon, golden swirls, peaked shoulders, with green bodice lines," and as she did, the words materialized in the air.

She repeated the words rapidly, and they stretched and became interwoven with each other. Their color changed from gray to purple as they swirled and spun around each other. The words moved closer to me, surrounding my body as they gained speed. I stood in the eye of a word-tornado, filled with awe as I watched them shift to streams of fabric that clung to my skin, pulling me in different directions. I struggled to keep my balance.

The spinning slowed, and the mist of magic began to fade. Now I wore a lavender, knee-length dress embroidered with golden swirls, like the markings of a pygsmy. Two curved, translucent triangles poked up over my shoulders, giving the impression of shimmering wings. Green accents wrapped around the body of the dress, accentuating curves that were non-existent on my stick-straight body.

"Wow," was all I managed to say as I felt the smooth fabric.

Tess beamed. "You like it?"

"It's incredible, Tess. Thank you. Your gift is fascinating. I haven't seen anything quite like it in Lingua. How does it work?"

Tess's brown eyes glistened with pride. "I can speak my designs into reality. Tonight, no one will be able to ignore the whisperer from Lingua." She winked. "Come on. We're running late."

My new high heels clacked against the bamboo floor of the endless hall. Tess kept hold of my hand, as much to drag me along as it was to keep me upright. I kept my eyes on my feet, trying not to fall. She came to an abrupt stop in front of a pair of natural wood doors.

"You should look up when you walk. It shows confidence," Aaron said.

My eyes snapped up to meet his. "You want to trade shoes and see how you manage in these things?" I held my leg out for him to examine the purple stilettos.

"I'll pass. I have a feeling you look a lot better in them than I would." He winked, and I couldn't help but blush.

I'd never seen him in anything other than scuffed jeans and T-shirts, but tonight he was in a well-pressed blue suit. His face was clean-shaven, and he'd put gel in his hair to contain some of his buoyant curls. His casual half-smile had my heart thumping in my chest.

"Thank you," I said, tucking some hair behind my ear. I turned to Tess, who watched us with raised eyebrows.

"Wow," she said flatly. "You need to work on your flattery, Aaron. That was far from sweep-her-off-her feet."

Maybe not for a girl like Tess. But for me—the home-schooled girl from Sedona—compliments from a boy were rare. As in, they never happened.

Tess continued. "Silas asked me to give you a rundown of the events tonight. The Presentation of Powers is all about intimidation. It's your chance to show the other Rooks what they're going to have to do if they want to beat you to the crown. The key is to flex a little, but don't reveal all your secrets. You want to keep some things in your bag of tricks. Show enough that they feel threatened and leave it at that."

"But I'm a low-level orator and a whisperer. What is there to show? I speak to pygsmies. It's hardly a show-stopper moment."

"You better find a way to make it one," Tess said, as if that settled it. "Your only other job is to learn as much as you can about the other Rooks. Can you do that?"

I nodded.

"Great, then it's showtime. The three of us will stand together on the Lingua platform. Laurelin, you enter last."

Tess opened the double doors that led into the stadium. A rhythmic pounding of drums filled my ears, drowning out the beat of my heart. I took a deep breath and then followed Tess and Aaron inside.

Chapter Seven

T he stadium was a large, bowl-shaped arena made of dark-gray stone. The stage sat in the center of the circular space, where four burly men pounded on drums with mallets half as big as my face. The stadium was divided into five sections, separated by flaming torches that lined the stairs between them. Everyone in my section would be from Lingua. My parents had been invited, and even though I knew they wouldn't be there, I found myself searching the crowd on the off chance they decided to surprise me. No such luck. I tried not to feel disappointed.

We stood on the platform above them while Silas was seated in front of the stage at a table with the four other judges, each wearing their province's official garb.

Tess and Aaron assumed the stance taken by the other teams —arms behind their backs, feet wide—and I did the same, standing between them but a step in front.

Each province's flag served as the backdrop behind the Rooks. I stole a quick glance at the one behind me. The purple pygsmy in the center of the banner brought me some comfort.

The section to my right was red for Amare. The Rook was a girl, wearing a red dress that gathered at the waist, accentuating her near-perfect figure. Her face was beautiful, with wide eyes and full lips. She looked straight ahead, her expression relaxed.

Orange for Fortis was next. The guy who stood in the Rook's spot looked too old for the competition, which was supposed to cap at twenty-one. He was well over six feet tall with bulging biceps that were visible through his orange, army-style turtleneck. He had a shaved head, and stared forward with determination.

The boy who stood in front of Creo's flag wore a green tunic and brown pants. He was the only Rook who smiled. He had dark, voluminous hair that was styled to appear wind-blown.

The final section was blue for Scentia, and their Rook was probably even younger than me. She wore a blue pantsuit with a white blouse underneath. Her hair was pin straight, brown, and came to a blunt edge at her chin. Her skin was pale, and her eyes were hidden beneath black-rim, square glasses.

The beating of the drums came to a crescendo, then abruptly cut off. With a collective "Ha!" the four men crossed their arms behind their backs, mallets in hand.

Queen Isadora's sister, Saundra Garcia, emerged from the mouth of the center tunnel and walked down the aisle that led to the judge's table as the crowd cheered. Everyone knew Saundra. She had been the palace's spokesperson as long as Isadora had been queen. She wore a green halter-top dress. Her thick hair was in a long braid with wildflowers woven into the sections. She took the stage, bowing and waving.

In the center of the stage, a podium rose from the ground, carrying the crystal diadem that belonged to Ausland's ruler. The crystal was woven together in long, thin strips. Nestled into the crevices were five glistening stones, each representing the five provinces' colors.

"Ladies and Gentleman of Ausland, welcome to Creo! Before we begin the Presentation of Powers, let us pause and remember my sister, our beloved Queen Isadora." Saundra bowed her head, and the audience did the same. "May she rest with the Matrons, watching over Ausland." Silence filled the stadium for a few seconds.

"Isadora will not be an easy monarch to replace, but as centuries of tradition dictate, one must be chosen to lead Ausland's five great lands. Each province has selected a young, gifted person who will best represent the province's values, as well as the skill and intellect needed to lead our kingdom. Tonight, these young warriors will give us a taste of what they have to offer Ausland, but it is the events of the Pentax that will truly determine which of them is most worthy of the crown."

Saundra walked to the diadem and stroked it fondly. "The Pentax is a centuries-old tradition based on the method the Matrons used to choose which kingdom would share their power. Our magnificent King Darius won the competition, and Ausland has sparkled with magic ever since. One of the five Rooks before you will have the honor of carrying on Darius's great example. The winner will wear the diadem and cross the meadows to be crowned king or queen by the Matrons themselves in their home, Everark."

My stomach squirmed with nerves at the thought of the crown being placed on my head.

"There are four rounds of competition, each held in a different province. We are honored to hold the first round here, in Creo, the home of the Great Isadora. The order of the other rounds was decided earlier today by random drawing. They will proceed as follows: The hosting province of round two will be Lingua. The hosts of round three will be Amare. Our fourth and final competition will take place in Scentia. We will be sad to miss out on Fortis during this Pentax." She bowed in the direction of Fortis's section.

Silas got his wish—round two would be held in Lingua. My heart felt much lighter at the thought of going home in just a few days. I might even be able to see my family.

Saundra continued. "At the end of each round, one Rook will be eliminated from the Pentax. This will be determined by a score awarded by the judges out of one hundred possible points. The scores from each round accumulate, so every performance matters."

"Now," Saundra lifted her arms to the Rooks, "let us get to the reason for our gathering: The Presentation of Powers!"

The pounding of the drums resumed. The flames along the aisles shot upward with such intensity that the heat reached my face. The lights from the glowing flowers pulsed with the beat. My heart felt like it would jump out of my chest and race out the door.

"Creo!" the green team shouted in unison, taking a carefully choreographed offensive stance.

"Fortis!" The orange team followed their lead, also with coordinated movements.

I looked at Aaron and Tess. "Were we supposed to plan something?" I hissed.

Tess bit her lip. "Silas never mentioned anything to me."

As Scentia and Amare chanted their own names, Aaron reached out to a vase of purple roses on the ledge of our platform. "On three, shout our name and copy one of the other teams' movements," he whispered. "One, two, three!"

"Lingua!" I yelled, feeling silly as I made a fist and extended my right arm above my left.

Purple rose petals showered our platform, drawing ooohs and ahhhs from the few rows closest to us, who were also covered in flowers.

Saundra's delighted laugh filled the stadium as the drums stopped playing. "Well done, very well done! I can tell we are going to have an exciting competition on our hands."

"Thank you," I whispered to Aaron, grateful for his gift.

"Just another role on my list." He smirked.

I nudged him with my elbow.

The green flower lights over the Creo platform glowed more vibrantly while the lights in the other sections faded.

"Ladies and gentlemen, from Matron Everly's province of

creation, the first Rook I present to you this evening is Owen Mendez from Creo!"

The spectators in the green section went wild, holding up signs of encouragement and chanting Owen's name. Owen ran down the stairs from his spot at the top of the stadium, shaking hands and giving high fives as he went.

"Hello, Owen." Saundra stretched out her hand as Owen took the stage. "How are you feeling tonight?"

The projection at the back of the stage changed to Creo's flag with a black raven in the center holding a piece of wheat.

Owen breathed out heavily. "It's a big night! Lots of nerves. It's an honor to be chosen to represent Queen Isadora's province, and I believe I can live up to the high expectations she set for not only Creo, but all of Ausland. I pray the blessings of Everly will be on me throughout the Pentax." He pressed his palms together and bowed.

Saundra chuckled. "I am sure you will make my sister very proud. Why don't you go ahead and show us what you can do?"

Owen held out his hands and swirled them together. He pulled in the air around him, creating a whirlwind that shot out sparks of red, gold, and blue. Saundra smiled but took a few steps back as wisps of hair fluttered around her face. Owen stopped and cupped his hands together. Then he thrust his palms upward and a magnificent, giant bird exploded into the air. Its back was black and belly blood-red, with white markings on its cheeks. It let out a piercing *kee-aah* as it dove over the section of the crowd from Scentia. They ducked, shielding their heads with their arms. The bird turned at the top of the stadium, and like a bullet, it darted toward the stage. Owen didn't flinch, though the bird was headed straight for him. Inches before it would have rammed into him, the bird stopped and floated down until it came to rest on the stage. Owen held up one hand. The bird cocked its head, watching his signals. It let out a chirp, which caused Saundra to stumble backward.

"There's no need to be afraid," Owen reassured Saundra and

the crowd. "I have him under control." The bird's black body and red-tipped wings stood at attention, waiting for a command. Owen scrambled onto the bird's back and clung to its feathers. The bird sprung into the air and circled the crowd as Owen hollered from its back.

Aaron leaned over and spoke in a low voice. "Owen is double-gifted, like you. He can create and control animal life, though only the ones he creates. Combined with his second gift, he's one of the most talented people in all of Ausland."

"What's his second power?" I asked, but Owen answered with his next move.

There were screams of shock as the stone benches seemed to have turned to rubber. They bubbled upward, following Owen as he circled the stadium.

"He can manipulate earth and stone," Aaron responded.

I whistled. "He's going to be very hard to beat."

"Don't sell yourself short, El," he said, staring at me intently. "Owen is talented, but I doubt he's any match for your determination."

I forced myself to look away and fiddled with the neck of my dress as if something needed to be rearranged.

As the bird passed over Creo's platform, Owen jumped from its back, landing in a somersault before he rolled to his feet. He held his arms up in triumph as the audience cheered.

"Magnificent!" Saundra cried from the stage. "Thank you, Owen Mendez!"

My palms were clammy with nerves. I was no match for Owen's showmanship.

The flag projection changed from Creo's to Scentia's. In the center of the blue flag was a white owl carrying a book in its talons. The blue flowers glowed brighter above her, putting a spotlight on the petite girl in the pantsuit.

"Please put your hands together for our second Rook who hails from Matron Seersha's province of knowledge. She is Faye Bennett of Scentia!"

Faye stepped to the edge of her platform as her supporters clapped. She kept her hands behind her back and gave several curt nods, her face unsmiling.

A sharp crack pierced the stadium. There was a flash of light at Faye's feet, then blue smoke filled the air. Her handler and trainer didn't flinch as Faye disappeared.

"My goodness!" Saundra exclaimed from the stage, holding her hand over her heart. Faye was standing patiently beside Saundra, waiting for the audience to notice her.

"The art of misdirection," Faye said, a smug smile on her face.

Saundra gave a genial chuckle. "Well done, Ms. Bennett. Well done. Please, show us what you have to offer Ausland."

Aaron leaned over again. "I'm curious about this one. The training book says Faye has one gift. She's able to perfectly recall anything she reads. Sounds like a total borefest for a presentation. In a province full of powerful seers and mind readers, I'm curious why she was chosen."

It was as if Faye could hear Aaron.

"Some people mistake my gift as weak because it doesn't come with a lot of flashy qualities. A lifetime of reading has taught me many things, though. I'm able to apply that knowledge to ingenuity. I've found that technology can mimic or surpass nearly any magical gift. There is no limit to what I can create, which means I have limitless power."

Faye reached into the pocket of her pantsuit. She withdrew a blue disc that was small enough to fit in her palm. The center appeared hollow but shimmered in the light. "I call it a paxum. I have many of them, and I'm able to program each one to hold the equivalent of between two to five magical powers. That is how I appeared on the stage so quickly. Allow me to demonstrate further." Faye held the device in her palm, and in dramatic fashion, she pushed one of the buttons.

Immediately, all the lights in the stadium were extinguished. Even the stars weren't visible through the vines above. I quickly reached for Aaron, wanting to anchor myself to someone or something in the darkness. My heart began to race, faster than if I'd been running at a full sprint.

"El, are you okay?" Aaron asked. He sounded winded, as if he was struggling too.

"I'm alright. I just— can't seem to— breathe."

Something brushed my ankles. A small squeal escaped me as I swatted at it. Whatever it was felt furry and small. A mouse? Another one brushed past me. Then another. My frightened squeaks were echoed by hundreds of others throughout the stadium.

"What is that?" Tess screeched. "Ew, I think there's twenty of them!"

"Ugh, why does it have to be spiders?" Aaron mumbled.

"Spiders?" I said. "I thought they were mice." I wasn't particularly fond of either option.

A whooshing sound rushed past my ear and I ducked, forgetting the possibility of mice or spiders for a moment. It was the noise of a passing arrow, and it had only been centimeters from my head. Another one flew past me.

"El, get on the floor. Now." Aaron yanked my wrist and pulled me to the ground. He put his large body over mine as a shield.

"What's going on?" I panicked.

Without warning, the lights in the stadium returned. I was prepared to see the floor swarming with mice or spiders or whatever Faye had unleashed, but there was nothing. The stone platform was just as it was before. No arrows were stuck in the wall behind us either. Aaron released his hold on me and I quickly stood.

The crowd was in chaos. People had ducked for cover between the rows of benches. They brushed themselves off and looked at each other in bewilderment. But the other Rooks and their teams were in the same confident positions as before— hands behind their backs, feet spread apart. Even their expressions were calm and collected, except for the girl from Amare who watched me with a smirk.

I adjusted my dress and cleared my throat. "Is everyone okay?" I asked my team.

Tess and Aaron swiftly resumed their stance, but I couldn't help glancing at Silas. He glared up at us, his lips pressed into a thin line. His face was red with embarrassment.

"You see?" Faye chirped from the stage. "Just a manipulation of technology sent the entire stadium scrambling. Even one of our brave Rooks was scared silly. Of course, she is from Lingua."

In the other province's sections, I heard snickers from the crowd. Feeling stupid, I kept my face expressionless and stared forward.

"Very impressive, Faye. Can you give us a simple explanation of how the paxum works?" Saundra asked. She had smoothed her dress and regained her composure.

"The paxum is essentially an emitter. First, it distributed esilia, the component of the nightcrawler plant that snuffs out light. Then, the paxum secreted a heavy dose of virulim, a scent that most mystical beasts put off. This caused an intense release of epinephrine in your body, which makes the heart race. Finally, the paxum manipulated the air currents in the room. Soft, lower gusts around the ankles made it feel like something was crawling around your feet. Our brains typically fill in the blank with something we fear, especially when panic has already been introduced. And lastly, stronger, higher bursts of air produce the sensation of being shot at with an arrow." Faye said all of this without a hint of regret for invoking fear in everyone present.

"Marvelous work. I believe any person—especially your fellow Rooks—will think twice before crossing you." Saundra beamed. "You may return to your team."

The audience clapped, but much less enthusiastically. They must have found being scared out of their minds hard to forgive.

"I have been told that our next Rook is positively fearless.

Please welcome, from Matron Ember's province of courage, Tobias Liang of Fortis!"

The stadium was flooded with orange light as Fortis's flag was put on stage. In its center was a crouched lion, its mouth stretched over pointy teeth.

Tobias made no effort to woo the crowd. He gave a stiff nod, then walked down the stairs, his eyes never wavering from Saundra on the stage. His handler and trainer, both wearing black from head to toe, followed behind him.

"Welcome, Tobias," Saundra said as the group took the stage. "I gather you've elected to use your entourage in your presentation. Please, introduce them to us."

Tobias motioned to the tall, slender female whose dark hair was pulled into a high ponytail. "This is Serenity, my handler."

She bowed, her long hair swinging to the front of her face.

"And this is Damon, my trainer."

The stocky, muscular man with sandy-blonde hair bowed as well.

"Excellent. Please, show us what you can do."

"You may want to join the judges at the table for now," Tobias said to Saundra.

Saundra gave a loud laugh before she realized Tobias was serious. She scurried off, standing next to the female judge dressed in red. I wondered what Tobias had planned that would require more distance than the previous two.

Damon pulled a black blindfold out of his pocket and wrapped it around Tobias's eyes. They all bowed to each other.

"Hi-yah!" Serenity shouted, and the fight began.

"Tobias has the gift of combat strategy," Aaron whispered. "He can see an opponent's move as soon as they've decided on it, and is incredibly quick at coming up with a counter-attack. His gift only works with human threats though."

Tobias's impressive skill sent a chill down my spine. It was obvious that both Serenity and Damon were excellent fighters, yet Tobias always escaped at the last second. In under two minutes, he had immobilized both of them.

"Well, I wouldn't want to cross you in a dark alley, Tobias," Saundra laughed. "Your skills and quick reflexes will certainly give you a leg up in the challenging rounds of the Pentax. I look forward to seeing you compete." She patted the giant on the shoulder, and Tobias left the stage.

"Our fourth Rook has caused quite a stir in her province with the recent revelation of her gift," Saundra said.

The flag changed to Lingua's purple pygsmy. My breathing stopped, and my feet grew heavy, like they were cemented to the floor. After sixteen years of secrecy, it was so strange to think about displaying my gift right here, in front of two hundred people.

"From Mother Mira's province of Language, the only Rook not from noble blood, I give you Laurelin Moore of Lingua!"

The cheers of the crowd sounded like roaring water to my numb brain.

I felt a hard nudge against my back. I wasn't sure if it was from Aaron or Tess, but I had to step forward to catch myself. And then I took another step. And another. Robotically, I moved down the steps toward the stage. I caught Silas's eye. He smiled broadly, motioning wildly to his lips.

Oh, he wants me to smile, I realized. My lips stretched into a cheesy grin. I waved to the crowd and finally reached center stage.

"How are you feeling, Laurelin?" Saundra asked. Her face was wrinkled and her skin was bare. No make-up tried to compensate for any perceived lack of beauty because of her age. Her chocolate eyes were kind as she smiled at me.

I gave a breathy laugh. "I'm nervous, but I'm grateful to be here. This competition means a lot to me."

"Because you want to be queen," Saundra finished for me.

I smiled. "Something like that."

"I've been told that you have a very special gift. I believe the entire audience is eager to see what you can do."

A jolt of nausea ran through me. I closed my eyes and breathed, trying to dispel my doubts. Pygsmies were very sensitive creatures. Asking one to come into this wild stadium full of people it didn't trust was going to be hard enough. It needed to feel like I was in control of my emotions. I had to be the safe place in the room.

I brought Pippin's face to the front of my mind. For a second, I counted the freckles I'd memorized a thousand times. I saw his green eyes, healthy and vibrant. I could almost feel his rough, red curls in my fingers. He was my purpose for being here. All I needed to do was keep that perspective. Stage fright was nothing compared to losing my brother. I could do this.

With a newfound confidence, I opened my eyes. I entered the vast space in my head where I could search for pygsmies and called, *Lyrun rach min baum.* For a long time, all I felt was blackness. I searched and searched, stretching out to the edges of my mind. Finally, I felt a prick of light. I connected to it and pulled through the distance, asking the gentle creature to come. Through a crack in the vine ceiling, a tiny, golden flutter was visible.

Then the pygsmy froze and fear entered his mind.

No, no, it's okay. I'll keep you safe, I said. I flooded my mind with peace and surety.

Slowly, the gentle creature lowered himself. The crowd began to stir with excitement. For most of them, this was probably their first sighting. The pygsmy darted back to the ceiling.

"Please, try to calm yourselves. The pygsmy is feeling very anxious in such a daunting space," I said.

I coaxed the mystic once more, throwing some force behind my request. With caution, he descended and finally landed in my palm. As his four legs connected with my hand, his body became fully visible. The crowd let out a collective gasp.

"Incredible," Saundra breathed. She took a step closer to

examine the pygsmy. "And you're not afraid to have its stinger so close to you?" She looked at his belly, hovering centimeters above my exposed skin. "One sting from a pygsmy will kill a person in less than thirty seconds," Saundra informed the crowd.

The thought seemed silly to me. The possibility of being stung never crossed my mind. I'd nearly forgotten pygsmies even had stingers. They would only use their poison if they felt extremely threatened.

"No, I'm not afraid," I answered simply.

Saundra laughed. "That's very brave of you. Can you show us more? What can you make this pygsmy do?"

I didn't like the idea of treating the pygsmy as if he were a common show pony, but I knew Silas would be disappointed if I didn't put in some effort to stand out. I thought about what I should do. The pygsmy's marking glowed, showing he had elixir, but I was not willing to extract it in front of the crowd. That could lead to danger for other pygsmies if someone stupidly tried to replicate the practice another time. The safest option would be to fly with the pygsmy.

I opened my mind and began my request, but I was interrupted by a woman who shot up from the Linguan section, third row back.

"Laurelin Moore doesn't deserve to be queen!" the blond-haired woman shrieked. "She won't share her gift with us! A Rook should be someone who's willing to sacrifice for her people! Laurelin only revealed her gift because she wants to be queen!" Two security guards descended on the woman, grabbing her by the elbows. "My husband is dying," she screeched as she was dragged down the bench, her face contorted in rage. "I've pleaded for elixir. I've slept outside her family's gates for days and she won't give me any! Selfish! Egotistical! Greedy!" The woman's voice faded as she was dragged up the stairs. She kicked her feet as she was hauled off by the guards, booing me the whole way.

A cold emptiness filled me. Someone she loved was about to

slip away, just like Pippin. The only difference between the two of us was that she was powerless to slow time. My heart ached for her.

This was not the first time I'd felt tremendous guilt for my greed. It was part of the reason I'd kept my gift a secret for so long. Before, at least I was only judged by myself. The woman was exactly right. I was selfish. I wouldn't—couldn't—lose my brother. And the plain truth was that I didn't seem to mind how many others died at his expense.

"Well," Saundra gave an uncomfortable laugh. "I'm sorry about that, Laurelin. Do you have anything you'd like to say? Any explanation for the woman's accusations?"

"I'm sorry," I said breathlessly. "I wish I was able to help everyone who needed it." I struggled to keep my emotions in check. A tear sneaked out of my right eye.

Without permission, I left the stage. I released the pygsmy and practically ran back up the steps to my stupid platform, hating the heels that slowed me with every step. I knew Silas would be furious, but he'd probably be madder about his Rook bawling on center stage, and at this point, that was the only kind of performance the crowd would have received if I'd stayed.

When I reached the platform, Tess said something I couldn't hear. Aaron gave me a sympathetic smile and squeezed my hand but remained silent. I wondered if he thought I was a monster, too.

"We'll move on then," Saundra said, her tone disapproving. "Our final Rook of the evening, from Matron Amiah's province of heart, I give you Amelia Allred of Amare!" she exclaimed.

"Amelia is another double-gifted Rook," Aaron whispered, trying to act like everything was normal. "She has heightened intuition that allows her to sense danger before it comes. She can also read and manipulate emotional bonds within relationships."

I couldn't speak, so I nodded to show my understanding. I kept losing my focus as I watched Amelia's trainer set up deadly obstacles for her to cross. Each had only one option that was safe to take. While blindfolded, she walked through the only metal hoop that wasn't burning, the tub of water with no electric eels, the glass of wine that wasn't poisoned, and on it went until Saundra brought the long night to a close. As impressive as Amelia's talents were, the main image that filled my mind was the agonized face of the screaming woman.

Chapter Eight

The knock on my bedroom door hit me like four taps to my skull. I ignored it, like I ignored the struggle to breathe with my face buried in a pillow.

I remained where I was, sprawled across the bed with my crumpled purple dress still on.

Tap, tap, tap.

Were all social norms lost on this person? I wasn't coming.

"Laurelin, I can see through the gaps in the vine. I know you're there."

It was Silas, the person I most dreaded to see. After a long pause, I decided I couldn't avoid him forever. I peeled myself off the mattress and yanked open the door. "There's nothing you can say to me that's worse than what I'm already thinking."

"I'm not here to criticize you, Laurelin. I came to give you something." Silas held a brown leather book at his side. "May I come in?" His eyes were droopy and he rubbed his temple. An unexpected pity washed over me. He probably spent the past hour defending his choice for a Rook to every journalist in Ausland.

Wordlessly, I moved to the side and gestured for him to step in.

Silas looked around the room, pausing at the open suitcase at the foot of my bed and the clothes spilling over the sides. His eyes narrowed slightly, as if my mess offended him, but he said nothing about it.

"I'm sorry about the woman in the crowd. I thought we had carefully vetted everyone who was invited. They all expressed tremendous support for you and for Lingua. I guess she fooled the interviewers. It won't happen again, I promise you."

I toyed with my dress, as if smoothing the fabric would somehow ease the ache in my stomach. "It's okay. I'm over it."

His eyes plainly communicated that he knew I was lying. "Well, I hope that is true, but either way, I'd like you to have this." He cleared his throat and handed the leatherbound book to me.

I ran my fingers over the pygsmy etched into the front. "Eva Evermore?" I asked as I read the loopy, cursive name written beneath the pygsmy.

"The last known whisperer, yes," Silas said. "When she was nearing the end of her life, she realized the next whisperer was not coming. Until then, Lingua's whisperers had always overlapped. They usually trained and worked with one another, at least to some degree. Eva didn't want to leave the next whisperer in the dark. She recorded some of the things she knew and left this journal with her family with instructions that we pass it onto whoever was next. We've been waiting a long time." Silas gave his first genuine smile in the time I'd known him.

It seemed like a gift of this magnitude deserved much more than a simple thanks, but all of the words I wanted to say were stuck in a jumbled mess at the back of my brain. "Thank you," was all I managed to say.

"You're very welcome. I figured you could use it after a night like this. Take some time to read a little and then get some rest. Tomorrow is a new day, and I expect my Rook to face it head on."

With the book clutched to my chest, I nodded. "I'll be ready. You have my word."

Silas turned to leave.

I stopped him. "Hey, Silas, do you know who the screaming woman was?"

"Yes, her name is Marcia Browning. Why?"

I disconnected the vial of elixir I kept around my neck and handed it to Silas. "Will you please make sure this gets to her?"

Silas watched me for a long moment before he said, "Yes, I can do that." He tucked the vial into his breast pocket. "Don't stay up too late. You need sleep."

He left, and I flew to my suitcase. I replaced the vial of elixir on my neck with one of the four I'd brought along with me. I knew that it was against the rules of the Pentax to use elixir before or during any rounds of competition, but I'd learned from experience that it was best to have a vial on me, just in case.

With the journal in hand, I slipped on a pair of cotton shorts and a T-shirt, then snuggled under the covers. Finally, someone who could truly understand my fears.

I flipped open the first page. Like the tongue of a snake, the crimson ribbon intended to be a bookmark flicked out and pricked my wrist.

"Ouch!" I said, peeved. I dropped the book and rubbed the place where the ribbon struck. The vein beneath my skin glowed angry red before it shifted to purple. The colorful streak spread down my forearm until it reached the midpoint. There, it stopped following the line of my vein and swirled around in a mesmerizing pattern until the outline of a purple pygsmy was complete.

My mouth hung open as I examined the new mark. It didn't fade or change with any amount of rubbing or wiping. I appeared to be permanently branded.

Could have warned me the journal was possessed, Silas.

I had tossed the book onto the bed in my panic. Its pages

were crumpled beneath its heavy cover. I stared at it, wondering if I dared touch it again.

Curiosity won out. Cautiously, I picked up the journal and flinched, waiting for a second sting. When none came, I exhaled and read the first page.

By opening this book, you have entered into a blood contract. This record is only to be read by Eva Evermore's direct family and is to be passed on to the next whisperer, whenever he or she is known. Violation of these terms will result in death. The book will know your intent.

You have been warned.

I looked down at the pygsmy marking. Did the book know I was the next whisperer? Is that what the mark meant?

If you're anything like me, you've wished a thousand times not to be a whisperer. For the first seventeen years of my life, I considered it worse than a curse. I was torn from my family and kept prisoner by a ruthless king in a cold castle. From my window, I'd watch the people below, walking the streets, and I'd wonder what my life would have been if the Matrons hadn't decided to burden me with such an infuriating power.

Life improved some when I met Julian, another whisperer who taught me more about my gift, but only marginally. I was still a captive, forced to collect elixir at the whims of King Tiras, and I had no say in how it was used.

When I earned my freedom, I was faced with a new burden—the cares of a whole kingdom and not nearly enough elixir to satisfy everyone who wanted it.

I wish I could promise you that you'll master balancing that burden someday. Maybe you will. But honestly, I never did. I can tell you it gets easier, and you will learn so much about life, death, and what it means to be a protector. After all, that's what pygsmies do best. They are beautiful, sacred creatures. If you let them, they will teach you more than you could possibly imagine.

Though my eyes were blurry with sleep, I kept reading. Eva wrote about new things I'd never heard of. Like the ability to see through a pygsmy's eyes when she was deeply connected with one. Or controlling more than one pygsmy at a time. She said that skill took a long time to master, but eventually, she was able to fly with her husband and children.

I read until I could no longer keep my eyes open. The flower lights on my walls faded as sleep clouded my brain.

That night, my dreams were filled with the faces of the other Rooks, an angry woman, and flying pygsmies.

Chapter Nine

Because the first part of my night had been full of nightmares, when the dreams stopped in the early morning hours, I slept very soundly. Too soundly. By the time I woke and threw on a change of clothes, breakfast was over. I grabbed a few leftovers from the cafeteria kitchen.

I was not lucky enough to avoid Silas.

"You should have been in training by now." His voice stopped me as I rounded the cafeteria door, my mouth still full of bran muffin.

I chewed and swallowed quickly, turning to meet him. "I know. I overslept. I am so sorry, but I am heading there now, and I promise to put in extra work before I leave."

"I am sure you're excited about Eva's journal, but you mustn't allow it to become a distraction. The Pentax is what's happening now, and I expect you to give it your all. Don't allow a repeat of last night. I won't explain you away to the media again."

"Understood." I continued down the hall.

"Laurelin?"

I cringed. "Yes?"

"Your training room is the other direction."

With a red face, I passed him, keeping my eyes on the floor. I'd have to ask Sofia to give better instructions from now on.

When I finally found the right room, there was no Aaron in sight.

I was irked. There was a note pinned to the wooden leg of a tall lean-to.

El,

You know trading is best when the market first opens and right at close. I'll be there soon, I promise. Forgive me? I'll take it off your bill. Swears.

—Aaron

If I didn't need him so badly, I would have fired him the second he walked through that door.

With a sigh, I examined the large room, if it could even be considered such. It was located behind the castle, really, in the courtyard. There wasn't even a make-shift roof this time, and the floor was straight dirt. The familiar vine walls separated each Rooks' training space and gave a semblance of privacy. The only shelter in the room was a wooden lean-to that covered random exercise equipment, most of which seemed entirely useless to me. We had two days to train. No significant amount of muscle or endurance could be built or lost in that time. These sessions were meant to be more about strategizing than anything else—at least for those contestants who were lucky enough to have trainers that showed up.

Well, I wasn't going to waste my time. What I wanted to practice didn't require Aaron's help anyway. Eva wrote about a much deeper level of connection with pygsmies than I had ever achieved. That was my goal today. I needed to know the full extent of my power.

I squeezed my eyes shut and exhaled, letting go of my

frustration with Aaron, the tension of the Pentax, and my irrational desire to slap the pretty smile off Amelia's face. Pygsmies were naturally gentle creatures. Eva explained that better connection would come if my emotions were in sync with theirs.

Reaching into the recesses of my mind, I opened the door that allowed the pygsmies to find me. I pushed the dark space outward, searching for that first prickle of light. After I found it, I didn't stop. Instead, I stretched out farther, testing the limits of my consciousness, pushing the black barrier until I was panting with effort. There were exactly eighty-four sparks, each one a different pygsmy. I was surprised by the precise number, but somehow, my brain knew. The black edges were pushing back, trying to narrow the field of pygsmies available to me. I fought it, working to hold the limits in place for no other reason than to strengthen my mind. There was no way to be sure, but I guessed I was searching about a five-mile radius—much farther than I had ever tried before.

With a snap, the edges of the field collapsed inward, until there was nothing in my head but my boring brain. It was as if I was holding a one-hundred-pound bar above my head and my arms suddenly buckled beneath the weight.

Sweat trickled down my forehead from both my mental effort and the bright sun beating down on me. I missed Lingua's cool climate. Creo was so hot and humid that the air never seemed to glisten with magic like it did at home. I pulled my T-shirt over my head. The heat was tolerable in my tank top.

Refocusing, I opened my mind and pulled in the nearest pygsmy. She came quickly, her thoughts eager. This pygsmy was less skittish than most. She fluttered around me playfully, excited to communicate with a human. This would be her first time.

No, there aren't others who can talk with you. I answered her question in her language. *Sorry. You're stuck with me.*

I suppose one human will do, the pygsmy said.

Seeing her bright markings made me crave elixir. Though it

wasn't my purpose today, extracting elixir was never a bad idea. I reached for the vial at my neck but stopped when an unexpected pain stung my forearm. I flipped over my arm and found the lines of the pygsmy marking shifting to words instead.

To build a connection, meet the pygsmy's needs first.

I was stunned. I'd never seen magic like this before. Were the words coming from Eva? But how, if she was long dead? Clearly, it was instruction intended to help me meet my goal.

I looked at the pygsmy, fascinated by her intelligent eyes. They weren't the eyes of an animal, but I already knew pygsmies were far more than that. I'd conversed with them before, but I'd never thought to ask about their needs. Typically, my interactions with them were always rushed, driven by the need to get as much elixir in as little time as possible.

I held out my palm and asked, *Do you want to come?*

The pygsmy cooed and then brushed my fingertips with her tendrils. *I've never touched a human before,* she thought. *This is exciting, but strange. You smell funny—kind of musty and like greasy food.*

That's not a compliment, I said.

I didn't mean it to be.

I blanched and then moved on. *Do you have a name?*

My name is Sun Petal because I like to fly high, close to the sun.

It's nice to meet you, Sun Petal. My name is Laurelin. Is that what you do with your free time? Fly?

The pygsmy laughed. The sound was like windchimes. *That's a very human question. There's no difference between free time and otherwise for a pygsmy.*

Okay, then. What do you do every day?

Migrate, of course. And then recover by eating and resting.

I knew this about pygsmies. Their flight patterns had been studied. Most lived in the same general area all their lives, but they made frequent trips from their homes to the meadows, where the Matrons were. They couldn't be followed beyond that, though. The meadows were far too deadly for any human to enter.

And do you like that?

Oh, yes. Pygsmies are protectors. It is our duty to keep the meadows safe, and we watch the humans, giving reports to our mothers.

Which Matron is your mom? I asked.

Sun Petal's mind was bubbly with excitement. *Everly, Mother of Creation. She's magnificent. She's interested in the human competition being held in her province.*

Suddenly, my own mind was flooded with warmth as an image of Everly filled my brain. Her long, brown hair was done in an intricate braid and capped with a crown of twigs, leaves, and wildflowers. She smiled, her brown eyes warm as she reached out to me.

I gasped when I realized what this meant. I had never seen Everly in any form other than gray statue, which meant this image came from Sun Petal's mind. It was a memory of a time when she had visited her mother. Excitement filled me.

"El? Er, what are you doing?" Aaron's voice punctured the sweet memory, breaking the connection. Sun Petal fluttered away.

I whirled. "You're an idiot, Aaron."

His eyes were wide. "Whoa, El. I'm sorry I wasn't here earlier. I thought you'd be okay with me doing some trading. If you remember, it was part of your sales pitch to get me to come along."

"That's not what I'm talking about." I sighed. "Never mind." I reached for my water bottle and drained half of it, making a note to bring extra tomorrow.

He looked at me with wary eyes. "Your hair is different with that silver stuff in it."

I raised an eyebrow, confused by his train of thought. "Yes, it's called hair color. It was Tess's idea."

"Hmm," Aaron said.

"What?"

"It's nothing. Just not the reaction I was hoping for," he said.

"What were you hoping for?"

"Well, Tess said I need to be more direct with my compliments."

"You didn't give me a compliment, Aaron. You made an observation."

His face scrunched, as if I was speaking a different language. Then comprehension dawned on his face. "Oh, you're right! Here, let me try again. I like the way your hair shimmers in the sunlight."

I snorted. "I suppose that counts as a compliment. So thank you."

"Am I forgiven?" His eyes were wide and innocent, his hands clasped at his chest.

He'd done it again. Somehow, he managed to cut through half an hour of frustration in thirty seconds.

"You are forgiven but conditionally. It's time to pay up. I asked you to be my trainer so you could tell me the ins and outs of the provinces. I've heard all the surface-level stuff a hundred times. I need to know what each province is *really* like. What unique gifts exist in Creo? What do people value? Tell me everything you know."

Unexpectedly, Aaron reached out his rough, weathered hand and brushed a scar beneath my collarbone. My cheeks grew warm at his touch.

"What happened here?" he asked.

Something flickered beneath the cool surface of his blue eyes. Something warm—something that caused my stomach to tighten in a way that was both painful and pleasurable. He dropped his hand.

"Umm, I was shot with an arrow when I was twelve. I was still new to my gift, or at least new to using it for anything other than an occasional flight around the forest. I was just beginning to collect elixir. A poacher spotted me in the woods. He shot me and stole the vial I was in the process of filling. At that time, I

71

didn't have enough command over my abilities to force a pygsmy to heal me. The one that had just given me elixir had been watching. I was only barely conscious, but I remember how relieved I felt when it wrapped its tendrils around me and shared its elixir. It didn't have enough left to heal me completely, so I've had the scar and a spare vial of elixir around my neck ever since."

"You know, you're kind of hardcore," Aaron said. "Way tougher than half the hawks on the black market."

"Now that's how you give a compliment." I smiled.

Aaron straightened an imaginary tie around his neck. "Why thank you. Make sure you tell Tess for me."

"If you're trying to impress Tess, you know you're joining a long line of suitors, right?"

Aaron scoffed. "Nah, Tess isn't my type." His eyes flickered from mine to the ground.

I cleared my throat. "We should really get to training. Time is running out."

"Right," Aaron said.

He walked to the shade of the lean-to, and I happily followed. I could feel my skin burning already. I still hadn't gotten my hands on a bottle of sunscreen, but a pygsmy would be able to heal me at the end of the day.

Aaron sat cross-legged in the dirt and pulled the large book Silas had given him into his lap.

"Did you really read that whole thing?" I asked.

Aaron beamed. "Sure did! You proud of me? It took all night."

I laughed. "I'm impressed. That's a lot of dedication."

"Couldn't have you lose on my account. Truth is, it was a lot of useless stuff. The overview it gave for Creo was nothing you don't already know. I could summarize it as saying the province is full of tree huggers, which is only three-fourths true. The only valuable thing I gained from reading the handbook was seeing a pattern. Most of the victors had one thing in common: they respected the perspectives of each province while competing there."

"So I need to act like a Creon would during the first round?" I clarified.

"Exactly. Here's what I can tell you about Creo from my own experiences. All living things are considered equal to humans, so killing an animal during the competition would be a definite no-no. That even goes for animals that may attack you or pose some other threat. You would need to find a way to immobilize or contain it without causing significant harm."

"I couldn't kill an animal even if it attacked me?" I repeated.

"That's right. Very different from the Linguan mindset, I know.

"The next thing to remember is that you have to use all your senses when analyzing a situation. There are a few Creons with an epic gift for creating illusions, so don't rely too much on sight. What you see may not be what's actually there. Strong illusionists can mimic sight, sound, and even touch, but they can't create convincing smell. Trust your nose.

"And remember that the structures in Creo are living, too. A room can change from one moment to the next. The province is full of people who can control plant and animal life, so be cautious around any living thing—they can do things you wouldn't expect. Basically, Creo is all about trusting your gut, not your external surroundings."

I nodded. "Don't kill creatures and follow my instincts. I can do that. In fact, I have an idea. Last night, Silas gave me Eva's journal. That's how I got this." I held up the marking on my forearm, which had shifted back to a pygsmy.

Aaron grabbed my arm. "A journal gave you a tattoo? I don't think your mom is going to buy that excuse."

"No, seriously. Somehow, it recognized me as a whisperer, and the even crazier part is, it just gave me some instruction. Eva wrote about being able to connect with pygsmies and use their senses, so I figured I'd give it a try today. When you walked in, I just saw a glimpse of Sun Petal's memory—"

"Sun Petal?" Aaron asked.

"The pygsmy that was with me. She's called Sun Petal."

"I'm sorry I interrupted. I can see why you were so ticked off," he said.

"The point is, pygsmies see differently than we do. I bet illusions wouldn't work on a pygsmy, and their eyesight is, like, ten times better."

"Well, I think we know what we should work on today." Aaron smiled and helped me to my feet.

"Actually, there's something different I want to try. It will still help me train, but I'll need you. You up for it?"

"Sure, sure. I believe that is the role of a trainer, after all."

I squeezed my eyes shut and searched the skies for a couple of pygsmies. First, I found Sun Petal, who was busy practicing the pronunciation of my name. It was a difficult one for a pygsmish speaker.

Lure-a-lyn. Lor-u-lyn. Lyr-a-lin, she said, as she hovered in front of us.

Not quite, but you're getting close.

When the second pygsmy appeared, I introduced myself. *What's your name?* I asked him.

I'm Stork, the pygsmy said.

Stork, meet my friend, Aaron. I gestured for Aaron to take a step toward Stork.

"You're sure it won't sting me?" Aaron asked. "I kinda like my life, you know."

Sun Petal laughed.

Scared human, Stork thought. If Stork was human, I was sure he would have rolled his eyes.

I snorted. "I'm sure he won't sting you. Pygsmies aren't like wild animals. They are very aware of themselves. Now go on, stretch out your hand for him. Pygsmies like to get a taste of humans with their tendrils."

Aaron put out his hand and took a couple of slow steps toward Stork, grimacing.

Do I have to do this? Stork asked.

Not if you don't want to, I said.

Oh, come on, Stork. How often do you get to interact directly with humans? Sun Petal said. *Lur-e-lun will protect you. She's nice.*

I will keep you safe, Stork, I promised.

Freveen, he sighed. It was equivalent to a human teenager's "fine."

"Ah!" Aaron jumped and pulled back his hand when Stork's tendrils brushed his palm.

I laughed. "It's okay. He's just getting a feel for you."

"Sorry," Aaron blushed and put out his hand again.

Nervous. Arrogant. But kind, Stork said, as he continued to feel.

Yeah, that pretty much sums him up, I laughed.

"Why are you smiling? Are you guys talking about me?" Aaron said.

"Of course not." Then I winked at Stork.

Well, what do you say, Sun Petal and Stork? Do you think you can help us fly?

Oooh, yay, yay, yay! Sun Petal said. *I love to fly!*

I suppose I could give it a try. I've heard it's difficult to fly with humans, though. I will need lots of direction, Stork said.

I'll do my best. Stork, you take Aaron. Sun Petal will fly with me.

"Are you ready to fly with a pygsmy, Aaron?"

His eyes popped wide. "You want me to fly? With that?" He jutted his thumb at Stork.

"His name is Stork. And yes. Eva said learning to control multiple pygsmies strengthened her connection with the creatures. I think it will help me a lot."

Aaron sighed. "I am not getting paid enough for this."

I smiled. "I'll take that as a yes."

Sun Petal flitted over to me and scooped me up with her tendrils.

Okay, Stork. Go ahead and pick up Aaron, I said. *Take us up, Sun Petal.*

My stomach flew into my throat as Sun Petal burst into the air, reaching the top of the green dome in a second.

"Whoa, El?" Aaron called. "Are you in control of this thing?"

I looked down to see Stork and Aaron tangled up in the vine wall of the practice area.

Yikes. *Go left!* I screamed. *Left!*

But instead of Stork and Aaron moving left, Sun Petal jerked to the left, and we slammed into the side of the dome. My vision popped with little black stars.

Meanwhile, Stork managed to extricate himself from the vine but was flying directly toward the stone castle walls.

"Laurelin, help!" Aaron yelled.

Pivot right and swoop to the ground, I directed Stork. But again, Sun Petal was the one following my direction. I couldn't seem to jump from Sun Petal's head to Stork's.

Stork and Aaron narrowly missed the castle and spiraled downward. Stork released Aaron, who crashed into the top of the lean-to that covered the exercise equipment.

Take us back to the ground, I told Sun Petal.

"Aaron, are you okay?" I asked as I ran toward him.

"I'm all right," he called.

Among the pile of rubble, I could see movement, which gave me some relief. I pulled broken boards off of Aaron and grabbed his bicep, helping him up.

He stood and shook dust out of his curly hair. "I'm going to call that experiment a failure."

I grimaced. "That would be an understatement."

I thought you said you'd be in control, Stork complained.

I'm sorry. I won't try that again. At least not until I have a much better grip on my magic.

Stork didn't respond and flew off in a huff.

Sun Petal landed on my shoulder and examined Aaron. *He seems all right. I don't think he'll need any elixir to heal.*

Thank the Matrons for that. And thank you for your help today. Maybe I'll see you again sometime.

I hope so, Sun Petal said. She brushed my neck with her wing before she flew off after Stork.

"I'm really sorry, Aaron. Are you okay?"

He swung his right arm around and massaged his shoulder. "A little stiff, but nothing that won't heal. I completely wrecked the lean-to though."

I frowned at the mess of wood and equipment. "Do you think Julio is going to be furious?"

Aaron wiggled his eyebrows. "All I'm saying is, this is definitely going to cost you extra." He touched the wood and another lean-to took shape. It was identical to the last.

"If it means avoiding the wrath of Aremia's butler, I can't complain," I said.

Chapter Ten

The bright light from the white flowers over the vanity somehow found its way through my eyelids, blinding me even with my eyes shut. The chair swiveled underneath me as Tess yanked me this way and that, pulling my hair into a complicated updo I could never hope to replicate on my own.

Working with the pygsmies left me more exhausted than I had ever been. Even the days Mom demanded I write ten-page essays in every core subject—including math—couldn't compare. This always seemed to happen when she had to focus more attention on Pippin. I tried to tell her I was perfectly content spending my days in the trees with the pygsmies, but Mom insisted she was not raising her daughter to be a monkey.

Tess yanked on a strand of hair, causing my eyes to fly open. She carried on as if nothing happened, unfazed by the way I glared at her reflection in the mirror. I would be glad when this was all over and my body felt like my own.

With an exhale, I closed my eyes again. I was getting used to using dress-up time as my chance to daydream. In my mind, Pippin was well enough to ride a horse again. Together, we tore through an open field, racing to the green barn that stood in the distance. He rode grandpa's black stallion and I was on grandma's palomino. Pippin was ahead of me, and I didn't mind. It was pure joy to see him look over his shoulder at me with a taunting smile.

Tess's voice caused the dream to crash down around me. "There," she trilled. "You look ready for a party."

"Are you sure I have to go?" I asked. Tess had squeezed me into black pants that were a size too small. My green shirt dipped lower than I was used to, but at least I had some coverage from the purple leather jacket she'd put over it. She'd applied a layer of light makeup that highlighted my best features. She really was a master of design.

"Yes, I'm sure. It's a required social event of the Pentax and there will be one in every province, so get used to it. This is your chance to get to know some people from Creo. You'll survive, I promise." She turned to the mirror to touch up her own makeup.

I was glad she hadn't pushed my fashion choices quite as far as her own. She wore black leather pants and a red shirt that left little to the imagination. I was certain all eyes would be on her tonight, and that was fine by me.

"Okay, let's go," Tess squealed. She pulled me from the dressing room.

The hard beat of deep, bass music hammered in my chest as we walked down the hall toward the ballroom.

"This doesn't sound anything like the music we have in Lingua," I shouted to Tess as we entered the overwhelming room. Lingua's music was focused on the beauty of language, and the instruments were little more than background noise. This music was the opposite—the instruments were loud and rhythmic. There were no words, just an occasional cry of a melody.

Tess shrugged. "Creons believe music should speak directly to the soul. You probably won't hear words in anything. Loosen up, kiddo. It's good to experience new things."

The ballroom was much like the other rooms in the palace,

with a wood floor and vine walls and ceiling. Flowers pulsing red, orange, and purple light hung from vines that varied in length above the crowded dance floor.

A handsome man with broad shoulders stood against the bar, making eyes at Tess.

"Speaking of new things, looks like you have your first suitor." I pointed in his direction.

Tess squeezed my arm. "Ooooh, don't mind if I do." She giggled, then left me alone to stand on the outskirts of the dance floor, feeling awkward.

I searched the pulsing crowd, trying to find Aaron or a group of people who looked friendly enough to join. The only familiar face I found was Silas's, but he was occupied. He sat in a blue booth along the edges of the room with an odd group of people: Arthur, the male judge from Fortis, and Faye, the Rook from Scentia. Silas's eyebrows were furrowed. He leaned forward and slammed his fist on the table. Arthur rose from his seat and left in a huff, with Silas glaring after him. Faye appeared bored by the exchange. She rested her head in her hand. I was beginning to wonder if she had any emotions. Perhaps Scentia really was as bland as all the jokes implied.

Silas and Faye spoke for a moment, until Faye caught my eye from across the room. She cut Silas off and walked in my direction, her blue sequin dress rippling like a wave with her movement. This ought to be good.

"You should tell your judge that groveling for help with your score only makes Lingua look more pathetic. Though I'm sure you're the one who sent him in the first place, so I suppose my advice is really intended for you." Faye sniffed.

Silas was asking for help from the other provinces? He hadn't discussed that with me. Embarrassment heated my cheeks.

"I don't know what you're talking about. And why would Silas come to ask you for help with scores? You don't have any influence over them."

Faye rolled her eyes. "Mariah is sick tonight, so she asked me to take the meeting for her. She said Silas wanted to discuss a coalition among the weaker provinces so we could help each other out. I suppose he wasn't asking for manipulated scores *directly,* but I got the message."

"That makes no sense. Fortis wins the Pentax nearly as often as Creo. Why would Arthur be involved if it's a coalition of the weaklings?"

"You're as bad at logic as I'd expect for a Linguan. I'll spell it out for you. Fortis is the province that got skipped as host. They may have a history of winning, but they're at a disadvantage this time around."

Her arrogance set my teeth on edge. "Well, since we're offering tips, allow me to give one of my own. Smiling has occasionally been known to make friends. You should try it sometime."

"I'm not here to make friends. I'm here for the crown, unlike you."

Faye's eyes glistened as the blood drained from my face.

"That's right. I know about your brother."

My family had kept Pippin's illness private intentionally. Mom had pulled us both from public school, and we rarely went out for anything more than grocery shopping. We didn't want people questioning how someone so sick continued to defy all odds and live. At some point, the question would have pointed to elixir and me, by extension. My secret was out in the open now, but I didn't like the idea of a competitor knowing my weakness.

"So what if I'm here for my family too? I'm sure everyone is," I said.

Faye's eye twitched. "Some of us are here to get away from our families." Without offering further explanation, Faye whirled and marched toward the dance floor.

Owen, the Rook from Creo, was near the center of the dancing, surrounded by a group of girls in opulent dresses and shiny jewelry. They were the kind of girls who usually gave me a twenty-foot berth.

Owen seemed to notice me staring. "Laurelin! Come join us!" he called.

The girls were shoving against each other, trying to push closer to him.

"I promise it won't kill you to let loose a little!" He winked.

Reluctantly, I wound through the sea of swirling bodies and joined the group. The girls watched me with hard eyes, evidently fooled enough by my fancy costume to see me as a threat. A week ago, a stuffy aristocrat like Owen wouldn't have noticed me if I was gum stuck on the bottom of his shoe. Now he took my hands and began dancing.

It felt strange to dance with someone to such upbeat music. My arms were like stiff twigs, and I wasn't entirely sure I still had control of my legs. They wouldn't move at my brain's direction.

Owen smiled down at me. "Are you always this high strung?"

His question irked me. There was every reason in the world to be 'high strung' right now, not the least of which was dancing with one of my rivals to music that sounded more like a bleating lamb than a melody. "Do you always keep your head buried in a bucket of self-praise? Or do you occasionally come up for air?"

Owen laughed. It was a deep, throaty sound that was entirely carefree. I wondered if he didn't take the Pentax seriously or if he was just so full of confidence that his body had no space for any negative emotions.

"Most girls find my confidence attractive." He smoothed the lapel of his garish green suit.

"Well, consider me a skeptic," I said.

"I'm sorry my question offended you." Owen attempted to bow. The motion was awkward with his hands still holding mine. "Allow me to try again. Are you enjoying what Creo has to offer?"

I ignored the double-meaning and answered with a half-truth. "I miss eating meat, but it's exciting to be in a place that's so different from home, and I certainly get a lot of fresh air here."

Owen threw his head back and laughed. "Spoken like a true politician. Maybe you are right for the queen thing after all."

"I'm pretty sure that was an insult disguised as a compliment, so maybe you're meant for politics too." I gave a sly smile. "Just not as king. That spot will soon be taken."

Owen chuckled. "I must admit, for a Linguan, you're a firecracker."

I let the conversation drop, and tried to enjoy the music. The longer I was on the dance floor, the easier it was to loosen up, and Owen turned out to be a good partner. He easily made up for my two left feet. Slowly, the girls surrounding us peeled away as Owen continued to focus on me.

"Hogging elixir not enough for you, Laurelin? Now you want the guys to yourself too?" Amelia appeared by our side, her skin sparkling with glitter. Her full lips were painted red, and her tight, curly hair had been ironed flat.

"There's no need to be nasty. There's plenty of me to go around." Owen's eyes slid to the plunging neckline of Amelia's red dress.

Amelia scoffed. "Don't be ridiculous. It's not that I want you, it's that I don't want Laurelin to have you."

The scene became more crowded as Tobias stumbled toward us.

"Great. Another idiot who can't take no for an answer," Amelia said under her breath.

But Tobias wasn't after Amelia. His angry eyes focused on me. "Lingua is so desperate to win the Pentax, they're willing to cheat to do it." His words were slurred, and the alcohol on his breath was pungent.

"Cheat? What are you talking about?" I asked.

Tobias rolled his eyes as he stumbled to the right. "Don't play stupid with me. I know what you're up to. Didn't think you could win on skill alone, I guess. I'm going to report you."

"Leave her alone, Tobias. You're drunk," Owen said.

"I have a right to speak with Laurelin just as much as you," Tobias growled.

"Well you don't have a right to cause trouble in my province. Get out of here."

Owen gave Tobias a shove, which was amplified by Tobias's tipsy state. He fell forward, knocking my eye with his elbow as he went. Then he turned and lunged for Owen.

I rubbed my hurt eye and watched with my other. The closest dancers scattered and Amelia screamed as a full on fist-fight broke out. The music came to a grinding halt.

I was relieved to hear Aaron's voice behind me.

"El, step back!" he called. A second later, his hand close around my wrist. He pulled, putting some distance between me and the fight.

Silas and Arthur appeared. Whatever disagreement they'd had earlier was put behind them as they worked to end the chaos. Arthur raised his palms and put an orange, dome-shaped shield over the four men, isolating them from everyone else. When a small break came between punches, Arthur managed to wedge a shield between Owen and Tobias, pushing them apart. Swiftly, Silas grabbed Owen's arms and held him back. Owen breathed heavily as he glared at Tobias.

Arthur approached Tobias, his hands raised in a gesture of surrender. "You're not well, Tobias. You're embarrassing our province. It's time to go to bed."

A chill ran down my spine as Tobias glared at me, flexing his muscles.

"I said it's time for bed," Arthur demanded through clenched teeth.

Tobias stood a full head taller than him, but the shield kept him carefully contained. Letting out a string of profanity, Tobias turned and stalked off. Arthur dropped his shield and followed closely. The crowd scurried out of his way, eager not to become the next target.

Owen straightened his clothes and dabbed at a cut on his right cheek.

"Are you okay?" Silas asked him.

"I'm better now that that maniac is out of the way. Laurelin, how are you?" Owen asked.

"Laurelin was hurt?" Aaron said. His hands fluttered over me, trying to find my injury.

"No, he only bumped my eye. It wasn't intentional."

"That's what started this mess, though. Tobias said something about Lingua cheating." Owen looked at Silas suspiciously. "Do you know what he meant?"

"Of course not. The boy was drunk. The competition must be getting to his head. If you're sure you're all right, Owen, I suggest we get on with the party," Silas said.

Like moths to a flame, Owen was immediately swarmed by a group of girls as Silas, Aaron, and I walked away. The music started up again and the mass of people slowly returned to their conversation and dancing.

"Are you sure you're okay, Laurelin? It looks like your eye could bruise," Silas said as we reached the outskirts of the room. "Here, let me get something for it."

An iced bottle of soda soared from the bar to Silas's open hand. He was a high-level orator. Unlike me, he didn't have to be touching an object to command it.

"Put this on your eye for now. I'd like to check in with Arthur and Tobias, but I did have a matter I'd like to discuss. It's about Eva's journal. Would it be okay if I meet you in your room in ten minutes? I'll bring you a proper ice pack when I come."

"Yes, that's fine." I was curious about what he might want to discuss, but I had questions of my own. "First, can you explain what you were doing earlier? I saw you speaking with Faye and Arthur. Faye told me you were talking about forming an alliance with Scentia and Fortis."

Silas gave an easy smile. "It's very common to make friends during the Pentax. That's my job as head of the team, and it's how you will win. Let me take care of building relationships. You worry about being ready for the competition, okay?"

Tobias's angry eyes and accusations replayed in my head. "As long as you aren't cheating," I said.

"Lingua needs you to win, Laurelin. I wouldn't jeopardize your chance by breaking any rules."

That was one thing we had in common—we both desperately wanted me to win.

"Okay. I'll see you in a few minutes."

I watched Silas as he walked away. I wasn't sure I could trust him, but I also couldn't trust Faye. She'd proven herself to be a master of misdirection. Maybe there was nothing underhanded about Silas's conversation with the other provinces. Faye might have told Tobias that Lingua tried to cheat when there was nothing going on.

I sighed and turned to Aaron. "Where the heck have you been all night?"

He wore his usual ratty T-shirt and jeans, standing out more than a mouse among snakes in this up-scale crowd. From across the room, I could feel Tess's eyes burning him.

"If you remember, when I agreed to come to this shindig, you said I could do all the trading I wanted when I was off duty. Besides, seems like I arrived just in time for the excitement." Aaron laughed, but his blue eyes were tight with worry. He touched the drink I held to my eye and it changed to an ice pack.

"Thanks, but why didn't you tell Silas you could make me an ice pack?"

"It's good for him to run some errands." Aaron smirked. "Are you really okay?"

"I'm fine, I'm just confused. I wonder what Tobias was talking about," I said as we walked to one of the booths on the perimeter of the room and sat down.

"He accused you of cheating?"

"Yeah, he said something like, 'I know what you're up to, and I'm going to report it.' The whole night has been weird, actually. I had an encounter with Faye, then Owen wanted to dance, and then Amelia came over, breathing fire." I shook my head. "I thought the hardest part of the Pentax would be the rounds of competition, but I'm thinking the social events might be equally dangerous."

"Owen wanted to dance?" With narrowed eyes, Aaron searched the crowd until he found Owen, who had a girl under each arm. Owen's face was animated as he threw punches in the air, apparently reliving his heroics.

I snorted. "That seems to be Owen's style. Don't worry, I had the situation under control until Tobias showed up."

"I don't know what to make of all of it, El, but I'd say keep your cards close to your chest. People will do crazy things when there's a crown at stake."

"You've got that right," I sighed.

Someone behind me caught Aaron's eye. He squirmed in his seat as a shrill voice said, "Aaron Gray! What are you doing here?"

A girl wearing a tight green dress and heels ran to our table. She pushed into the booth next to Aaron, batting unnaturally long eyelashes at him.

"Karessa, I didn't expect to see you here," Aaron said.

The girl linked her arm with Aaron's, then seemed to notice me for the first time. Her face fell. "Oh, who are you?"

"Hi, I'm Laurelin. Aaron and I ... work together."

I studied Aaron's face, trying to gauge his reaction to Karessa. His cheeks were red, but I couldn't tell if it was from embarrassment or attraction. Karessa's body language was easy to read. A wave of jealousy washed over me.

"I'm going back to my room—"

"You don't need to rush off, El," Aaron interrupted.

"No, really. I've got that thing with Silas anyway. You two have a good night."

Karessa looked as if I'd just presented her with a bar of solid gold. The jealousy grew stronger.

Without caring what Tess would think, I took off my heels and made my way through the crowded room with bare feet.

When I entered the corridor that led to my bedroom, I saw Amelia standing halfway down it with her back to me and a black note in her hand. I wondered what she was doing there. Amelia's room was in a different hall.

I cleared my throat and she whirled, dropping the note to her side. I braced myself for another verbal assault, but she only stammered and then marched off with a small "hmph," tossing her hair over her shoulder as she went.

That was strange.

Once inside my room, I pulled out the journal and sat on the edge of my bed. To distract myself from thoughts of Aaron and Karessa, I read and waited for Silas. I didn't get far before there was a knock on my door.

"Come in!" I called.

Silas stepped in. "May I pull up a chair?" he asked.

"Of course."

Silas flicked his wrist and the wooden chair from the writing desk swooped over to the side of the bed. "Have you enjoyed what you've read so far?"

He held out his hand for the journal. With some hesitation, I handed it over. He flipped through the pages while I spoke.

"It's been incredible. I spent the morning trying to strengthen my connection with pygsmies so I can use their senses, like Eva describes. It didn't go too well." I thought of Aaron crashing onto the lean-to and frowned.

"My understanding of what it takes to be a whisperer is limited to what I've read in this journal, but there seems to be one common thread among the group of you: strength. My great-grandmother had it in spades. I believe you do too."

Silas's compliment made me blush. "Thank you."

"How is your wrist?"

"So you did know the journal would attack me. A warning would have been nice." I pulled up the sleeve of my jacket and held out my forearm.

Silas's eyes grew wide. "That's very unique. The journal must have recognized you as a whisperer. This is all I've got. It's been the same for every member of my family." He held out his right wrist. The veins were raised, red, and irritated.

"Does it hurt?" I asked.

"Not terribly. It was beginning to burn after I learned about you but hadn't yet passed on the record. It's been better since giving it to you. I rather hoped it might go away entirely, but it appears I'm stuck with it."

"Sorry," I said. "So you had something to discuss?"

"Yes, I suppose I should get on with it. You need to get plenty of rest tonight, so I won't be long. I wondered if you might translate something for me. There are a few lines written in pygsmish near the end of Eva's record. I've always wondered what they say, but I've never been able to read it. I kept telling myself I should wait to ask you, but my curiosity got the best of me." He gave a crooked smile, then flipped to the page and passed it to me.

The cream paper was worn, as if someone—or generations of someones—had spent a lot of time here. Four lines were written in black ink. Beneath them, the page was torn. I ran my fingers over the words. It was strange to see pygsmish written out. It didn't flow quite as naturally as the language did in my head.

"Can you grab me that pen over there?" I asked, motioning to the writing desk.

Silas flicked his pointer finger and the pen flew to him.

"Do you mind if I write in the margins?"

"Not at all. That would be helpful," Silas said.

My forehead scrunched as I worked to translate the lines.

Five stones, their colors bright.
Magic given for man's delight.

89

Powers protected in crystal form.
From it, Ausland's provinces born.

After I finished, I read the words aloud. "What do you think?"

"It's satisfying to finally know what it says. It's a creation poem. It's about the Matrons creating the crystals that allow us to share their magic."

"Do you know what happened to the rest of the page? It seems like there should be more."

Silas frowned. "No, it's been like that as long as I've had the record."

"I wonder why Eva wrote it in pygmish. The lines don't rhyme that way. It seems like it's intended to be read in our language."

"Strange. Sometimes I wish my great-grandmother was around to answer all my questions. Ah, well. Someday I might figure them out." Silas stood and directed the chair back to its place. "Thank you for allowing me to assuage my curiosity tonight, Laurelin. I'll let you get some rest now."

He crossed the room and I shut the door after him. Then I walked back to the journal and re-read the lines several times. Nothing about them struck me as remarkable enough to translate to pygmish. It's as if Eva wanted to keep them secret, but their message was common knowledge. The Matrons' crystals gave Ausland its magic.

I sighed. "Eva Evermore, you are quite the mystery," I said as I placed the journal on the nightstand.

Chapter Eleven

A heavy knock pounded on my door. "Laurelin, wake up!" Aaron called from the other side.

My eyes flew open. I grabbed a bathrobe off the desk chair and wrapped it around myself as I crossed the room.

When I opened the door, Aaron marched inside, wringing his hands—an odd sign of tension from him.

"What's going on?" I asked.

His blue eyes were like stone. "Tobias is dead."

"He's dead?" My voice came out an octave higher than usual. "What do you mean?"

"I mean he's dead. Gone. Finished off—"

"Okay," I held up my hand, "I get it. I just can't believe it. Do you know what happened?"

"It's not good, El." His expression was grave. "Tobias was found on his bedroom floor ... dead from a pygsmy sting."

My stomach dropped to my toes. "A pygsmy sting? Pygsmies don't just come indoors and sting people, Aaron. They're mild creatures."

"I know that. And so do the police." Aaron paused. "I'm sure you can guess who the primary suspect is."

Dread filled me. "The suspect is ... me."

Aaron nodded. "You're a whisperer who had a very public encounter with Tobias a few hours before he was killed."

"Wait, you don't think I did it, right?" I asked.

"Of course not. You're the kind of girl who would greet a kidnapper with pepper spray. But you have to admit it looks pretty bad."

"I would have no problem killing a kidnapper, thank you very much," I snapped.

Aaron grabbed the tops of my shoulders. "El, you're not seeing the problem here. Someone wants to frame you for murder, which means you're in as much trouble as Tobias."

"I think I need to sit down," I said, feeling lightheaded.

Aaron caught me as I stumbled on the way to the bed. He helped me down and then sat next to me.

I took a few deep breaths. "Well, I'd say the best place to start is to figure out who has motive to kill Tobias. There were definitely some fishy things happening last night."

"Fishy like what?"

"Well, I think Faye might have told Tobias that Silas and I are trying to cheat, probably to create trouble. And when Tobias first approached me last night, Amelia said something about how he didn't know how to take 'no' for an answer. Then later, when I was heading to bed, I saw her in this corridor, but her bedroom is in the east hallway. It's only Tobias and me on this side."

Aaron ran his hand down his face. "Remember what I said last night about keeping your cards close to your chest? I mean it even more now. Don't talk about any of this with anyone else, okay? If Amelia or Faye have something to do with this and they believe you're onto them, you're definitely next on the list."

Amelia or Faye a murderer? I didn't particularly like either of them, but murder felt like a leap. Aaron was right though. Someone was behind this, and their weapon of choice did communicate something to me. I just wasn't sure what.

"What does this mean for the Pentax? It's not being delayed, is it?" I knew I sounded horribly insensitive for asking the question, but Pippin didn't have a day to waste.

"I don't know for sure, but Ausland takes this competition very seriously. I think we should carry on with our morning schedule as if nothing has changed. At least as best as we can."

I let out a sigh of relief. "I was hoping you'd say that. What happens to Fortis? Will they send another Rook?"

"I don't know, but I'm sure we'll find out soon. Get dressed. After breakfast, you have a three hour training session with me, then you get an hour with Tess to prepare for your media interview."

I groaned. "I was dreading the interview enough without being a suspected murderer while I gave it. Not even Tess will be able to save this train wreck."

Aaron grimaced. "You'll think of something. You always do."

Apparently, my suitcase was fresh out of clothes that said, *I'm not a murderer*, because I couldn't find anything to wear. In the end, I settled for tan shorts and a white T-shirt. As I changed, my mind played over the events last night in slow motion, trying to piece it all together. Silas, Arthur, and Faye at the table. Faye's confrontation with me. Owen's eagerness to keep me occupied. Amelia's jealousy and that strange note in her hands. Somehow, it was all connected.

The halls and common area buzzed with conspiracy as I walked toward the cafeteria. Everyone stopped and stared at me as I walked by, then resumed their gossip when my back was to them.

When I entered the cafeteria, Faye and her trainer were the only ones there. Faye held a book in one hand as she shoveled food into her mouth with the other, watching me the whole time.

Eager to sit down, I walked briskly toward the serving bar

and put some plain oatmeal on my tray, a cup of fruit, and a handful of nuts.

I sat alone at a corner table, but I wasn't left undisturbed for long. Amelia came into the room with her muscular trainer at her side. Immediately, her fiery eyes zeroed in on me.

"Let's see, we already knew you were selfish, power-hungry, and a flirt." She ticked the words off on her manicured fingers. "But even I was surprised murderer was next. I don't know what Tobias found out about you, but you won't get away with cheating. Or murder."

"I haven't killed anybody, Amelia. Obviously, someone's trying to frame me."

"That excuse might work in other cases, but there's only one person who could force a pygsmy to kill and that's you."

Heat flooded my cheeks. "Well perhaps when the police get around to questioning me, I'll have to mention that I saw you near Tobias's bedroom last night."

Aaron would kill me if he knew what I said. But seeing the fear flash through her eyes was worth it.

Amelia scoffed. "Come on, Leo. Let's eat before I completely lose my appetite."

My stomach was clenched so tight I had no room for the flavorless oatmeal. I left my dirty tray at the table and decided to head for the training room. At the door, I was stopped by an officer who looked like he'd never said no to a cookie in his life.

"Laurelin Moore?" he asked.

"Yes, that's me."

"I'm officer Jackson. I need to ask you a few questions. Please follow me."

I bit my lip. "Umm, I think I'd like to speak to Duke Evermore first."

"You'll come now. That's an order."

The entire way down the hall, I glanced over my shoulder, hoping to catch sight of Silas, Aaron, Tess, or even Sofia—any familiar, friendly face that might help me. I found no one.

Officer Jackson opened the door to a room that had stone walls on all sides. The space was empty except for two black chairs that were placed across from each other. He took the chair facing the door and I sat in the other.

The officer prepared his notebook, then looked at me for a drawn-out moment, as if he hoped *guilty* would be scribbled across my face. Finally, he asked, "What was your relationship with Tobias Liang of Fortis?"

I forced myself to stop spinning the lifestone ring on my hand and cleared my throat. "We were both chosen as Rooks to compete in the Pentax. I didn't know him personally."

"Is that so? Several individuals have mentioned that Tobias confronted you at the party last night. They say he accused you of cheating. What was he referring to?"

"I don't know. He was very drunk, and I'm not sure he knew what he was saying. I haven't cheated, and I don't intend to either."

The officer studied me. The only sound was of him breathing deeply, in and out, while I waited for him to say more.

"Tobias Liang was found dead this morning. The cause of death has been determined to be a pygsmy sting. Not only was pygruim found in his system, there was a burn mark around the sight of injection, consistent with a direct sting from a mystic. There are no documented incidents of pygsmies entering human dwelling spaces to kill. You are a known pygsmy whisperer. Do you have an explanation for this coincidence?"

I swallowed and reminded myself to breathe normally. "It would be incredibly stupid of me to kill someone in a way that so directly points to myself, wouldn't you say, Officer Jackson? More likely, someone is trying to draw attention to me in order to keep themselves out of the spotlight. You're wasting your time. I don't know Tobias, and I don't know why someone would want to kill him."

Officer Jackson let the silence sit again, hoping it would pressure me into saying something else. I kept my mouth shut.

"Very well, Ms. Moore. We know where to find you if we have more questions. You may leave."

———

"What took you so long?" Aaron asked as I ran into our training room.

Between the police interrogation and my jog, my heart was racing. I put my hands on my knees and breathed. "Sorry, an officer pulled me in for questioning."

Aaron's expression changed from one of annoyance to concern. "How did it go?"

"It was intimidating. The officer was looking for answers, but I had none."

"That's good. Keep communication to a minimum. You never know what kind of stunt those guys will try to pull."

"You really have an issue with authority, don't you?"

"Never liked cops before, and I'm not about to start. Now, it's time for us to focus. I'm flying with a pygsmy before we leave today."

I felt exhausted just thinking about it. "We can give it a try, but I really think my time will be better spent trying to use a pygsmy's senses. I had more success with that yesterday, and during the competition, the chances of needing to fly someone alongside me are slim."

"I hate when you're right. Okay, fair enough. What do you need from me?"

"Silence, mostly."

"And here I thought you asked me to be your trainer for my expertise. Turns out I came along to eat rabbit food and bake in the sun."

"And flirt with Karessa," I added.

Aaron's face turned red. He held his hands up in surrender. "I'm shutting up—going to my corner. I'll be relaxing in that sweltering patch of dirt if you need me."

96

It was harder to calm my emotions with Aaron around. Something about him brought out a nervous energy in me. I took several deep breaths of air and filled my mind with thoughts of rain storms, pine trees, and Lingua's purple mountains. When I felt appropriately relaxed, I opened my mind to the pygsmies. Close by, I felt Sun Petal, but I pushed farther out, testing my limits. The pygsmies' sparks of consciousness hit me with more speed and force than usual, each one like a flick to the forehead. I found myself flinching against the bright spots of light, but I kept going, reaching out into the sea of darkness.

A few pygsmies seemed to call to me, their light shining brighter than the others, but the strongest draw was backward—toward Sun Petal. It did make the most sense to continue working with the pygsmy I'd already built some connection with.

I pinched Sun Petal's spark and chanted, *Lyrun rach min baum*, pulling her toward me.

Sun Petal's thoughts became clearer as she drew closer. *Yippee!* she said as she zoomed into the practice arena. *Do we get to fly today?*

I laughed. *Maybe in a while. Has Stork recovered from the shock of yesterday?*

Sun Petal reached up with one of her feet and scratched her long nose. *I'm not sure. He wouldn't speak to me this morning.*

I'll guess that means no. I felt bad to have created such a negative memory as Stork's first human interaction.

Pygsmies are resilient. He'll get over it soon enough, Sun Petal said.

I hope so. And how are you? Did you have a good night?

Sun Petal did a backflip. *A better night than you, I'd say.*

How do you know? I asked, feeling tense.

I've been keeping tabs on you, of course. You're interesting. Humans have such strange traditions. Like that guy, for instance. Sun Petal pointed a tendril at Aaron. *It's obvious you like him. If you were a pygsmy and you wanted to form a clan with him, you'd have said so already. Instead, you keep batting your eyes at him.*

I do not bat my eyes at Aaron.

You do. It's like you think your eyelashes are fans and he's overheating in the desert. Sun Petal flapped her wings in imitation of me and giggled.

My face burned red. *Can we talk about something else?*

Sun Petal did a few more flips before saying, *Sure. What do you want to do today?*

Well, I was hoping I might try something with you. The last whisperer said she was able to use a pygsmy's senses—you know, see what they see, hear what they hear. If I can learn how to do that, I think it would help me a lot in the Pentax.

Sounds awfully intrusive, she said.

You don't have to do it if you don't want to.

Sun Petal zipped around my head a few times. *I suppose there's no harm in trying. Who knows? Maybe I'll be able to do the same to you.*

The thought made me squirm. I suppose if I was expecting Sun Petal to do it for me, I'd have to be okay with the reverse.

Okay, Sun Petal. You go ahead and fly but stay nearby. I'll be working on putting my mind in sync with yours. I guess I'll know it works when I see something other than the practice arena.

You're a little crazy, you know, Sun Petal said as she zoomed away.

I know, I thought, mostly to myself.

I kept a tight hold on Sun Petal, following her vibrant spark of energy as she flew. I could feel the tenor of her thoughts, just like I could any pygsmy that was nearby. But that was the end of it. I didn't know how to force myself deeper into Sun Petal's head. I danced around the edges of her consciousness but couldn't find an opening.

My forearm burned. This time, it didn't shock me—it excited me. More instructions.

The pygsmy marking on my arm was gone, and purple words took its place.

You can't force your way in. Turn off your own mind and let the pygsmy guide you.

Turn off my mind. Okay. I could do that, right? Just switch it off. Easy peasy.

Right now.

Go ahead and power down, brain. It's your day off.

"You okay, El?" Aaron asked.

I waved him off. "Fine, yeah," I mumbled.

For a moment, I let go of Sun Petal and breathed deeply. I pictured Pippin and allowed myself to get lost in his freckles. I thought of long days lying in the grass as we counted the glimmer of pygsmies as they fluttered by.

With a smile on my lips, I opened my mind again and quickly found Sun Petal. I imagined how it would be to soar, flip, and twirl through the air. I could feel Sun Petal's body moving in the sky, the wind poignant on the tip of her long nose, then spilling over onto her cheeks and to her wings. A laugh of exhilaration escaped me.

For a second, my vision was black. Then it burst open with the vibrant green of Creo's forests. The trees formed a mossy blanket beneath my tiny body as I rotated in the air, feeling the wind slip over me. Though I flew at incredible speed, my eyes were sharp, catching all the small details, like a ladybug on a leaf below, or a squirrel, hopping from branch to branch, an acorn in one paw.

I'm doing it, Sun Petal. I can see through your mind, I said.

Hey, that was pretty fast! And speaking of speed, what do you think of mine? Sun Petal sped up, dropping low to weave in and out of trees, missing branches by millimeters.

I laughed. *Very impressive. And nauseating.*

"How are you, Laurelin?"

Abruptly, I was yanked from Sun Petal's mind.

Silas entered the room with Tess at his side.

Irritation burned hot inside me. "I'm fine," I grumbled.

Silas's brow furrowed. "There's no need to be rude. What is going on here anyway?" He looked toward Aaron, who hurried to his feet. "Proving yourself useful, I hope, Mr. Gray. It's never too late to replace Laurelin's trainer."

"He's been very helpful, thank you very much. We have a solid understanding going into the competition tomorrow. There's no need to worry about me," I said.

"Very well. I came to inform you of some developments. I'm sure you're aware of what happened to poor Tobias."

I grew tense. Being in Sun Petal's mind had allowed me to forget the disaster happening at the castle for a while. "Yes, I heard. It's tragic."

"Indeed, it is. The judges and I had a meeting, and we've decided it is in the kingdom's best interest for the Pentax to continue as planned. Ausland has never allowed the competition to be derailed before, even in times of war or natural disaster. We want to uphold that tradition now." Silas's dark eyes were hard, not revealing his feelings about the events.

I knew I was wrong to feel so much relief. "That's good news."

"Arthur says Tobias's brother, Crede, is prepared to take his place as Rook. He's a fifteen-year-old boy with the gift of strength. He'll arrive with enough time to give his interview this afternoon. As you can imagine, it's going to be a difficult time for him. And considering the circumstances, I would suggest you give him space. I doubt he will want to hear from the girl his family believes is responsible for Tobias's death."

I raised my eyebrows. "This ought to be exciting if nothing else. Thank you for the info. I'm glad to hear we're still on schedule."

"Almost on schedule. You were originally planned to be the final interview of the day, but they've swapped Lingua and Fortis to give Crede some extra time to get here. You're on in forty-five minutes."

My eyes felt like they'd pop out of my skull. "Forty-five minutes?"

"Tess, I'll let you take over from here." Silas bowed and walked to the door.

"This is so exciting!" Tess clapped her hands together. "And it's never been more important for you to nail your interview. We have a lot of work to do. Starting with a shower." Tess scrunched her nose as she looked at my sweaty face.

"Oh, Aaron," Silas poked his head back into the room. "I've arranged to have you join Laurelin for the interview. I think it will be best for her to have a buffer. We all know she's innocent, but the media never passes up an opportunity to stir up drama."

"Uh—I—Umm, okay. I don't think I'll be any good at it, but I can give it a try." Aaron turned to me, panicked.

I shrugged one shoulder. "Don't look at me. We're in the same boat."

"And it's taking on water fast," Aaron said, shaking his head.

Chapter Twelve

Tess worked her magic and spun me another incredible dress. This one was designed to convey innocence. The fabric was shimmery white with a faint purple undertone beneath the top layers of the dress. Where the gown gathered at the waist, purple detailing mimicked the spread of a pygsmy wing, splashing across my right side. The neckline was high and wide, following the line of my collarbones. It was a comfortable length, ending at my knee. The only part of the outfit I wasn't thrilled about was the heels, but I knew they were inevitable when Tess was in charge.

The curtain of the dressing room rustled behind me. In the mirror, I saw Aaron emerge, and my jaw dropped. He wore a sharp black tux with a black bowtie and shiny shoes. His tan face was clean-shaven, and his brown curls were styled with gel.

"Can you help me with these cufflinks?" he asked, holding out a pair of purple and gold ones.

My mouth snapped shut. "Sure," I said. My fingers were trembling embarrassingly, so I concentrated on holding them steady as I threaded the tack through his sleeve.

"I never thought I'd see the day authority would force you into a tux," I teased, avoiding his eyes.

"That makes two of us." Aaron grabbed at the neck of his white shirt and pulled a face.

I laughed. "Well, you look great." My eyes flashed up to meet his.

"If that's what you think, then I guess it's worth it." He winked, and my pulse increased. "It doesn't matter what I look like, though. With you next to me, no one will be paying attention."

I snorted. "Probably, but only because they think I'm a murderer. They'll wonder how you dare to sit by me."

I finished the last cufflink. Gently, Aaron took both my hands in his. I could hear my pulse hammering in my ears.

He chuckled. "Well, there is that to consider. But it's not what I meant. You look beautiful, Laurelin." His blue eyes burned with sincerity, twisting my stomach in strange ways.

"Okay," Tess called loudly as she re-entered the room. "Time to get you two coached up."

Aaron gave a half smile and dropped my hands. I stood still for a moment, trying to make sense of what had just happened. It felt distinctly like something had shifted between us, from friends to something new. Aaron helped Tess pull a few chairs into the center of the room. He looked up at me and smiled.

After a few deep breaths, I joined them, taking the chair next to Aaron and across from Tess. She started speaking, but I was distracted by the way my knee touched Aaron's as we sat close together. I noted the way that simple touch put butterflies in my stomach.

"Laurelin?" Tess's sharp voice asked. "Are you listening?"

My head snapped up. "Sorry, what did you say?"

I glanced at Aaron for a moment. He smiled knowingly. Was he feeling this too?

"I asked if you'd given any thought to your key message points," Tess said through tight lips.

"Er, message points?"

She let out a sigh. "The stuff you want people to know about you. Why you're competing in the Pentax, why you'd make a good queen, how you can use your gift for good. Those are message points. You want to direct the conversation rather than allowing the interviewer to control you."

I didn't know how to answer any of those questions. All I knew for sure was that I couldn't tell the truth. No matter how well I handled the competition, the judges wouldn't give me any points if they knew I didn't want to be queen. The Pentax wasn't about the wish. For most people, that was nothing more than a side note. Most winners used it to grant themselves wealth or additional magic. A few rulers used their wish to improve life for the general population, but that was rare. All I wanted to do was save my brother.

Tess stared at me, waiting for an answer.

"I'll have to think about that," I said.

"You better think fast. You'll be on live television in fifteen minutes. It's always safe to talk about wanting to unite the provinces. Make sure you don't indicate that you'd treat Lingua with any preference."

"But every king or queen favors their province."

"That's not the point, Laurelin. It doesn't matter what you actually do once you are queen. It's about saying the right stuff in the interview."

"Right. Politics," I sighed.

"You could talk about wanting to share elixir with people in need or using it to bolster the powers of the guard when the kingdom faces external threats."

I nodded. Tess had no idea what went into obtaining elixir, let alone deciding who deserved to receive it and who did not, but I couldn't expect her to. It was the burden of a whisperer. She'd never understand.

"Okay, next pointer. If a tough or uncomfortable question is asked, redirect the conversation. You can try answering the question with a question of your own, or you can pick a part of the question that's easy to answer and address that, or you can answer the question you wish you were asked." Tess leaned forward in her chair. "The interviewer can ask whatever they want, but you don't have to answer anything. You control the conversation, okay? And the most important thing to remember is to smile. People will relate best to you if you can relax and be yourself."

"So lie? About everything? But act natural."

"It's not lying, Laurelin. It's called being savvy. Now let's get you to the stage."

"Ready or not," Aaron sighed.

The interview was happening in the stadium where the Presentation of Powers had been. A heavy, black curtain closed off half the stage, and a pretty blonde woman in a blue dress sat on a chair with her legs crossed in front of it. A daunting camera loomed behind her, pointed at the two chairs across from where she sat.

"Come in, come in," the woman called when she saw us at the mouth of the low tunnel. "I'm Stacey Saunders. It's a pleasure to meet you, Laurelin. And you ..." she trailed off, looking at Aaron.

"This is my trainer, Aaron Gray."

"Ah yes, Duke Evermore let me know he'd be joining you. That's different from the norm, but everything about today has been different, hasn't it?" Her eyes sparkled with the thrill of the gossip. I'd guess a media woman like herself couldn't dream of better circumstances than a Rook being murdered the day before competition. "Please, have a seat."

I climbed into one of the tall, uncomfortable chairs and fidgeted with my ring.

"We're live in three, two, one," a man said from behind the camera.

Stacey straightened in her chair. "Welcome back for our fourth interview of the day. I'm joined by Lingua's Rook, Laurelin Moore, and her trainer, Aaron Gray. We have so much to discuss in this interview, so I'll jump right in.

Janilise Lloyd

"Laurelin, can you shed any light on what happened the night of the Presentation of Powers? A woman accused you of being unwilling to share your gift to help others. That's obviously not a quality Ausland wants in their queen. The public has expressed concern. Can you explain yourself?"

I stared into the lens of the camera, which reminded me of a dragon's eye. My mouth was dry, like I'd swallowed a handful of sand. "I ... I ..." The right words wouldn't come out. Blood rushed to my face.

Aaron jumped in. "I met Laurelin about four years ago, and I've known she's a whisperer for most of that time. One night, when I first suspected her ability, I followed her, wondering if she might prove my suspicions right."

I watched Aaron, curious where he was going with this. Whether it was a true story he was sharing or something he was making up, I wasn't sure.

"She left me with some elixir for a ... need I had."

He smiled at me and I mashed my lips together to keep from laughing. I suppose his "need" on the black market would count under a very loose definition.

"But I knew she had more. That night, I decided to follow her, and I learned a lot about Laurelin Moore. She stopped at the homes of nine families, leaving each of them with vials of elixir. No note, no explanations, and no desire for credit. I didn't recognize most of the places she stopped, except for one. It was the home of a mother with sick twin babies. A few days later, I intentionally bumped into that woman and asked her about her girls. She told me they'd been healed. She didn't tell me how, of course, but I knew it was Laurelin."

I blushed at Aaron's flattery.

"The woman who spoke up last night is going through something terrible. I can't imagine how it must be to lose the one you love. The Matrons know I couldn't handle it." He smiled crookedly at me. "Laurelin has been given an incredible gift, but it's not something that can cure every ailment in Ausland, and it

106

would be wrong of any of us to assume that's her responsibility. I know Laurelin. I know she's a good person—good to the core. I'm confident she'll always help when she can, whether as queen or otherwise."

The feelings I'd been having for Aaron doubled in that moment. I'd never received such a sincere compliment, and somehow, it gave me the confidence I needed to get through the interview.

"Well, I don't think Aaron could have been kinder if you'd paid him to be." Stacey laughed, but I didn't miss her insinuation.

"Aaron has given me too much credit, but he is right about one thing. I do want to help." I bit my cheek and stared at the black curtain for a moment, gathering my thoughts. "I'm trying to work through the best way to go about that. I'm sorry for that sweet woman and her husband. Seeing her heartbreak hit home in a very personal way."

Stacey kept a polite smile on her face, but her eyes betrayed her dissatisfaction with the direction the topic had taken. She pivoted, trying to stir up controversy. "You are the only Rook who is not from a noble family. Despite that, do you believe you have the right skills to be successful as queen?"

"I don't believe being a good ruler is about knowing the right way to dress, talk, eat, or socialize. I may not have perfect manners. I may not be the best party planner, and I would absolutely embarrass myself if I tried to waltz at a ball. But I do know what it's like to work hard for every penny. I know how it feels to be judged because of where I live. I know what it means to fight for family. These are situations that the majority of people experience at some point in life. In the end, I think not being part of the nobility would make me a better leader of Ausland."

Stacey guffawed. "You must not be afraid of making enemies among your competition. That's a bold claim to make."

I shrugged. "I didn't come here to make friends."

"Perhaps you made enemies faster than you expected." Her eyes sparkled with anticipation. "Tobias Liang was found dead this morning. A pygsmy sting was the cause of death. As the only whisperer in Ausland, people are naturally suspicious that you are responsible. Did you kill him?"

I knew this question was coming. Still, the pressure of being in front of the camera had my mind in a scrambled mess. "I—I did not, and I express my condolences to his family."

"Sources tell me you had an argument with Tobias last night. Is that true?"

"You don't have to answer her," Aaron mumbled.

I ignored him, knowing it was best to get the truth out in the open. "Tobias confronted me at the opening social and accused me of cheating. The encounter was very brief, and I don't have any idea what he was referencing. I haven't cheated to get to this point and I won't cheat going forward."

"Well, Laurelin. You've certainly given our audience a lot to think about. Thank you for joining me today."

"It was our pleasure," Aaron lied, rushing us off stage before Stacey or anyone else had a chance to pull us back for more questions.

Tess waited for us behind the stage curtains. Overall, I was feeling okay about how things had gone until I saw her face. The corners of her lips twisted downward, and her eyes were balls of fire.

"Did you not listen to anything I said before the interview?" Tess hissed.

"I listened. I thought it was pretty good."

"The only good part was Aaron's story at the beginning. We should have had him do all the talking." Tess pressed her hands over her eyes. "This is a disaster."

"What did I do wrong?" I asked.

"Let's review, shall we? I told you to think of message points. You had none. I told you to control the conversation. You let her ask all the wrong questions. I told you when a tough question was asked that you didn't have to answer. You spilled the beans. I should have scheduled the entire morning for interview prep. Even though you're a commoner, I didn't realize you were going to be so inept."

"You're going a little overboard on the drama, Tess," Aaron spoke up. "It wasn't that bad. I'm sure a lot of people will appreciate El's honesty."

"The wrong people, Aaron. It doesn't matter what the average folks think of Laurelin. They don't control the competition or the media. She gave legitimacy to the gossip surrounding Tobias's death by confirming an altercation with him, she brought up the possibility of cheating, which wasn't a widely discussed topic before, and she offended the entire nobility—AKA the judges who will be scoring her. I don't know how I'm going to face Silas. He's going to be furious." She threw her hands into the air and stormed off, mumbling as she went.

I stared after her in shock.

"Is it awful of me to be glad she's mad at you instead of me?" Aaron asked out of the side of his mouth.

Tears prickled at my eyes for a moment, but instead, a laugh burst out of me. Suddenly, the whole debacle didn't feel so bad. Sure, Tess made a good point. I appealed to the wrong crowd. But looking back, I couldn't have handled it any other way. I spoke the truth. Now I just had to trust that truth wins out, like Mom and Dad always said.

"Eh, she'll get over it," I said. "I'm just glad it's done. Now I can focus on preparing for tomorrow."

Through a gap in the curtains, I saw Arthur walking toward the stage with a boy who looked like a miniature Tobias, except for his hairstyle. Crede had long black hair gathered into a bun at the base of his neck. He walked with his hands behind his back, his eyes fixed on the floor.

Though I knew I was innocent of any crime against Tobias, a surge of guilt washed over me. For some reason I couldn't explain, I felt responsible for his death. The way he was killed seemed to send a message directly to me, like the murderer was telling me it was my fault.

As he took the stage, Crede saw me through the gap. His eyes narrowed, shifting from grief to anger. "What is she doing here?" he asked Arthur.

Arthur wrapped his arm around Crede, turning him from me. "Will someone please ask Miss Moore to vacate the stage?"

"Come on, El. Let's go," Aaron said.

Two members of the broadcast team walked toward us. Aaron pulled me through one of the low tunnels before they could reach us.

"I feel awful for him," I said as we walked toward our bedrooms.

"Me too. Such an unexpected way to lose a brother. One minute, he's in the running to be king, and the next he's gone. But it's not your fault, El. Someone is responsible, but it isn't you. Remember that."

I nodded. "I'll try."

We walked in silence for a moment before I said, "Tell me the truth. Did you make up that story about the elixir? Or did you really follow me home one night? Because if you did, that's kind of creepy."

Aaron's face turned red. He undid his black bowtie and the top button of his shirt. "Yes, I followed you, but I promise it was only the one time. You have to understand, you came into my life so out-of-the-blue. You were like a shooting star blazing across a pitch-black sky. I'd only been a hawk on the market for eight months, and it was tough going for a fourteen-year-old. The people I dealt with were thieves, cheats, and sometimes worse. I was drowning in dishonesty, and I felt like I couldn't escape."

"Why did you become a hawk if you didn't like it?" I interrupted. "I thought you loved what you do—the freedom it gives you."

"Well, I like it now, but that's because I know how to handle all the cheats. Plus, I've made a few decent contacts, and that helps. But in the beginning, I got into it out of necessity. My dad hadn't been in the picture for a long time, and my mom dealt with drug addiction since before I was born. She was sort of a hawk, only she rarely had anything to offer, and she always gave up anything good for drugs. I became a hawk because it was the only way I could survive after she died. I never went to school like a regular kid. I didn't know what a normal life was like."

I'd never heard Aaron speak a word about his parents, which had been enough for me to assume it wasn't a happy story. But I always thought he wanted to be a hawk because his gift was perfect for it. I didn't realize it was the life he fell into out of desperation.

"What happened to your mom?"

"She overdosed. I tell myself it was bound to happen." He shrugged, but I could see the pain in his eyes. "This is all I have left of her now."

He held out a necklace from under his shirt. The charm was a yellow moon connected to a blue star. I'd seen the thin, black band around his neck many times, but I never knew the significance of it.

"I'm sorry," I whispered. "That's awful."

"Yes, it was, and it taught me to stay far away from all that stuff. I'm still a hawk, but I never deal with drugs, and that's thanks to you."

"Me?" I asked. "How did I help?"

We stopped in front of my bedroom door.

"I survived because of you. No one trusted me until I had your pygsmy elixir. Suddenly, I was one of the most sought-after hawks in Ausland."

Selling elixir to Aaron had always bothered me some. I knew he was different than the other hawks, but still, it felt greedy. Now I understood that he and I were a lot the same. I sold it because my family needed the money to get by. Aaron was just a kid forced to grow up too soon, doing the best he could.

"I followed you because you made me curious. I wanted to know how you had such a steady supply of elixir, and I was even more curious why you were so different from everyone else I dealt with. When I saw you giving elixir freely, without any return or recognition, it gave me hope. No one ever reached out to help just because. No one gave without wanting something in return. No one except you."

"Aaron, that might be the saddest story I've ever heard. I'm sorry you never had family or friends you could count on."

Aaron reached up and tucked a lock of hair behind my ear. A corner of his mouth turned up in a smile. He rested his hand on my shoulder and stroked my cheek. My heart pounded in my chest.

"I wish my childhood had been different. I wish my mother had been better—for both of us. But I'll never regret meeting you because of it."

"Aaron, I—"

"I know," he cut me off. "You need to focus on the Pentax, and I want to help. I'll meet you in the training room in half an hour, and I promise I'll be on my best behavior." He leaned in and kissed my forehead. "I'll see you soon, El."

Wordlessly, I watched as he walked away.

My head was dizzy. My heart was like pudding. And I wasn't sure my arms were attached to my body anymore. There were at least a dozen reasons I should resist everything I was feeling. But for one moment, I allowed my mind to fill with thoughts of Aaron.

Chapter Thirteen

I stood in my starting place, moments from the beginning of the first round of the Pentax. A dark, scratchy fabric was tied securely over my eyes. My body shook with each beat of the deep, bass drums that surrounded me. Beyond that, I could hear birds chirping and monkeys grunting. The air was humid and smelled like moss. Near me, I could hear human breathing.

I knew I wasn't supposed to see where I was, but Sun Petal had followed me here. I could feel the spastic pygsmy zipping through the air above us. Just a smidge more concentration and I could slip into her mind and see for myself ... I wasn't great at the skill yet, but I had improved in my last training session with Aaron.

I tugged on the collar of my purple flannel shirt and wondered why Tess had chosen to dress me in such thick material. I readjusted the straps of the bag on my back and tried to be patient, fighting the urge to cheat.

Suddenly the drums stopped playing, and my heart stopped along with them.

Saundra Garcia's voice came through a speaker. "Welcome to Creo. Today, we start our search for a suitable replacement for my dear sister, Queen Isadora. She was generous, brave, and honest in all she did. The judges are seeking similar qualities, and they will incorporate that into their scores." She paused. "Rooks, you may remove your blindfolds."

I stood on a flat, purple stone at the bottom of a round outdoor stadium in the heart of Creo's jungle. The stadium was much smaller than the one they used for the Presentation of Powers, but it was packed with people who sat shoulder-to-shoulder. In front of me, on the second row of stone benches, Aaron was next to Tess. He was on the edge of his seat, his leg bouncing up and down. On his right side, there was an arch that was repeated five times around the stadium, each adorned with a different province's flag. The other Rooks were spread out in a circle behind me, facing their own tunnel entrances. Owen caught my eye and gave me a stiff nod. Then Amelia glared at me.

Saundra's face was broadcast onto a large screen at the top of the stadium. "Deep inside Agrasa Cavern, a beast is loose. Our Rooks are to navigate the obstacles within the cave network and find the beast. They must subdue the creature while striving to keep themselves and their fellow competitors safe. Each Rook is allowed to use the materials found in their black bag and any advantage their magical gift affords.

"Now," Saundra rubbed her hands together in anticipation. "The first round of the Pentax will begin in three ... two ... one ..."

A piercing beep rang through the stadium. I kissed Pippin's lifestone, then ran toward my tunnel entrance, throwing one last look at Aaron as I passed. His expression was stoic, and he was gripping his knees.

"You can do this, El!" he shouted as I ran by.

First, I took off my pack and rifled through its contents. There was a knife with a five-inch blade, a skein of rope, a flashlight, a bow, and a quiver with ten arrows.

I slung the bag over my shoulder and pushed forward. A

drone followed close behind, broadcasting my movements to the watching audience. The tunnel was dark, but flower lights had been placed sporadically along the walls, allowing me to see enough of the rocky sides to navigate the first twists and turns. Soon, I smelled sulfur in the air, and the musical sounds of water tumbling over rocks reached my ears.

The noise and smell grew stronger as I wound through more twists of the cave floor. Mist prickled my face, and then I saw the edge of the wide stream. The water moved swiftly, sending white rapids into the air as it collided with shark tooth rocks jutting upward. I wasn't a very strong swimmer, and the speed of the current scared me. I dipped my hand into the water, testing out its temperature. I was surprised when my vision turned completely black. Startled, I withdrew my hand and my vision returned. I breathed a sigh of relief.

Okay, so swimming across the stream was a bad idea. I thought about the other Rooks. Owen already had the advantage competing at home, and with his gifts, he could make his own tunnels to navigate the cave or create a bird to soar past all of it.

But he wasn't the only one who could fly.

Through my thoughts, I searched for a pygsmy and found Sun Petal, of course.

Would you like to help me? I asked in pygsmish.

I was hoping you'd ask, Sun Petal said as she zoomed toward me. Almost instantly, the pygsmy hovered in front of me, her green tendrils flowing, waiting to help.

Do you understand that today is very serious? I asked. *It could be dangerous.*

Absolutely. Sun Petal gave a salute with one of her tendrils, then giggled. *That's something a human would do, right?*

I was concerned Sun Petal didn't know the meaning of the word serious. Still, I'd much rather work with a pygsmy who already trusted me. *Will you get me across the stream?*

Probably to show she could be somber, Sun Petal said nothing and immediately lifted me into the air.

"Wahoo!" I yelled as we soared over the rushing stream and my eyesight remained.

Will you take me farther? I'll be much faster flying than on foot.

You know me. I'll never pass up a chance for a good flight, Sun Petal said, pushing forward.

My hopes for easily soaring through the caves came to a grinding halt as the rocky space narrowed into a hole so minuscule I'd have to army-crawl through it.

Put me down, please, I said.

Sun Petal released me. As I got down on my stomach, she said, *Can I come too? I promise to be nothing but helpful.*

Sure, but get in my bag. You'll be safer there. I don't know what's ahead. I opened the latch and Sun Petal hopped inside, turning the inside a glowing gold.

Smothering the overwhelming sense of claustrophobia, I got on my hands and knees and stuffed myself into the rocky hole. A jagged piece of rock snagged my calf, cutting through my jeans to my skin. I ignored the trickle of blood and continued forward. Soon, the space became so narrow I had to remove my pack and shove it one pace ahead of me, then drag my body using my elbows and toes. The entire time, I kept Pippin's face in my mind. It was the only thing that kept panic from crushing me.

Finally, the tunnel began to widen until I was able to crawl and eventually stand. But as I walked out of the tube, the sight that met me made me crave the safety of the tunnel.

A twenty-foot snake with black scales and a red diamond on its head was wrapped around a stalagmite only a few steps in front of me. It unhinged its jaws and hissed, spraying me with spit and venom. Its fangs were inches from my face. I screamed and jumped back. Beyond it, the cavern floor was littered with garter snakes, some even larger than the one in front of me. There were so many hissing at once, it sounded like air leaked out of a hundred punctured tires. The only break in the sound was the chilling rattle of the diamondbacks.

I had told myself I could do anything for Pippin, but could I really cross fifty feet of snake-strewn floor? Somehow, there were snakes hanging from the stalactites above the floor as well, so flying wasn't even an option.

I didn't have long to think. The red and black snake snapped at me again, and the entire floor seemed to be slithering toward me. I backed up until I was almost pressed against the stone wall, my heart racing.

Then I remembered. Snakes didn't move in unison, and they had a distinct smell. But the cavern didn't have the cloying scent of garter snakes, or a rattler's musky odor.

Aaron had told me that illusionists couldn't imitate smell. Only sight, sound, and touch.

A diamondback coiled inches from my leg. Fighting every instinct to run, I slung the bag from my back but before I could pull out Sun Petal, the snake struck, its fangs sinking into my flesh. I screamed from the pain of it.

If this was an illusion, it was a darn good one. The fire from the venom spread up my leg.

Sun Petal, fly with me, I begged.

Sun Petal wrapped her tendrils around me and lifted me in the air. The rattler came with us, its teeth still buried in my flesh. I kicked my leg until it released and fell onto a pile of writhing snakes below us.

With every ounce of discipline I'd gained during my training, I worked to calm my mind. Slowly, the hissing of the snakes began to fade into the background as I focused on a memory of Pippin beating me at chess, his face glowing with triumph.

The memory calmed me enough to allow me to shift my mind to Sun Petal's. Again, I felt the exultation of flying. First Sun Petal's wings became my own, and then her vision was mine. Just like I hoped, the illusions had no effect on the pygsmy. Relief tore through me as I saw the cave as it really was—empty except for the dripping stalactites and bubbling stalagmites. The pain from the snake bite was also gone.

Let's move on, I told Sun Petal, keeping myself firmly in her mind instead of my own.

Sun Petal shot across the wide cavern, dipping as we reached the chamber that would let us out. It was a tall but narrow tunnel. As we neared the end of it, Sun Petal's mind froze with fear.

What is it? I asked.

She responded with one word: *scrawl.*

I should have seen this coming. The judges would have designed the obstacles to challenge our specific gifts, and scrawl were a pygsmy's biggest predator, with bodies half the size of my own. Their beady black eyes were trained to find the pygsmy's translucent figure in flight, and with their own wings, they were more than capable of keeping up. They had sharp teeth designed to tear through the pygsmy's surprisingly tough skin—and they'd happily feed on human flesh as well.

The tunnel opened up to another wide cavern, this one twice the size of the snake pit and with fewer lighted flowers. I wouldn't have been able to see much of anything through my own eyes, but Sun Petal could see fairly well in the dark.

A second after we entered the cavern, the haunting call of a scrawl punched the air and was quickly echoed by innumerable others.

What do we do? Sun Petal asked. *Can we go back?*

I think it's too late for that. They'd follow us, and being stuck in an even smaller cavern wouldn't help.

Sun Petal let out a terrified squeak.

My blood ran cold as the stalactites and stalagmites of the cave began to ripple, but I knew rock couldn't move. The cave pulsed with leathery black as at least two hundred scrawl unfurled their wings and took flight, circling the top of the cavern, zeroing in on us.

Quick, put me down, I told Sun Petal.

As the pygsmy swooped downward, I detached the bow and arrow from the side of my pack. I had been shooting scrawl in the woods behind my house since I was six years old and could nail them blindfolded. I threaded the first arrow and took aim at a scrawl in mid-descent, its beady eyes set on me.

A heartbeat before I released the arrow, I stopped, recalling Aaron's instructions.

In Creo, all living things are considered equal to humans, so killing an animal during the competition would be a definite no-no. That even goes for animals that may attack you or pose some other threat. You would need to find a way to immobilize or contain it without causing significant harm.

No Linguan would ever consider the death of a scrawl a tragedy, but I wasn't in Lingua now. If I wanted to win this competition, I had to play by Creo's rules.

Do something! Sun Petal shrieked as the scrawl swooped down on us, its talons extended.

I snatched Sun Petal and clutched her to my chest as I dove behind a pile of flowstone. The scrawl's talon grazed my cheek, but I considered myself lucky to have avoided worse.

You'll be safer inside here, I said as I shoved Sun Petal into my bag.

Thank you. Sun Petal slumped against the side, exhausted.

Without Sun Petal's vision, I couldn't see much of anything. I heard the whoosh of leathery wings and ducked. Another scrawl let out an exasperated shriek. I dug the flashlight out of the bag and pointed it up.

It would have been better to remain blind.

The sight of so many scrawl, their eyes red with bloodlust, made my stomach heave. But there was no time for throwing up. A string of scrawl descended, and my only thoughts were born of instinct. I swung my bow like a baseball bat, smacking the scrawl at the head of the line into a column of rock that crumbled under its weight.

One after the other, I struck at the beasts while I tried to come up with a plan. There was a divot between a group of stalagmites that looked like it might offer me better protection, but a scrawl caught my back as I dove for cover. Its razor-sharp talons dug into my flesh, and it lifted me off the ground until my weight was too much for its hold. I felt my skin rip off in its claws and fell to the ground, narrowly missing a serrated rock that would have impaled me.

I'm so sick of small spaces, I thought as I wiggled into the hollow between stalagmites, enclosing myself in a protective cage. The scrawl wouldn't be put off for long. They swooped down on my makeshift enclosure and snapped at the tips of the stalagmites with their teeth. Strings of stinky, slimy saliva dripped down on me as I began to feel woozy from blood loss. The back of my shirt was soaked with it, which would only increase their appetite.

I closed my eyes, trying to block out the hungry scrawl, and raked my hands across the ground, desperately searching for something other than damp rock. My eyes flew open. I could hardly believe my luck. I traced the rough feel of a dry root, following it as it twisted up and around the stalagmites. I directed the beam of the flashlight across the floor. Hope rose in my chest. Dry root covered everything.

"Burn," I commanded the piece of root. Red and orange flame burst upward.

"Yes!" I screamed. Scrawl were afraid of fire.

The creatures above me stopped snapping at the rock and pushed off, their wings fanning the flame into a brighter column.

Staying low, I crawled across the jagged cave floor. Every piece of root I passed, I commanded to burn. The scrawl flew above me but didn't dare come closer to the flames. Soon, nearly the entire bottom of the cavern was alight with fire.

It's getting hot in here, Sun Petal said. *What's going on?*

I've got it under control, I said.

With sweat pouring into my eyes, I pushed forward. It was a small price to pay. I wiped it away with my sleeve and felt dizzy with relief when I reached the narrow opening that led out of the cavern. I scurried down it, ignoring the pain from my bloodied knees. That was nothing compared to the terror behind me.

The tunnel widened, and eventually, I was able to stand again. I leaned against a rock, panting and wincing. Little black dots popped in my vision, like tiny gnats swarming around me. If I didn't act soon, I'd pass out.

I opened my backpack. Sun Petal burst out. *Whoa,* she said, seeing the red and orange light behind us. *You set the whole place on fire?*

I gave a breathy laugh. *Had to get us out of there somehow.*

Filthy scrawl, Sun Petal said. Then her mind turned softer. *Thank you for saving my life.*

You wouldn't be in this mess if it wasn't for me, I reminded her.

A wave of nausea turned my stomach. I leaned against the wall for support and brushed the wounds on my back with my fingertips.

Yikes! That looks really bad, Sun Petal said. *Can I heal you?*

Immediately, I wanted to say yes, but my wrist burned with the memory of Eva's reminder: put the pygsmy first.

Are you sure you're okay to part with your elixir?

Sun Petal looked down at her body, seeing the vibrant, golden swirls. A feeling of sadness rushed past her mind. Then she said, *For a friend? Of course.*

Thank you, Sun Petal.

I undid the top buttons of my shirt and pulled it halfway down my back, knowing I'd heal faster if she could contact the wounded area. All six of her tendrils glowed a vibrant green. They stretched over my back, wrapping around my shoulders, my ribs, and my waist. Sun Petal laid her body flat against my spine. I felt warmth that started on the surface of my skin, then sunk deeper, into my muscle, and finally my bones.

When Sun Petal released me, I was whole again. The pain was gone, and my body was re-energized.

Thank you.

You're welcome. She fluttered happily around me. *I've never used my elixir on a human before. It feels good to heal, and I still have some left!* She flipped in circles around my head.

I laughed, but the moment of peace didn't last long. A thunderous roar echoed through the tunnel up ahead.

Please, Mira. Let this be the beast I'm supposed to find. Let this be the end, I prayed.

Chapter Fourteen

I took a deep breath, steeling myself for the next challenge, and glanced at Pippin's lifestone. The splash of red in the bottom corner gave me the courage to put one foot in front of the other. Soon, the stone would be as full and vibrant as his red hair. All I had to do was face my fears.

The roaring grew in intensity, and flashes of flickering, orange light accompanied each one. I could see the end of the tunnel up ahead. It dropped off into a deep cavern of red rock. I slowed as I reached the edge, not wanting to fall into the pit that contained the beast without a plan.

The roaring continued, and now that I was close enough, I felt heat rising with each burst. Whatever animal was waiting for me down below could breathe fire. I grabbed the rope from my backpack and tied it around a rock with an hourglass shape. Giving the rope a few hard pulls to make sure it would hold, I slowly lowered myself to the edge of the tunnel.

Something black, spindly, and segmented whipped past my face. I quickly turned my head to the right, missing the object by a hair. Another roar let off such intense heat I had to close my eyes to protect them. I might have lost my eyebrows in the blast. Tess would be mad about that.

The beast was clearly telling me to back off, but I needed to see what was waiting for me.

Can you fly in to get me a visual? I asked Sun Petal.

She sighed. *I suppose whatever it is can't be any worse than scrawl.* The brave little creature took flight, twisting up into the height of the cavern. Her translucent body seemed to avoid the beast's detection.

After calming my mind, I was able to slip into Sun Petal's thoughts. The sight below was grisly. A twenty-foot manticore paced around the bowl-shaped cavern with hatred in its eyes. It had the body of a lion, the tail of a scorpion, and a human face with a tangled red mane around it. Obviously agitated with its trapped condition, the beast opened its mouth and torched one of the red boulders that lined the outer circle of the cavern.

I knew little about manticores. Creo was the only province stupid enough to let them live. They'd been hunted to extinction everywhere else, and with good reason. Humans were their preferred source of food. There were probably a few manticores in the meadows, too, but that place was a free-for-all as far as mythical creatures go. It was common knowledge that to enter the meadows was akin to suicide.

My time for observation came to an abrupt end when Crede suddenly appeared at the mouth of another opening across the wide cavern. With horror, I watched as he prepared himself to jump.

"Crede, no!" I shouted. "You'll get yourself killed!"

The boy hesitated, then launched himself through the opening and landed on the beast's back. He wrapped his arms around its neck, trying to crush its throat with his gift of strength. With a fiery roar, the manticore's scorpion tail whipped around, catching Crede in the stomach. His body flew through the air and collided with the rocky side of the cavern, bringing a pile of boulders down on him. I scrambled to the edge of my tunnel. Crede's eyes met mine for a brief second before they closed. He was in serious trouble. The manticore prowled toward him, its head ducked low, ready to strike.

I acted without thinking.

"Hey!" I shouted as I slid down the length of rope to the ground. "Hey, over here!"

This is a bad idea, Sun Petal said from above.

I ignored her and picked up a loose stone. As hard as I could, I chucked it at the back of the beast. It hit the manticore's left flank. The scorpion tail unfurled, sending an eight-inch stinger flying through the air toward my chest. I dove behind one of the boulders. The stinger whizzed past my head and shattered as it hit the rock wall behind me.

My stunt did not distract the manticore. It continued its slow, steady approach toward Crede, opening its mouth wide. I shouted again, but was helpless to stop the beast from torching the pile of rubble with Crede buried just beneath the top.

"No!" I screamed.

I ran until I reached a boulder by the side of the beast. I pressed both my hands against it, focusing my magic into my palms. Commanding an object of this size would take a lot of focus.

In my mind, I imagined the boulder pinning the beast against the wall. What I really wanted was for the boulder to crush the monster, but I tried to remember Aaron's instruction. Don't kill, no matter the threat.

"Roll!" I pushed the rock, sending a burst of magic from my heart, through my arms, and into my hands. The five-ton boulder rolled forward, gaining some momentum as it went. Just like I envisioned, it forced the beast against another boulder and the wall. It roared with frustration, but its fire was directed upward as it ricocheted off the rock.

I ran to Crede, struggling not to vomit at the sight of his charred flesh. I could only imagine how his family was feeling as they watched this moment on screen. One son dead with the other inches from joining him.

Furiously, I touched the rocks that buried his legs and torso, commanding, "move" repeatedly. Crede's left leg was broken, bent at a sickening angle. While I worked, one half of my brain was keeping tabs on the manticore, who was making progress shifting the rock with its hind legs as it kicked over and over again.

Sun Petal, do you have any elixir left?

I might have enough to heal the boy.

I felt selfish for having used any of the elixir on myself, but Sun Petal's markings were still shining gold. I hoped it would be enough for Crede's extensive injuries.

With a forceful kick, the manticore moved the boulder at least six inches.

Hurry, please, I said as I ripped open Crede's shirt.

Just let me work, Sun Petal said as she wound her glowing tendrils around Crede, stretching one up to his charred face. They glowed green, then shifted to gold as the elixir ran through them. With satisfaction, I saw Crede's broken leg return to its normal form. The raw, angry flesh on his burnt face changed from red to a puckered pink before it became his healthy original color.

As Crede's eyes began to flutter, the manticore leveled one final, powerful kick at the boulder that kept him bound.

Uh oh. Time was up and I had no plan.

That's as much as I can heal, Sun Petal told me. *He will live, but he's weak.*

Thank you, Sun Petal. You've been magnificent, I said.

I tugged at Crede's arms, trying to pull him up, but he didn't budge. My heart raced as the manticore shot another poisonous dart, which I blocked with my backpack. It stalked toward us, baring its teeth.

"Come on, Crede," I yanked at his arms. "Wake up!"

There were twelve feet between us and the beast. Then ten. Then five. The monster lunged for me, and I ducked, covering my head with my arms.

Ke-kaw! The piercing cry of a bird echoed off the walls.

"Hang in there, Laurelin!" Owen said as he swept into the cavern, riding a giant, black and red bird. He drew his bow and shot the manticore in its back leg. The beast whirled, directing a stream of fire at the bird. The tip of its wing caught the flame. It began to fall, spiraling toward the ground with Owen still on its back.

I cringed, but the instant before they collided with the earth, the bird popped out of existence, and Owen landed smoothly on the rock floor. With a flick of its tail, the manticore sent a stinger at him. He lifted his palm, flinging a stone into the air, which knocked the stinger from its path. The beast roared, directing fire at Owen again. He dove behind a boulder.

I gave my attention back to Crede, who was finally regaining consciousness.

"Crede, can you understand me?" I asked.

His brown eyes met mine. His pupils were dilated, but he gave me a slow nod.

"I'm going to hide you somewhere safe." I pulled his arms, and this time, he was able to help carry some of his weight. I put his arm over my shoulder and dragged him to a crack in the cavern's wall. "Wait here until you either feel well enough to help or this nightmare's over, okay?"

"Mmkay," Crede said.

I turned to face the beast.

"Thanks," Crede slurred. "You saved my life."

I didn't know how to respond other than tipping my head to acknowledge I'd heard him.

I slipped out of the crack and joined Owen in the cavern. His current plan was a good one—with his gift, he opened holes in the ground beneath the manticore's feet, causing it to trip. The beast was learning, though. Instead of stepping where Owen next expected, it swiveled to the left and sent a stream of fire at him in one lithe movement.

"Aaargh!" Owen cried as the fire caught his arm. He ducked behind a boulder for cover.

Sun Petal, let's fly!

The pygsmy scooped me up and I pulled out my bow. As I threaded an arrow, Amelia dropped into the cavern, her eyes wide with fright as the manticore whirled at the noise.

"Now would be a good time to shoot, Laurelin!" Amelia cried as she scrambled for her own bow.

I closed one eye and took aim at the manticore's front, right paw and released. The arrow plunged into the monster's foot. A perfect shot.

It appeared not to notice.

"You missed its heart!" Amelia screamed at me.

The manticore's tail flicked and a stinger soared toward her. With a shriek, she ducked for cover, but the manticore prowled toward her with angry eyes.

Owen ran toward Amelia to help, holding his burnt arm in pain.

Running from boulder to boulder, I saw Faye charging toward the beast, her knife drawn. Without giving any indication it even knew she was there, the manticore flicked its tail, sending a dart at Faye. She moved to the side, but it brushed her right arm, leaving a long, bloody gash where it hit. She stared at it, her mouth open wide, as if she couldn't believe it had the gall to strike her.

Take me to her, Sun Petal.

The pygsmy dipped, dropping me next to Faye.

"Ahh!" she screamed, her hand at her chest as I suddenly appeared. "Oh. What do you want, Laurelin? Now's not the time for chit chat."

"I want to know everything you can remember from reading about manticores."

She looked at me in disbelief. "And why would I tell you? That information is my advantage."

"This isn't about having the upper hand, Faye. The only way

we're going to beat this animal is by working together. Trust me, you don't want to end up like Crede. He almost died trying to take it on by himself."

"I don't want to end up like Tobias, either. Look what happened to him after crossing you."

I rolled my eyes. "I'm not a murderer."

Though still busy with Owen and Amelia, the manticore managed to send fire at us. We dove in opposite directions. My forearm, elbow, and side scraped along the rock floor, stinging my skin. Faye's pant leg was on fire. She rolled on the ground, trying to smother the flame.

"Please, Faye, just tell me what you know. We can end this together," I shouted as I ran back to her side.

Faye looked at me through the shattered glass in one of her lenses. "Fine. There's a main artery that extends from the bottom of its right, front paw up the back of its leg. If we slice that, it will be dead in half a minute."

"No, no. What other weaknesses does it have? We don't want to kill it."

"We don't want to kill it? You're insane!"

"Come on, Faye. There has to be something else. Think!"

"I don't need to think," she snapped. "I already know. Its tail can only sting periodically, but there's not a set time between its activity. Sometimes it's as little as ten seconds, sometimes up to two minutes. Its fire-breathing can be squelched by the water ranunculus plant, but it has to be swallowed to be effective. In nature, its biggest rival is the hyena. And it's a very deadly beast. That sums up what I know," she rattled off.

"Okay, okay. Let's think. Amelia can warn us when it's about to sting. Owen could create some hyenas to distract it. And I think I can get the pygsmy to retrieve some water ranunculus for us. If we take away its fire, it will be much easier to subdue."

"Tell me again why we don't just kill the beast?" Faye asked.

"Creo values life. All life. We're supposed to play according to their rules."

Faye's eyes flashed. I could tell she didn't like it when I was right.

"So it's settled," I said. "I'll tell Owen and Amelia the plan. Then, you work with Amelia to distract the manticore if it gets too close to Owen, okay? She'll be able to warn you before it stings."

"I'm pretty sure this is a set-up to kill us all except you," Faye mumbled, but she walked in the direction I pointed, so I took that as her way of saying yes.

Hopping from boulder to boulder, I made my way to Owen and Amelia and shouted out the plan.

"You mean we're not going to kill it?" Amelia asked, her eyes angry.

"No, Laurelin's right. We have to capture, not kill. That's the Creo way."

Amelia's face was a snarl, but she said, "Fine. Tell me what to do."

"Owen will be the main distraction with the hyenas. We just have to step in if the manticore gets too close. Your job is to warn any of us when a stinger or fire is coming our way. Tell us which way to go."

"Sounds like a solid plan to me," Owen said.

Amelia stalked off, spreading out from me and Faye as Owen produced a pack of four hyenas.

Are you up for another adventure, Sun Petal?

Her reply was simple. *I'll help you.*

Great. There's a plant I need you to find in the forest. It's the water ranunculus. Do you know where to find a pond nearby?

Oooo, pretty. I like that one. Be back in a jiffy.

My mind returned to the battle before me.

Owen jumped from boulder to boulder, directing the hyenas that ripped at the manticore's legs.

"Stinger for Owen. Move left!" Amelia called.

Owen dove off the boulder, using his gift to move another rock to catch him as a stinger whirled past his head.

Angry, the manticore spun around and spewed fire at Amelia, but she was already safely around the side of a boulder.

"Stinger for Faye. Duck!" Amelia said.

Faye laid flat on the ground as the poisonous dart flew over her.

But Amelia missed the manticore's move for Owen. It swiped its giant paw as Owen leapt to the top of the next boulder, sending him crashing into the side of the cave.

Amelia screamed as more fire was directed at her. Distracted by it, she gave no warning about the stinger coming for Owen, but I saw the tightening of its tail that seemed to precede its attack. Owen was on the ground, groaning.

I threaded my bow and touched the arrow. "Block!" I commanded as I released. Obediently, the arrow adjusted its trajectory as it flew toward the stinger headed for Owen. It pierced the center, sending shards of stinger raining down on Owen.

"Thank you," he breathed as he made eye contact with me.

Sun Petal zoomed back into the cave. In one of her tendrils, the drooping blue bells of the water ranunculus plant were dangling. Knowing the plan, Sun Petal scooped me up. Manticores have poor vision, so it was unlikely it would see us in our translucent state. On the other hand, they have an excellent sense of smell, especially for their prey.

Gripping the slimy ranunculus in my right hand, I waited until the hyenas attacked the manticore again.

Now's our chance, Sun Petal. Dive right for its mouth.

I can do this. I can do this! Sun Petal chanted to herself.

As we got closer, I felt the manticore's hot breath on my hand. Hope filled me. Then, at the last second, it detected us and snapped at me, then released a wave of fire. I jerked to the left, and Sun Petal screeched in terror, retreating from the hot flame. The hyenas bit at the manticore's legs, drawing its attention for a moment.

"Amelia, Faye," I shouted as I hovered above. "Provoke it to sting, then I'll go in for another try. Be ready to tie it up!"

Amelia lunged for the beast's tail, which rippled in response. With a piercing roar, it released a stinger and breathed more fire. Amelia sheltered behind a rock, panting.

This was my chance. "Come on," I whispered. "Right in its mouth."

Sun Petal dove, coming at it from the side this time. I stretched out my hand and dropped the blue plant into its throat, slicing my palm on its sharp teeth as we passed. The manticore sputtered and shook its head, trying to force the plant out. Finally, it swallowed. Its black eyes found me. They were filled with vitriol. It knew who had disabled its best weapon.

"Laurelin, stinger! Get down!" Amelia called.

Drop! I shouted at Sun Petal, who dipped just in time for the stinger to soar over us. Then she gently set me on the ground.

"Ropes!" I yelled. "Get its legs!"

Faye held one end of a long rope and Amelia dove underneath the beast with the other. They pulled it tight, then ran to the flank of the manticore. Faye took Amelia's end and pulled, binding both of the creature's back legs. It roared in anger, but no fire came out.

"Stinger aimed at Faye!" Amelia said. She jumped out of the way, using the beast's own leg as a shield.

Owen tossed me the end of another rope. Like Amelia, I rolled beneath the beast, then brought the rope around the front. The monster's teeth slashed at me, but it couldn't move forward with its back legs bound. Owen finished off the knot as the beast snapped at him. It managed to take a chunk of his shirt but missed his skin. With all four of its legs bound, the manticore rolled to its side. It growled but lay still, finally surrendering.

I dropped to my knees and couldn't help but smile. Somehow, I'd made it to the end of the first round of the Pentax. I could only hope my performance was good enough for the judges.

Chapter Fifteen

T hrough a gap in the green privacy curtains, I could see Crede's parents gathered around his bed. I waited on my own medical cot to see Dr. Perez, like the other contestants. No one but Crede had curtains around them—an indication of his serious condition.

At my request, Silas stepped in to see Crede. "Laurelin would like to offer her abilities to help your son. She wasn't able to fully heal him during the competition, but she has elixir she can share. It would have him in perfect condition."

I bit the inside of my cheek, hoping they'd accept my offer.

Mr. Liang's voice was full of acid. "No, absolutely not. I don't want that girl anywhere near Crede."

"Mr. Liang," Dr. Perez said, "your son needs serious medical attention. Much more than I can offer here. He will have to be taken to a hospital, and he will likely face permanent injury. Elixir could heal him fully—"

"Aren't you supposed to be a doctor? It is your job to heal, not that common girl from Lingua. We want nothing to do with her. That is my final answer. Now please, do your job and see to my son."

Mrs. Liang's eyes flashed to me, pleading. "Can't we—"

"Stop it, Minna," Mr. Liang said. He followed her eyes, seeing me. Angrily, he walked over and yanked the curtain closed.

I sighed and laid back on my pillow, squeezing my eyes shut.

Another ten minutes passed, and a medical team gathered to take Crede to the hospital. He shot me one wistful glance behind his parents' backs.

Sorry, I mouthed.

Dr. Perez moved onto examining the rest of us.

"Why doesn't Laurelin have to take one of these stupid tests?" Amelia asked the doctor as she peppered her with basic questions like, *how old are you?* Or *how many fingers am I holding up?*

Dr. Perez glanced at me. "I will administer her examination once I'm finished with the other contestants. Laurelin is of least concern to me. She's already been healed by elixir."

"I was told the use of elixir is grounds for disqualification," Amelia grumbled.

Dr. Perez kept her face neutral. "My understanding is that each Rook is afforded the use of their gift during the competition. Since Laurelin can use a pygsmy to heal directly, I assume it is viewed differently than taking elixir beforehand. But I am not a judge. That will be decided among them, I am sure. Now please, let me do my job. I need to check on the others as well."

Amelia continued to glare at me over Dr. Perez's shoulder as she answered the questions.

Finally, it was my turn. The other contestants had left the tent after they'd been seen, so it was just me and Dr. Perez now. As she bandaged my minor injuries, she checked over her shoulder and said, "Thank you for saving Crede. I wish his parents would have allowed you to heal him completely. Of course, I *should* hope our next ruler will be from Creo. But between you and me, I wouldn't mind a commoner on the throne for once." She gave me a wink.

I blushed at her unexpected praise. "Thank you," I said.

"Laurelin, come on," Silas called from the mouth of the medical tent. "The crowd is anxious to hear the scoring."

I hopped down from the cot, my stomach full of butterflies. I followed Silas down a dirt path back to the stadium. When we got to the end of the trail, he paused. "You made Lingua very proud today, Laurelin. Very proud." He placed his hand on my shoulder and squeezed.

"I hope I made my family proud too," I said.

He smiled. "I have no doubt. Now get out there." He gave me a gentle nudge toward the center of the arena, where the other contestants waited in black chairs.

I walked into the stadium and the crowd erupted with cheers. I knew it was only because they were excited to finally hear scores, but I pretended the applause was meant for me.

I caught a glimpse of Aaron before I took my seat. His forehead was wrinkled with worry, but he managed a half smile and a thumbs up.

The drums at the top of the stadium stopped beating as Saundra's face appeared on the screen. "Ladies and gentlemen. What an incredible display of bravery and teamwork we have witnessed today. There is still much to be decided, but I think it is clear that among this group, we will find a warrior who will rise to the challenge of leading our beloved Ausland.

"Now, let us proceed with the judgment. Keep in mind that the score I give for the Rook is the average score of each judge's assessment out of 100 total points. The judges were looking for wisdom in the use of magical gifts and other available resources, the speed with which the Rook found the manticore, and Creo's fundamental belief that all life must be valued and protected, including creatures that may be dangerous in a given moment."

Out of the corner of my eye, I saw Faye shift in her seat. I gave her a look that said, *I told you so.*

"First, Faye Bennett of Scentia. Praised for her knowledge of the water ranunculus as a harmless way to eliminate the threat of fire, she earns a score of 79."

The crowd cheered politely.

"Next, Amelia Allred of Amare. The judges were impressed with the use of her gift, which kept her out of many dangerous situations and was used well to protect the other Rooks from the manticore. Amelia's score is 76."

Amelia smiled and waved at the applauding crowd, but when she looked at Faye, her smile disappeared.

"Third, Owen Mendez of Creo."

The crowd went wild as the drummers pounded their mallets. Saundra waited with a victorious smile.

I twisted the lifestone around my finger and tried to stay calm.

When the crowd quieted some, she continued. "The judges saw the use of his gift as essential to the success of subduing the manticore. Owen fearlessly protected the other Rooks, though this often came at great danger to himself. We have awarded him a score of 89."

Owen punched the air. "Yes!" he called.

My heart sank. That would be a very hard score to beat.

"Fourth, Laurelin Moore. The judges were pleased to see a stronger-than-expected demonstration from Lingua."

I didn't miss the insult in her remark.

"For the use of her healing abilities to save a fellow Rook and her clever plan to tackle the manticore, Laurelin is given a score of 80."

Nine points behind Owen. I was disappointed. With his talents, making up that difference in future rounds felt impossible.

"Boooooo!" A deep voice called from the crowd.

I braced myself for the accusations that would follow. Something about being a murderer or a selfish hog of elixir. But I was surprised to find Aaron standing up.

"They all would have died if it weren't for Laurelin!" he shouted. "She deserves to be in first place!"

My face flushed with embarrassment.

Saundra didn't wait for the crowd or Aaron to quiet, raising her voice to speak over them. "Regrettably, I must inform you that Crede Liang of Fortis will not continue in the Pentax. His parents elected to withdraw him before the judges were able to give him a score.

"I extend my most sincere congratulations to Amelia, Faye, Laurelin, and Owen as you will each move on to the second round of the Pentax. I suggest you take the evening to pack your bags and rest. The Rooks and their teams will be transferred to Lingua in the morning."

Saundra gave a deep bow, then the screen shut off.

Owen gave my shoulder a playful punch. "Good job today, Lingua. Your trainer isn't wrong. If it weren't for you, we'd probably be smoldering piles of ash right now. And I saw you heal Crede. That was cool. I wouldn't say no to some elixir." Owen raised his heavily bandaged arm. "But Saundra would kill me if I tried. And that woman can be scarier than a manticore, believe me."

I snorted. "I'll have to take your word for it. After today, I'm not sure there's anything scarier than a manticore. You deserved a big score. Maybe not an 89," I smirked, "but a big score."

Owen laughed. "I'll see you in Lingua. It's time I learn what real music sounds like." He winked, then walked off to talk with his team.

"That was insane, El!" Aaron wrapped his strong arms around me, pulling me into a bone-crushing bear hug.

"Aaron," I squeaked, "I just survived round one of the Pentax without any major injuries. Please don't break a bone now."

"Oh, sorry." He set me back on the ground looking sheepish.

"It's okay. I just wish I were in first place."

Aaron frowned. "Yeah, the judges are crazy biased. But there are plenty of rounds still to come."

I gave a shaky laugh. "I guess. I just ..." I looked down at the lifestone. "I really want this."

Aaron caught my hand and touched the ring. My pulse quickened.

"I know you do, and I hope you'll tell me the whole story sometime. Just know I believe you can win this."

I sighed. "I wish I were as confident as you."

Chapter Sixteen

P acking my bags was easy since I never really unpacked
in the first place.

While I worked, a note slid under my door. Through
the gaps in the vine, I thought I saw Silas hurrying down the
hall. I picked up the paper and read:

*Well done today, Laurelin. I've sent payment to your family, like
we agreed.*

—Silas

I smiled. 150 darics. That was more than Dad brought in
from his carpentry in four months. Hopefully that would ease
my parents' burdens for now. They could focus all their attention
on Pippin.

Exhausted and satisfied, I reached for Eva's journal. It had
been a while since I had time to read. I flipped it open and
began where I left off.

*Pygsmies are protectors. The Matrons created them for this
purpose. Their first responsibility is to guard Ausland's magic.*

*They do this by defending the meadows, which is why the
meadows are so deadly for humans. If one enters that sacred space
without the protection of the diadem or the approval of the
Matrons, a pygsmy will quickly sting, and death will
immediately follow. Second, pygsmies protect humanity. Their
elixir can heal and strengthen us, and they are the eyes and ears of
the Matrons. The sooner you understand pygsmies' natural
strengths, the better your connection will be. A pygsmy can be
fiercely loyal when you earn their trust.*

I thought of Sun Petal. I never would have made it through
the competition today without that spastic little pygsmy. I
opened my mind, curious to know if Sun Petal was close by. Just
outside the castle perimeter, I felt her twisting and flipping
through the air. I smiled and kept reading.

*As a whisperer, these same responsibilities extend to you. You are
a guardian of Ausland's magic and a protector of humanity. In
ancient times, when Ausland's magic was new, many sought after
the Matrons' crystals. These thieves were called Stone Seekers,
and they wanted to steal the magic for themselves. Whisperers
directed armies of pygsmies as Stone Seekers tried to sneak past
them to Everark, home of the Matrons.*

*For centuries, this battle went on, but no one was successful.
Finally, after so much death, the ways of the Stone Seekers were
forgotten. Until my trainer, Julian, abandoned his role. He
visited the great seer, Baltazar, for instructions about how to
steal the crystals. Then he killed King Tiras in order to force a
Pentax. For reasons I'm forbidden to write, the Matrons are
particularly vulnerable during this time. While the competition
was underway, Julian used his gift to cross the meadows, but I
knew what he was after. Like many whisperers before me, I had
to fight and protect our magic. In the end, we were victorious,
and Ausland's magic was saved.*

Remember, pygsmies are protectors. You should be too.

I had never thought of myself as a protector of anyone besides Pippin. If I'd been alive during Eva's time, would I have had the courage to fight against Julian? I wondered what she meant about the Matrons being vulnerable during the Pentax.

A knock on my bedroom door interrupted me.

"El, it's me," Aaron said.

Hurriedly, I placed the journal in the bottom of my suitcase and covered it with some folded clothes. When I yanked open the door, Aaron bowed and held out a rusted fork.

"For you, my future queen."

Still thinking about the journal, I took the fork.

"You okay, El? I just handed you rusty silverware as a gift, and you didn't react."

I shook my head. "Right. Er, thanks, but you can keep it."

I tried to pass it back. He laughed and touched the fork, changing it to a silver bracelet with a pygsmy charm dangling from it.

I smiled. "That's more like it. Thank you. It's beautiful."

"Everyone's in a weird mood tonight. Guess I can't blame you Rooks. The competition was intense," Aaron said.

"Sorry, I was still thinking about something I read right before you came." I put the bracelet on my wrist. "Anyway, what do you mean about everyone being weird tonight?"

Aaron jutted his thumb toward the hall. "Amelia practically attacked me just now," he said.

"Attacked you?" I gasped.

"No, not like that." Aaron's face turned red. "She tried to kiss me, but I think she was only trying to distract me. I don't think she expected to run into anyone. There's no reason for her to be in this hallway."

I balked. "And did she ... 'distract' you?"

"No." Aaron looked like he'd rather trim a grandmother's

toenails than have this conversation. "I pushed her away and she just ran off."

"Hmm. That is odd. The last time she was hanging around here, Tobias was found dead the next morning."

Aaron's eyes grew wide. "You don't think she's after you now, do you?"

"I'm not sure. It's possible. I can't see a reason why she'd target me, but I can't figure out why she would have been after Tobias either."

"I don't think you should stay here alone tonight," Aaron said.

My mind swirled with thoughts about the journal, Stone Seekers, and Amelia. "You might be right. I'll see if Sofia can stay or something."

"That's a good idea."

I nodded. "So what's up?"

"Well, I was coming to ask if you had plans this evening, but it looks like you're ready for bed."

Embarrassed, I looked down at myself. I'd already changed into cotton shorts and a loose tank top. I crossed my arms over my chest.

"Clearly, I do not have plans. Do you have something in mind? I can get dressed again."

"I have something to show you outside, if you're up for it."

My stomach twisted with anticipation at the idea of being alone with Aaron and not because we were training. "Yes, give me two seconds and I'll be ready to go."

I undid any progress I'd made in packing as I frantically dug through my bags. I pulled on a pair of jeans and put a jacket over my tank top.

I opened the door. "Ready!"

Aaron led the way to the back doors that went out to the gardens. "Okay, time to cover your eyes."

"What? No, I don't want to do that. I'm not good with surprises."

"My game, my rules," Aaron insisted. Without waiting for permission, he walked behind me and cupped his hands around my eyes.

It wasn't all bad. I enjoyed the woodsy scent that came off his skin.

"I'm trusting you to keep me from falling. The ground in Creo is all over the place."

"I've got you," Aaron promised.

We walked for about a minute before Aaron stopped. "Okay, you can open your eyes now."

I put my hands over my mouth. It was like seeing home again. Aaron had taken us to a small alcove of trees where he'd strung purple lights through the branches above. A blue blanket sat on the ground with a picnic basket on top of it.

"We're going back to Lingua tomorrow, but I know you've missed home. I figured I'd try to bring a little piece of it to you. So, behold—electric-powered lights and the color purple. Do you like it?"

"I love it. Where did you get the lights? Electricity's like a cardinal sin here!"

"Enjoy it now because we have about five minutes before the authorities show up to arrest us." Aaron's straight face was betrayed by a small twitch at the corner of his mouth.

I put my hand on his arm. "Worth it. Definitely worth it. I love purple. It's such a great color. Seriously, how do the lights work? I haven't seen a lightbulb or an outlet the whole time we've been here."

Aaron sat on one side of the basket. I hesitated, wondering if I should sit close to him—like I wanted to—or if it was better to keep my distance. I decided to play it safe and sat on a pillow across from him.

He began to pull out food as he answered. "Ah, now that was the tricky part. I couldn't find any materials to spin into lights myself, so I had to resort to the black market. Very hard commodity to come by in this province, mind you. You'll never guess what finally got my contact to give up battery-powered lights." Aaron wiggled his eyebrows.

"Yep, no guesses. I'm not well versed in your criminal ways."

"Don't worry. You'll learn in good time. I got the lights by promising Jed something signed by the great Laurelin Moore."

I snorted. "Fine. Keep your secrets."

"No, seriously." Aaron took a bite out of his sandwich as he passed one to me. "That was the only item that got his interest. I have to get it to him before we leave tomorrow or he gets to take my ruby encrusted fish hook, so don't hold out on me."

"You're really serious? Why would anyone want something signed by me?" The idea of someone wanting my autograph made me uncomfortable—those were for famous people. I was just a regular kid from small town Sedona.

"Dead serious. Well, his first demand was elixir, but I told him I couldn't have the future queen breaking the law during the Pentax, duh. So yeah, your signature was the next best thing. People believe you're going to win this thing, El. Something with your autograph is about to become pretty expensive on the market."

I bit into my own sandwich, reveling in the flavor of smoked ham. Four days on a vegetarian diet felt like an eternity. "People are nuts," I said.

"They're nuts about meat, that's for sure." Aaron held up his sandwich. "This stuff was crazy expensive too. Guess not everyone in Creo is on board the vegetarian train."

I sucked in a sharp breath. "Now that's a scandal if I ever heard one. We should write an exposé about it. We could be rich."

Aaron scrunched his nose. "Nah, journalism would be too straight-path for me. I'll stick with hawking. But hey, if this whole queen thing doesn't pan out, you've got a back-up plan for your career. Better make the switch to Creo permanent though. There are too many writers in Lingua already."

"I'd rather drink scrawl blood than live in Creo for good." I took another bite of food and chewed slowly. "Besides, I really need 'this whole queen thing' to work."

"You know, you've never told me why that is. You say you're not after the crown, but what else could be worth risking your life?"

My eyes wandered to the purple lights above. Aaron deserved an explanation, and I wasn't afraid of him knowing the truth anymore. After hearing his own tragic story about his mom, I knew he'd understand. Still, talking about Pippin would probably make me cry, and there was a part of me that didn't want his pity.

"You can trust me, you know." Aaron scooted around the basket. He reached up and touched my cheek, gently tipping my face up to meet his eyes.

We'd never been so close before—at least, not like this. But somehow, it didn't feel close enough. My whole body hummed with excitement.

I exhaled. "I know I can trust you, it's just ... hard to talk about."

Aaron's fingers brushed the lifestone, then he grabbed my hand. "Someone you love is dying. You want the wish to cure them."

"Yes." I could barely speak past the lump in my throat. "My little brother, Pippin, has cancer. He's hanging on by a thread. Daily elixir is the only thing keeping him alive."

Aaron kept his eyes on the lifestone. "I'm sorry, Laurelin. I had no idea. That explains why you stopped bringing elixir over these last months."

"Yeah, I haven't had any to spare lately. We found out about the cancer four years ago. He started to decline really quickly, so Mom quit her job at the hospital to care for him. Dad does carpentry, but it's not enough to keep the family afloat. So that's when I started selling elixir to you."

"I wish I had known. I should have been paying you double

for your elixir instead of trying to get the best price. Is there something I can do to help?"

I wiped a tear on my sleeve. "No, there isn't anything that can be done for him anymore. It's just so unfair, you know? He was so young when he got sick. Just ten. He's barely left the house in three years. What kind of life is that? He deserves more."

"Life really is unfair." Aaron's thumb rubbed the charm on his mother's necklace. "What is Pippin like?"

Imagining Pippin brought a smile to my face. "He's competitive. When we were kids, we used to visit my grandparents a lot. They had a few horses and Pippin loved to race on them. He was little, so I usually let him win. It wasn't worth the tantrum he'd throw if I beat him, though the foot stamp before he'd storm off was adorable.

"He's always been jealous that I have two gifts when no one else in my family has any, but he's gifted in other ways. He's crazy smart. I haven't been able to beat him at a game of chess since he turned eight."

Aaron chuckled.

"He likes comic books and rainstorms and ice cream. He can be brutally honest, so he helped me develop some thick skin, which is coming in handy these days." I laughed. "He's my best friend, and I can't stand to lose him. That's why I have to win the Pentax. The Matrons can heal him. I have to get that wish."

Aaron squeezed my arm. "Well, my bet is on you. Always has been."

"Thank you," I whispered.

I rested my head on his shoulder and allowed myself to truly relax for the first time in years. For a moment, I could pretend I wasn't a Rook with the pressure of the Pentax hanging over me. I could imagine Pippin was healthy and my family was whole. For now, I could rest.

Chapter Seventeen

T he green vine slithered around my waist, releasing me on the top of a wooden platform. I was not sad to say goodbye to Creo's transportation system. Through the tunnel that connected Creo and Lingua, I could see a railcar waiting. The familiar sight filled me with comfort. At least this leg of the Pentax would be manageable. And in a few hours, I'd have a chance to see my family again.

Each team had their own railcar. I felt sorry for Arthur as he boarded with only one servant boy to accompany him. I hadn't heard any update on Crede.

With seven people in our railcar, it was a squishy ride. But it pushed Aaron closer to me, and I spent most of the trip wondering why something as simple as our touching legs had my stomach in knots.

Above us, I could feel Sun Petal following our railcar.

Since when are you interested in visiting Lingua? I asked.

Oh, I'm not. I'm interested in helping you, Lur-a-lin, Sun Petal said.

I smiled. *You almost got it right. And thanks.*

We flew through Meadow, and Mira's daunting statue came into view. At her neck, a purple crystal glistened. My mind went back to Eva's passage I'd read last night.

"Hey, Silas," I said as we passed the statue. "I was wondering if you knew what Eva meant about the Matrons being more vulnerable during the Pentax. It was in the section where she talked about Julian and the crystals."

Silas's eyebrows knit together. "No, I don't remember her mentioning that. It's been a long time since I read all of her journal though. Do you have it? I'd like to take a look."

I walked to the back of the railcar where the three servants sat with our luggage. The dark-haired boy helped me unbury my case. I unzipped it and dug to the bottom. There was no journal. Strange. I sifted through the clothes more carefully. Panic began to rise in my chest. Where was the journal?

"El, you okay?" Aaron asked.

I turned. "The journal is gone. I can't find it."

"What?" Silas's voice cut me like a knife. "That's a priceless family heirloom. Please look again, Laurelin. My family will be devastated if it's missing."

I tossed around the clothes without hope. It wasn't there.

I bit my lip, trying desperately to keep any tears from escaping. "It's gone. I'm so sorry, Silas."

His furious glare burned worse than a pygsmy sting.

"When did you last have it, El?" Aaron asked.

"Last night, right before you came. I was reading it, and I remember placing it in my suitcase before I opened the door. I never checked to make sure it was still there before we left." How could I have been so careless?

Silas took several deep breaths, then cleared his throat. "I will contact the palace staff and ask them to check your room thoroughly. Hopefully, they find it."

"I really am so sorry," I said as I returned to my seat.

Silas gave a tremulous smile. "I know you didn't mean to lose it. I'm sure it will turn up, but when it does, please return it to me immediately."

Deservedly, I'd lost his trust. But Eva intended the journal to be for the next whisperer, not her family. I didn't feel like I could argue. Instead, I mashed my lips together and nodded.

"I have another matter to discuss with you. The other judges were ... less than thrilled with your use of the pygsmy during the first round. I was able to convince them you didn't deserve to be disqualified, but they have decided that from this point forward, you are not permitted to use a pygsmy to heal."

"What? That's crazy!" Aaron's voice filled the car. "No other Rook has their power restricted. Laurelin is a whisperer. That's her gift, and she should be free to use it, just like the others. Not to mention it saved Crede's life. There has to be some way—"

"Believe me, Aaron, I have tried. I argued all of the same things. I'm overruled. It's four against one. There is no higher governing body for the Pentax. Everything comes down to the five judges. You're still able to use pygsmies to your advantage. You simply can't use them to heal. The others say it is the same as drinking from a vial of elixir, which has always been prohibited during the competition. I'm very sorry."

"I get it. They don't want Lingua to win." I exhaled.

"That's true. You've surprised all of them. I warned you that you came to this competition with extreme bias against you, and it was obvious in the way you were scored after the first round. Perhaps that helps you understand why I was trying so hard to form an alliance with Scentia and Fortis when we first arrived. I hoped it might even the playing field. But alas, we must fight on without anyone in our corner. I know you can do it." Silas reached across the aisle and patted my knee.

Tess startled all of us as she let out a high squeal. She'd been engrossed in her sketchbook since we pulled away from the station. "I've got it! The perfect outfit for the social tonight." Proudly, she held out her design for me to see, completely unaware of the tense conversation around her.

"That looks very ... fancy," I said. "What will we be doing?"

"It's a concert and poetry reading at the Careen with a mixer afterward. You're going to look fabulous." She beamed.

I worked to keep myself from rolling my eyes. "I always do when you're in charge, Tess."

"Not always," Silas grumbled. "Your media interview was a disaster."

"No one remembers it now," Aaron said. "She healed Crede. That's the only thing people are talking about."

"Let's not get ahead of ourselves. Appearances matter, and there are plenty of people who still believe Laurelin is responsible for Tobias's death—including Tobias's parents. It would be easy to feel complacent because you're in second place and this round is happening in your home province. I can assure you the task will still test you very much," Silas said

I nodded as we pulled into the main rail station in Meadow. Outside, a crowd waited for us. I was relieved to see that this time, most of them were cheering, happily waving Linguan flags. On the far right side of the platform, though, a group of people held signs splattered with negative messages.

Aaron's low voice tickled my ear. "Don't worry about them, El. They don't know your story."

"Silas, do you mind if I stay on? I want to go see my family before my training session."

"That would be an example of the complacency I was just referencing," Silas sighed.

"So ... yes?" I smiled.

"You may do what you wish with your free time. But make sure you're back for training at noon. Your room number is 303." Without another word, Silas exited the train with Tess on his heels.

I turned to Aaron. "Do you want to come with me?" I was nervous he'd think I was weird for asking, but I didn't know how much time Pippin had left, and I wanted Aaron to meet him.

Aaron smiled. "I was hoping you'd ask."

"Sedona," I commanded the railcar.

The car detached itself from the others in the line and sped toward home. And this time, I got to hold Aaron's hand all the way.

"Have they been out there the whole time I've been gone?"

People clung to the bars of our iron gate, stumbling over each other as they yelled for elixir. Just to reach the house, Aaron and I had to make a wide circle around the block and then cut through the Johansen's yard to reach our back door.

"Every day, all day," Mom sighed. "It's probably best Pippin sleeps through all of it. He's been feeling guilty about using the elixir."

"That's ridiculous. It's my gift that got the elixir and I can choose how to use it." I wished I believed it as firmly as I could say it.

"I know, sweetie, and I'm so glad." She poked her thumb at Aaron, who sat with Dad at the oak table. "Aaron Gray? The black market boy? I'm not sure he's the right fit for you."

I rolled my eyes. "Mom, he's a lot more than some low-life hawk, and he's the only one keeping me sane right now."

Mom sighed. "I never liked you selling elixir to him in the first place. Our financial problems were never yours to solve, and that's not a crowd I want you mixed up in."

"Give him a chance. Please. I know you'll like him."

She squeezed my arm. "We'll see." Then she walked back to join them in the kitchen.

I watched the faces of the angry mob, wondering what was right. How could I ever help all of them? The demands would never stop. Frustrated, I yanked the curtains closed, but that did nothing to block the noise. With a sigh, I joined the others in the kitchen.

Mom handed me a cup of tea, then reached up to the cupboard where we stored the elixir. There were only a few vials left.

151

"Why is the supply so low?" I panicked.

"Oh, we've had to increase how often Pippin has elixir. He's taking it every fourteen hours now," Mom said as she poured the contents of a vial into a teacup.

"Every fourteen hours? You'll never make it through the Pentax with that supply. Why didn't you send a message to let me know?" I turned to Aaron. "I'm not going to be able to train today. I've got to build up a better supply for Pippin."

"This is why we didn't tell you," Dad said. "You know I didn't want you to enter the Pentax, but now that you've made your choice, that's where your focus should be. Winning is what will give Pippin a long-term solution. Not the elixir."

"The wish can't bring someone back from the dead, Dad. I want to see Pippin, but it will have to be brief. I have a lot of work to do."

Dad gave Mom a knowing look. "I told you this would happen."

Mom swatted his arm as she passed. "Come on, let's give Pippin his tea."

Dad had to stay downstairs because of his wheelchair, but Aaron and I followed Mom up the stairs.

I grabbed her arm as we reached his door. "Can I have a minute alone with him?" I asked.

"Of course," Mom said. She handed me the cup and kissed my forehead.

As I approached Pippin's bed, his face was paler than I'd ever seen it. The bright red blood smeared across his cracked lips was a gruesome contrast to his grayish hue. Was he already gone? I panicked, wondering if we'd waited too long for the tea.

"Pippin," I said as I shook his shoulder. "Pippin, wake up. I have elixir for you."

There was no response, but I could see breathing in his chest.

"Hey, Pip. It's Laura. Wake up. I want to see you."

Pippin remained still. I held the teacup under his nose,

allowing him to inhale some of the elixir as it came off the steaming cup. Finally, he roused enough for me to prop him up and put the tea at his lips. His drinking was labored, producing a bubbly gargle as he tried to swallow. I wiped liquid as it leaked from the corners of his mouth.

"We're almost there," I whispered as I waited for him to wake fully. "Give me just one more week. Please."

Slowly, Pippin's green eyes opened. He licked his dry lips and smiled. "Laura," he breathed.

"Hey there, kiddo. How are you?"

"Not so good. Everything hurts."

"Even with the elixir?" I asked.

"It helps a little, but not for long."

I knelt at the side of his bed and took both his hands in mine. "Just think. A year from now, this nightmare is going to be a distant memory. Keep fighting, Pip. We both have to. It will be worth it."

"The only thing that keeps me going is thinking about beating you at chess again." Pippin laughed, but it came out as a gravelly cough.

"It's good to live off a dream, but remember, it is just a dream. There's no way you're beating me again." I laughed. "Hey, there's someone I'd like you to meet, but then I've got to go get more elixir."

Pippin nodded and struggled to sit up.

"Come in!" I called toward the door as I helped pull him up in bed.

Mom stayed by the door, but Aaron came to stand by me.

"Hi, Pippin. My name is Aaron. I'm Laurelin's trainer in the Pentax."

"Did you teach her how to beat the manticore?"

Aaron laughed. "No, she did that all on her own. You've got one tough sister."

"Do you like her?" Pippin asked.

I blushed and turned my face to the window.

"Pippin, that's not polite to ask," Mom said.

"I don't have time to waste on manners," Pippin grumbled.

The tips of Aaron's ears were red. "I don't mind you asking. Yes, I like your sister very much." His blue eyes met mine for a second before they snapped back to Pippin.

"Good. At least I know you aren't stupid." Pippin settled into his pillow as if that established everything he needed to know about Aaron.

Below, the yells from the mob grew louder for a moment. Pippin looked toward the window, his expression pained.

"Mom, maybe we should turn some music on for Pippin," I said loudly, trying to drown out the noise.

"That's a great idea." Mom rushed from the room.

"You can't shield me from everything, Laura. I know they're out there. Lots of people could use the elixir and be healed, but instead, I'm up here escaping death by an inch every few hours. Wouldn't it be better to—"

"Stop," I said. I couldn't let him finish that sentence. My breathing came in shallow gasps. "You will be healed, and then I'll share the elixir. Just give me a little more time. You promise?"

Pippin rolled his eyes. "I promise."

Mom came back to the room with an old radio.

"Keep the music going for him whenever he's awake," I said. "I need to go now, but I'll be back with more elixir later."

I leaned down and kissed Pippin on the forehead. "Keep being strong, Pip. I love you."

"Love you too," he said.

As I walked out of the room, I left a piece of my heart behind. Watching Pippin struggle had been hard, but I always believed he wanted to keep fighting. Today, I wasn't so sure.

I needed to win this competition, and fast.

Dad had been busy preparing a box of empty vials for me. I grabbed it from the kitchen table with a hurried, "Thanks," and headed out the back door, with Aaron at my heels.

"Wait, El." Aaron caught my arm. "Can I come with you? I can help."

"I'm sorry, but no. Pygsmies get very nervous around humans. I don't have the extra time I would need to calm them down and get the elixir."

Aaron nodded. "Okay. Just be careful, please. Guess I'll go see if your brother's up for a game of chess."

I laughed. "Be prepared to lose. I'll meet you back at the Careen."

I rushed into the woods at the back of my house.

How can I help? Sun Petal asked, appearing by my side.

I was so glad to see her. *Can you help me find some pygsmies with elixir? I don't have much time.*

I'm on it, Sun Petal said as she swooped off into the trees.

I glanced at my watch. Only six hours until the social would begin. I hoped there would be enough time.

Chapter Eighteen

Finding pygsmies with enough elixir to spare proved harder than I expected. Now, I had twenty minutes to be ready for the evening social. I could only imagine how annoyed Tess was going to be when I got there.

As the railcar slid to a stop, I shoved my way through the other passengers and rushed to the Careen, but the doors were locked. "Open," I commanded with desperation. Thankfully, they weren't password-protected. The doors glowed purple and let me through.

The Rooks were staying in rooms on the third floor. I tore up the steps and searched for number 303. When I walked through the door, there were sixteen minutes left until the concert began.

Tess would have been less frightening if she could breathe fire. She launched herself at me, screeching, "Where have you been? Do you think just because I have a magical gift for design that I can throw something together at the drop of a hat? I hope you don't plan on looking good because I'm not a magician."

I didn't dare point out that, technically, she *was* a magician. She dragged me from the bedroom area to a spacious, bright closet with marble flooring.

With a *humph* she handed me a lavender gown. "The dresses

always turn out best when I can make them on you. I had to form this to a mannequin, so don't complain when it isn't a perfect fit."

"Thank you, Tess. I'm sorry I was so late." I took the dress from her and slipped it on.

It felt like Tess was using a beating stick instead of a brush to comb my hair. I winced with every stroke. She twisted my white hair into a simple bun, then slapped some mascara on me. "That's as good as it gets tonight. Don't be surprised if the judges score you lower tomorrow."

"Yes, I'm sure my ghastly appearance will reflect in my score." Although with the judges searching for any reason to knock off some points, she might be right.

Tess stormed off as I rolled my eyes. I quickly put on my shoes and rushed to the first floor of the concert hall.

"You're very late," Silas hissed when I squeezed past him to my seat in the third row. The first song had just ended.

"I'm sorry," I whispered.

Silas stared straight ahead with his lips pressed tight.

"Are you mad at me too?" I asked Aaron as the group on stage began the next song.

"No, I was just worried. I'm glad you're safe." He squeezed my knee but quickly pulled his hand back to his own lap.

The program helped relax me as it alternated between gentle songs and poetry. Several different performers took the stage, and their songs were familiar. The language was flowery, the music soft. It was so unlike the music in Creo with its wordless, harsh rhythm. I glanced down the row and saw Owen's head bobbing as he struggled to stay awake.

When the concert ended, Silas directed us to an upscale restaurant on the second floor of the building. The walls of the Careen were made of glass, and below, the city was bustling despite the late hour. Railcars whizzed in and out of stations with people tumbling out of their doors before they rushed off into the night.

I stood alone at one of the tall, metal tables spread out across the carpeted, navy-blue floor. Aaron had been pulled into a trainer huddle and Tess and Silas were too busy glaring at me from across the room to chat.

"Aren't we in your home province? What are you doing here alone?" Owen asked as he approached from behind.

I turned to see him in his usual green suit that complimented his skin tone nicely. "I may be in my province, but I'm definitely not among my people. Remember? I'm not part of the nobility like the rest of you, and that's who is invited to these things. But if you want to have a barbecue on Maple Street, I'll be right at home there."

"Ah yes. I heard about your scathing interview where you said as much. You really don't know these people?" He gestured to the sea of swarming bodies. They wore opulent dresses, dapper suits, costly jewelry, and expensive watches.

"No, I don't know anyone here beyond the covers of magazines, brief appearances on TV, and occasional PR visits to local schools—the ones their own children would never attend. They're the upper class. The ones who know nothing of how it feels to stress about making it to the end of the month. These are not my people."

Owen passed me a glass of soda, then sipped from his own cup. "They're your people now, like it or not. Even if you don't win, being a whisperer will lift your family to prominence. You might as well get to know them."

My eyes narrowed as I scanned the crowd. "You're wrong. They will never be my people, and whispering has only brought my family sadness since my gift has been known." I thought of Pippin's regret as he heard the cries from the mob, and I hated them for forcing themselves onto my family. Couldn't they leave us alone? We had enough to deal with.

Owen's brown eyes softened. "I'm sorry, Laurelin. I hope it gets easier for you."

I dropped my gaze, feeling strange about the way he looked at me. "Thank you."

Amelia joined us at the table, wearing a pink dress and wide eyes. "You were so late tonight, I wondered if you weren't going to show up. I thought you were running scared, afraid of tanking at the competition in your own province."

I scoffed. "If this is your attempt to intimidate me, you're failing."

Amelia turned her hungry eyes on Owen. "I'm surprised you're standing here chatting with a murderer. You know what happened after the last social event."

"I also know Laurelin is the only reason we made it out of the first round alive and with decent scores. Although some scores seemed fairer than others." Owen raised his eyebrows.

Amelia pulled a face. "You know what? This table is too crowded for me," she said. "You two have fun." She lifted her handbag from the table and knocked over Owen's drink as she made to leave. It spilled all over his suit. "Oops," she said with a smile.

"Can you believe her?" I asked as I dabbed at the spots on Owen's suit with a napkin.

"She's not as mean as she seems," he said as he examined his suit. "It's the competition. I knew her before all of this, and she was a lot nicer then."

"I'll have to take your word for it."

"Thanks for your help, but it's no use. I'm going to change," Owen grumbled as he walked away.

Somehow, my drink escaped unscathed. I sipped as I watched Amelia flirt with Evan Hilton. Over her shoulder, he shot me a cold look. I guess he wasn't over the fact that I'd taken his spot in the Pentax.

"Don't look too happy." Aaron wrapped his hand around my waist. "You might give someone the impression you're having a good time."

I smiled and pulled away. "What are you doing? Silas will kill you if he expects anything is going on between us."

Aaron clasped his hands in front of him. "My apologies, ma'am. I simply could not help myself. My compliments to your designer."

"You mean the latest in the string of people who hate me."

"Never mind Tess. She'll get over it by morning. She just hates missing a chance to display her full skillset."

"I'm sorry I missed our training session. Anything we should discuss before tomorrow?"

"You know the province well enough. My best guess for the task is that you'll have to solve a puzzle—you know, find deeper meaning in words or something like that. Remember the key to every round of competition is to respect the heart of the province. If you had to summarize what's most important to Lingua, what would it be?"

It was an easy question to answer. "Lingua most prizes the ability to use language to influence for good. And pygsmies. Always pygsmies."

"Ever the optimist." Aaron shook his head. "I don't know that the 'good' part matters to someone like Silas. More like influence for *his* good. But yeah, I'd say that's a decent assessment. So look for a way to show that's important to you, too."

"Silas hasn't been that bad to work with," I said.

Aaron picked at a spot on his jacket lapel. "You're only saying that because he gave you Eva's journal."

"It was very helpful. Until I lost it." I grimaced.

"Sure, Laurelin. Just don't let one kind act blind you. He's the same stick-up-his-butt kind of guy he's always been."

"Very eloquent." I rolled my eyes.

Aaron shrugged. "Never claimed to be. I'll never fit in with this crowd, El. I'm only here for you."

My breath caught in my chest. "Is that the real reason you

agreed to be my trainer? You didn't only agree because of the trading opportunities?"

Aaron squinted. "I mean, it was a pretty close toss up."

I elbowed his ribs and he laughed.

"Yes, that's the real reason. I wanted a chance to spend time with you in a way that wasn't completely contraband. So far, it's worked out better than I hoped. You're really going to do it, El. You're going to be queen."

I stuck out my tongue. "Don't remind me. Besides, I have to survive tomorrow first."

"Neither of us have any doubt you will. Whatever Lingua has up its sleeve has to be easier than a manticore, right?" Aaron asked.

"It's the Pentax, Aaron. You never know."

Chapter Nineteen

L ong purple stage curtains separated the Rooks from the noisy crowd on the other side. They blew in the breeze, either blocking out the chatter of the crowd or amplifying it, depending on which way they swung. As I waited, I bit my nails. I'd been feeling lightheaded all morning, and as the stage curtains wiggled, I swayed with them.

"Are you okay?" Aaron asked as he steadied me.

I took a deep breath. "I'm not feeling great. It's probably just nerves."

Aaron eyed me with concern.

"This is Lingua," Amelia scoffed as she spoke to her trainer a few yards away. "How hard could the competition be? They'll probably have us write a song and judge which one is best."

"Don't pay any attention to her. She's trying to get under your skin," Aaron whispered.

"She's good at it." I leaned forward and caught a glimpse of Dad sitting in the front row of the audience. I was excited to have him here, but it also added some pressure. I didn't want to disappoint him.

"Rooks at the ready," a woman called to everyone backstage.

"Time to shine," Aaron whispered. "You can do this. I'll see you when it's all done." He gave my hand a squeeze, then disappeared behind a set of stage curtains.

I made my way over to the line of Rooks. Amelia fiddled with a lock of hair, her leg bouncing. Faye straightened her glasses, and Owen leaned behind the row of others to wave at me. His goofy smile made me laugh despite myself. I waved back.

Saundra would be emceeing this event. From the stage, her voice boomed over the crowd. "Please put your hands together for Ausland's fearless Rooks!"

Owen led the line and I took up the rear.

The amphitheater was on the east side of Lyre Square in the heart of Meadow. It was strange to see the place so empty. Other than the hundred spectators who sat in the amphitheater's seats, the area beyond had been cleared for today's competition. As the crowd cheered, I looked down at Dad. His face beamed with pride from his front row seat. It was hard to see him there alone, but I knew Mom had to stay with Pippin.

Saundra continued. "We are very excited to see what our Rooks have in store for us today. We have a group of talented young people, and I'm sure they will exceed expectations once again. As a reminder, Crede from Fortis went home after the first round. Today's scores will be added onto the Rooks' existing totals, and the person with the lowest score will be eliminated from competition."

My stomach turned and sweat began to drip down my forehead. I hadn't felt this awful before the first round. Something about competing in Lingua had ratcheted up my nerves. I had to get control of myself.

"Silas Evermore, Duke of Lingua, will give our Rooks some instruction. Then we'll let the games begin!"

The audience erupted in cheers and chanted, "Laurelin! Laurelin! Laurelin!"

It would have been flattering if I'd had enough head space to concentrate on them. Instead, I was fighting to keep down my breakfast.

Silas walked onto the stage in his Linguan uniform. His purple jacket reminded me of pygsmies with its swirly, golden embroidery; it helped calm me some. I wished I could use one to help me feel better now.

"The people of Lingua receive their gifts from Mira, Matron of Language. We use these gifts to express ourselves through song, writing, and poetry. We can command and persuade with our words, and we are natural leaders because of it. Here, we truly believe the pen is mightier than the sword.

"Today, the Rooks will be asked to solve a riddle and accomplish the task contained therein. Each riddle was created by the judge from the Rook's province with oversight from the full panel. They are similar, yet unique to the individual's knowledge and skill set. Each one will point the Rook to the same goal, which is to retrieve a specific object and return it here, to this stage. This round of competition has an hour time limit. Should any Rook not finish the task in time, he or she will automatically receive a forty-five point deduction from their score."

Black dots filled my vision as I strained to comprehend Silas. I blinked furiously and concentrated on breathing deeply.

Next to me, Faye whispered, "Are you okay, Laurelin? You look like you're going to pass out."

I was surprised by her concern. "I'll be fine once we get started."

She looked at me through her glasses. "As long as you're sure."

The dots began to fade as I continued to take deep breaths.

"Each Rook will head to their province's flag." With the wave of his hand, four large banners unfurled in the distance. Lingua's purple flag hung off the side of a dress shop about two hundred yards to the right. "The riddle is hidden nearby. Rooks, take your mark."

As my mind focused on the flag, the other distractions faded away.

Silas counted down. "Three ... two ... one ..."

A bell rang. I sprinted from my place on the stage, down the stone steps. The crowd gasped as I tripped on the bottom stair. My hand skidded across the brick ground as I caught myself, leaving a trail of road rash.

I wasted no time assessing my injuries. I ripped myself off the ground and pushed forward. Mentally, I searched for nearby pygsmies in case I needed to use one for flight or sight. I knew healing was strictly off limits. I didn't agree with the rule, but I'd abide by it. Saving Pippin was too important.

It was comforting to find Sun Petal close by, as usual. I was beginning to expect her to follow me.

The flag fluttered in the breeze as I approached the shop, searching for any clues that would indicate where the riddle was hidden. Nothing on the sidewalk, street, or brick building caught my eye.

The wind calmed for a moment, allowing the flag to hang still. I studied the pygsmy and lyre branch detail in the middle. I followed the curve of the pygsmy's long nose, which pointed at the dress shop's brick facade. I ran my fingers over the rough surface, feeling for any loose spots.

"Open," I repeated over and over as I touched each one. Finally, a brick glowed purple as my hand passed. It slid out from its place in the wall, falling into my palm. On the inside was a piece of folded paper with these instructions: *Write the translation below, then follow the steps.* The rest was in pygsmish.

Some of the dizziness began to creep back into my head, but I shoved it aside. With my fingers shaking, I undid the clasp on my leather backpack. This time, we were afforded the use of a bow and arrow, a notepad, and a pencil. Across the paper, I scribbled the translation.

Through the meadows one must go

Matrons waiting kept in stone
Seize the magic but beware
Mystics must be used with care
Only one will leave with power
Unite the stones atop the tower

The words ran through my mind in a steady loop. *Through the meadows* would probably refer to the city, Meadow, since it was named after the meadows.

Matrons waiting kept in stone seemed to refer to a statue of the Matrons, but which one? There were so many, especially in Meadow.

Seize the magic. So once I found the statue, something related to magic would be there—probably stones, like the last line indicated.

But beware, mystics must be used with care. Pygsmies were often referred to as mystics. Silas said each riddle would be unique to the individual. He was probably reminding me not to use them to heal.

Only one will leave with power. That was definitely referring to the winning Rook. Only one of us would become king or queen.

Unite the stones atop the tower. I had to retrieve the stones and bring them back to the metaphorical tower—the stage—like Silas said.

Black spots returned, dotting my vision as I looked over the city. Owen was on the back of a bird, flying off across Meadow. Amelia was running from Amare's flag toward the Careen. And Faye was nowhere in sight. It was time to get going.

I wracked my brain, trying to decide which statue I should target. *Matrons,* I repeated, which meant at least more than one of them together. Lingua was full of statues of Mira, but not many of multiple Matrons. In fact, I could only think of two in Meadow. There was a statue of Everly and Mira at a fountain on the other side of the amphitheater. And then there was a relief of all the Matrons on the pediment of Mira's Temple on the east side of Meadow. That seemed like the better fit for the riddle since I would have to cross Meadow to get there and all the Matrons were "kept in stone."

The fastest way to get across Meadow was by flight.

What do you say, Sun Petal? Are you in this with me?

Always, always, Sun Petal said as she twirled toward me. She wound her tendrils around me and lifted me into the air. *Where are we going?*

Mira's Temple. I'll show you the way, I said.

For a moment, I thought about the poem's warning. *Mystics must be used with care.* But I couldn't win this competition without using a pygsmy. It was only a warning about healing, I was sure of it.

Normally, I enjoyed feeling the wind in my face as we soared through the sky. Today, the rush of the ground below made me sick. I kept my eyes tightly shut as we flew for several minutes with only the hum of the camera drone to accompany me.

Oh, not again, Sun Petal said as her mind filled with panic.

My eyes popped open. In the distance, a pack of scrawl were heading toward us.

Stay calm, Sun Petal. We can get through this.

Fortunately, we were no longer in Creo, and killing scrawl was fair game here.

I unclipped the bow and took my shot, commanding the arrow to kill before I released. Despite my poor aim, the enchanted arrow found its target. With a piercing screech, a heavy, black scrawl fell from the sky. I repeated the action, littering the ground with puddles of black blood that looked like oil spills.

The pack's numbers were falling, but they were also getting closer. I shot as quickly as I could, but at least twenty remained airborne and I was running low on arrows.

"Replicate." I touched each of the five remaining arrows. With a quiet *pop,* they doubled. The scrawl were so close now that I could feel each beat of their leathery wings.

I told Sun Petal to drop lower. Winding between buildings would slow us, but I hoped it would help lose the scrawl. Their bodies were too large and cumbersome to fly through small spaces.

Sun Petal zigzagged, taking a winding path toward the temple. The scrawl were determined though. A few, in particular, were better flyers. Skillfully, they arced between buildings while managing to dodge the arrows I continued to send. Occasionally, my arrow would strike one of the worse flyers in the rear, but the frontrunners would not be deterred.

Our twisting and turning flight took a toll on my queasy stomach. I heaved, and my breakfast made its second appearance on the street below. Too embarrassed, I didn't dare look to see if it hit someone, but that was just enough time for the nearest scrawl to attack. It dug its razor-sharp teeth into the tendrils that bound me to Sun Petal.

Oh, no. Sun Petal!

The pygsmy screamed in pain, but the scrawl had no pity and snapped again. I whacked it with the bow sending it spinning backward. It knocked into the scrawl behind, and they spiraled downward, making an audible thud as they hit the earth.

The remaining three scrawl were too close. One tore into Sun Petal's tendril on my other side. She screamed again and the sound ripped my heart. I'd never been one to cause a pygsmy pain, but it was even worse when the creature was my friend. Sun Petal was only in this position because of me.

Release me and hide. I threw every bit of force behind my command, not wanting Sun Petal to stay out of some silly sense of loyalty.

Sun Petal withdrew the only tendril that bound me to her. I fell ten feet, landing on a lush patch of grass between a tall building and the street. Pain shot up my legs as they absorbed the rough landing.

I'm sorry, Sun Petal, I said, hating myself for the terror I had caused her. I hoped she would get away from the scrawl. She stood a good chance without me as baggage.

Instead of chasing Sun Petal, one of the three remaining scrawl dug its talons into my side as I scrambled to collect my bow and an arrow. I felt its hot breath on my face as it screeched and lunged for my throat. Swiftly, I blocked the scrawl with the handle of the bow. Its fierce eyes met mine as its jaw snapped the shaft. In the same moment, I brought both legs up and kicked its stomach, sending it hurtling behind me. It wailed as it skidded across the ground. Its wings thrashed in its struggle to get on its feet.

My mind was a jumbled mess, operating on instinct alone. I grabbed my last arrow and dove for the scrawl. Its teeth pierced my wrist as I plunged the arrow into its chest. It let out a final, grisly squeal before its body slumped to the ground, black blood pouring from its wound. The blood smelled sour and caused my stomach to heave again, but this time, it was already empty.

I had flown far enough from the starting point that the streets were filled with bystanders. They stared with open mouths and gave me a wide berth, probably because I was covered in a putrid mix of scrawl blood and my own. Stars popped in my vision, and my legs wobbled beneath me. Still, I forced myself to trudge on. The temple was in sight, just a few hundred yards in the distance. I could make it. I had to make it.

By the time I reached the temple steps, my vision was so blurry I couldn't distinguish any shapes around me. I had to rely on my sense of touch alone. On my knees, I felt the cold, stone steps and dragged my body up toward the doors. Blackness filled my mind. My body was sluggish and then unresponsive.

"Pippin," I whispered. "Please, Mira. Let me finish for Pippin."

Then the darkness swallowed me up.

Chapter Twenty

I couldn't make sense of my surroundings. It felt like my body was floating in water, but there was no liquid around me. In fact, there wasn't anything around me. No floor, no walls, no sky. Everything was white. The only concrete sensation was a lyrical, female voice that chanted:

> *Through the meadows one must go*
> *Matrons waiting kept in stone*
> *Seize the magic but beware*
> *Mystics must be used with care*
> *Only one will leave with power*
> *Unite the stones atop the tower*

It was Mira, the goddess of language, and she was turning her breathtaking, green eyes on me. Face-to-face, she was so different than the gray, stony statues I'd looked at all my life. Her cheeks were warm, her skin soft, and she had the long nose that was characteristic of the Matrons. She wore a simple purple dress that ended just above her ankles. Her red hair fell around her heart-shaped face in thick ringlets. She extended her hand to me, smiling. I reached out, but as our skin connected, Mira was washed out in a blaze of light.

I sat up, sucking in sharp breaths.

"Whoa, hold on a minute there."

I knew it was Aaron, but I couldn't see him. My eyes were still blinded by the bright light around me. It was as if I stared into the sun.

"Just lay back for a second." He pushed my shoulder as his arm cradled my head.

The ground beneath me was cold. The hiss of whispered voices filled my ears. I struggled to put the pieces together, to understand where I was. Then the memories hit me.

"How much time is left?" I gasped. "Did I miss it?" I sat up again as my vision slowly returned. Aaron's face hovered above mine. Then Mira's temple came into focus behind him. And at the bottom of the white steps, a gathering of onlookers stared and mumbled to each other—the source of all the noise. "Please don't tell me I missed it." Before I could stop it, tears began to fall down my face.

Aaron's eyes were sad, his lips tight. "I'm sorry, El. There's less than five minutes left until the hour is up, but it doesn't matter now. I ..." His eyes dropped to the ground and he took a deep breath. "I know you're going to be mad at me, but I gave you elixir from the vial around your neck. You're going to be disqualified."

The lump in my throat was too large to speak. I failed. Pippin would die because I failed. I squeezed my eyes shut and let the waves of pain lick my heart.

A hand gripped my shoulder. I turned and was surprised to see Owen.

"Owen completed the competition about the time you passed out," Aaron explained. "We were watching on the screens at the amphitheater. He offered to take me here, and it's a good thing he did—"

I found my voice. "No, it isn't." Anger came spewing out of

me like lava. "You shouldn't have come. Owen only offered to help so he could knock me out of competition for good. You should have known better, Aaron. Now I'm disqualified."

"El, I don't think you understand how serious your condition was. I had to use elixir to bring you back, and it almost didn't work. You would have died."

"Don't call me that," I snapped. Something about the use of his silly nickname felt like sandpaper against my skin. We were not friends. We couldn't be. Not after this.

Aaron's eyebrows knit together. "Don't call you what?"

"Don't call me 'El.' My name is Laurelin. And you're wrong. I would have woken up because I had to. I *had* to, Aaron. This was Pippin's last chance, and now it's over." I buried my face in my hands. I didn't know how to cope with this level of pain.

"I'm sorry, El—Laurelin. I'm so sorry." He placed his hand on my knee, but I pushed it away.

"Please, just leave me alone. I can't stand to see you right now."

A railcar pulled up on the tracks across from the temple. Officers and medical staff came pouring out with Silas behind them. The officers worked to disperse the onlookers. A female medic in a blue uniform raced up the steps and shooed Aaron and Owen away. I was glad to have them gone.

The woman checked me out, examining my pulse and my breathing as two other medics hauled a stretcher up to us.

"I don't need that," I insisted. "I'm perfectly fine."

"It's our responsibility to make sure that's the case, ma'am," one of the men said.

He and his partner loaded me onto the tan stretcher, but at that point, I no longer cared what happened to me.

"Laurelin," Silas said as we reached the bottom of the steps, "I'm very sorry to see things end this way. I know you were hoping for so much more. We all were." His eyes dropped. I hated to see his disappointment. "How are you feeling?"

His simple question brought on a new round of tears. The

medics rolled me past him and into the railcar without an answer. I stared at the bright, white lights on the ceiling and seized the numb feeling, pulling it over my mind like a blanket.

"Why do you torture yourself like this, Laurelin?" Dad asked as he rolled into the front room.

I'd been home for a week, and the mob outside the gate only seemed to grow larger every day. I stared out the window at them, hating myself for revealing my secret when it amounted to nothing.

"They'll always be there. They'll always want more from you. You have to learn how to shut them out. You'll find ways to share your gift in your time and in your way."

I pulled the curtains closed, but it made no difference. The real demons lived in my mind, reminding me constantly of my failure. I was nothing like the great whisperers of the past—Eva, who saved Ausland's magic. Maybe I was more like Julian ... he used his gift to cross the meadows. I could do the same.

"Mom is about to bring Pippin some tea. Do you want to go with her?" Dad asked. He kept his face arranged in a carefully composed mask, but his eyes betrayed him. He had no hope I'd say yes.

I'd refused to see Pippin since I returned home. It was too painful to confront my failure so directly. I stared at the rose pattern wallpaper without really seeing it. "Sure, I'll go with her," I answered.

Dad tried to hide his surprise, but it slipped through in the twitch of his lips.

"That's great, honey!" Mom called from the kitchen. "He'll be so glad to see you."

She rounded the corner, and I dropped my gaze. I couldn't look at her. A week ago, she'd been full of hope. She tried to convince me she was proud of me for trying, but I knew the truth.

I was a disappointment to us all.

Dread filled my heart with each stair I climbed. Could I bear to look into Pippin's eyes knowing I had failed him? My hand froze at the doorknob. "You go ahead, Mom. I need a second," I breathed.

"Sweetheart," Mom said as she cupped my cheek. She forced my eyes up to meet hers. "Pippin wants to see you. He's been asking every day. Please don't make him wait any longer."

What she meant to say was that he didn't have any longer to wait.

I nodded and Mom smiled. She opened the door. My feet felt like they had resistance bands wrapped around them as I forced them forward. Finally, I reached the chair by his bed and collapsed into it.

Pippin surprised me. His eyes opened, even without the tea. "Hey, Laura." He smiled. "Thanks for coming."

I searched his face for signs of anger, hatred, even mild disappointment. I found none. A tear fell down my cheek.

"Hey, Pip. I'm sorry it took me so long to get up here. I just couldn't ..." I choked up, unable to speak past the lump.

"Here, honey." Mom handed Pippin the cup of tea, which he quickly drank.

His smile grew wider as the elixir took effect. "So, chess?" he asked.

I smiled slightly. This kid. How could he sit there, acting like everything was fine? Didn't he know how much I ached?

"You really feel up to it?" I asked.

"Oh, I get it. You're still scared of losing," he teased.

I rolled my eyes. Playing games was the last thing I wanted to do, but I could do it for Pippin. "You're crazy, you know. If you think I'm going to take it easy on you just because you're dying, think again."

"Well, if you think I'm going to let you win so you don't feel like such a loser, think again."

"Pippin," Mom scolded.

"Ouch," I laughed. "Now I've really got to put you in your place."

I pulled the old chess set out of the bottom drawer of his dresser and set it on a table by his bed. Pippin propped himself into a sitting position. Already, I could see his mind at work, calculating his moves.

"Hey, Pip," I said when we were nine moves in. I'd already lost three pawns, a knight and a rook. Pippin was down two pawns and a bishop. "I need you to know something, but you can't say anything to Mom or Dad, okay?"

Pippin scrunched his eyebrows as he continued to examine the board. "Okay," he hesitated. "What's up?"

"I have an idea—another way I can save you."

He looked at me. "Not this again, Laura. There is no other way. It's time to let it go."

"No, listen. The Matrons can still save you. If they can give a wish to the winning Rook, they can give a wish to me. I'm going to do it. I'm going to cross the meadows and demand one."

Pippin's mouth hung open. "Laura, that's crazy. Nobody makes it across the meadows."

I believed that too—until I learned the pygsmies made it impossible to cross. I didn't want to muddle him down in the details, though.

"I just needed you to know so you'd keep fighting, okay? Don't give up. I'm going to fix this for us."

Pippin stared at me for a long moment. Then he looked at the window. "Is the crowd still out there?" he asked.

I shrugged. "Yeah. It's no big deal. They're always out there."

He nodded, then made his next move. "Don't you think it would be better to share the elixir? I've had my turn—four long years that shouldn't have been mine. There are others who need it too. Just think how different Dad's life would be if he had elixir when he was trampled by that horse. You could make a real difference for people. You could save lives."

His talk had my breath coming in anxious gasps. He was giving up. "The only life I'm interested in saving is yours, Pip, and I will do it. I know I can do it. Just promise me you'll keep fighting." I moved my knight to H5.

"If that's what you want me to do, Laura," he said as he snatched up my knight with his rook. In six more turns, he had me in checkmate.

"Well played, Pip. But to be fair, I'm very out of practice." I winked.

"I think I need to sleep again, Laura," Pippin said as his eyelids drooped.

I kissed his forehead. "Thanks for a fun morning. I love you, kiddo."

His words were badly slurred, but I still understood. "Love you too," he said as he snuggled into his pillow.

I rushed down the stairs and grabbed a jacket from the back closet. There was no time to waste.

"Hey, where are you going?" Dad called after me.

"Library. I'll be back later!" I said, already half out the door. It slammed shut behind me.

I sprinted to the side yard and placed my hand on the iron fence. "Move," I commanded, and the metal bent enough for me to slip through. I managed to make it across the Johansen's backyard without being seen by the mob. From there, no one was watching. I ran the rest of the way to the rail station without being stopped. I had to find any information I could about the meadows and the Matrons before I left tomorrow.

Chapter Twenty-One

For hours, I'd been curled up at the top of my bed, poring over the ten books I'd checked out from the library. So far, nothing had struck me as particularly helpful. Most of the books warned about the dangers lurking in the meadows with its many mystical beasts and gave flowery descriptions of the same facts I already knew about the Matrons. I began to nod off as I read yet another explanation about turngrass—a plant that was common and harmless on the floor of the meadows.

A knock on my bedroom door roused me. "Come in!" I called, hurrying to cover the books with my blue quilt.

Mom walked into the room, chewing on her cheek like she always did when she had bad news. She wore a ripped, floral-print apron. Its pockets bulged with Pippin's medicine and empty vials of elixir. Her brown hair, now streaked with silver, was pulled back into a braid with flighty strands surrounding her face.

I despised the way life had stolen so much joy from this gentle woman. I was supposed to be the one to share her burden. I was the reason to hope that her baby would be saved. If I couldn't deliver on that most important wish, what good was I to her? Suddenly, I found myself unable to meet Mom's eyes.

She grabbed my chin. "Laurelin, how are you, my sweetheart?"

"I'm okay, Mom. What did you have to tell me? Is Pippin all right?"

Mom shrugged. "Pippin is the same. I came to update you about the Pentax."

I cringed. I'd been working hard to avoid the news. A couple days after I was eliminated, I accidentally overheard two women outside say that Owen had been cut after the round in Amare. That was a shock for everyone. Of course, in the back of my mind, I had been keeping track of the days. Today would have been the final round.

I braced myself. "Go ahead and let me know who's our next queen."

Mom tucked a strand of hair behind my ear. "It's been announced that Faye Bennett has won."

I nodded. I suppose out of Faye or Amelia, Faye was preferable, but only mildly.

"I wanted to tell you how proud your father and I are. You've been so brave, and not just through the Pentax. The last few years have been tough, and you've handled it so well. Now it's time to make plans for yourself."

"My only plan is to see Pippin healthy again, Mom. Please don't tell me you're giving up too."

Mom smiled. "I'll never give up on either of my kids. I just hope you can find something that makes you happy, that's all I'm trying to say."

"I am happy," I lied.

Mom wasn't fooled. "What about Aaron? Have you responded to the letter he sent?"

My eyes darted to the desk, where I'd stashed Aaron's letter after failing to throw it in the trash. At least I hadn't caved so far as to open it.

"Not yet," I sniffed.

"He's a great friend, Laurelin. Don't push good people away."

I raised my eyebrows. "You've come a long way from calling him black market trash."

Mom frowned. "I never said that."

"You implied it."

"Well, I'm sorry if I did. I judged too quickly, and I think you should write to that poor boy."

I did not want to talk about this. I faked a yawn. "I'm really tired, Mom. I think I should get some rest."

Mom paused before she leaned in and kissed my forehead. "Goodnight, Laurelin." She rose from the bed, giving me a last look before she shut the door.

Everyone in this house claimed they weren't giving up, but I could feel it. I was the only one holding out hope. I'd prove them wrong. I would find a way to save Pippin.

With renewed determination, I returned to my reading. I would find something useful, and even if I didn't, that wouldn't stop me. I'd cross the meadows blindfolded if I had to.

Ausland's provinces get their power through crystal stones created by the Matrons. The five crystals act as a conduit for the Matrons' powers, projecting magic to the people of Ausland.

I sighed. More of the same information. The books couldn't tell me anything I didn't already know. Five crystal stones, like in Eva's poem.

Five stones, their colors bright
Magic given for man's delight
Powers protected in crystal form
From it, Ausland's provinces born

Such common knowledge. I wondered again why Eva had felt the need to write the lines in pygsmish.

179

Tap, tap, tap.

A green finch was perched on the other side of my window. It slammed its beak into the glass again. I hoped it would leave soon, searching for some bug to eat.

I returned to my thoughts.

Tap, tap, tap.

The bird hopped around the windowsill, chirping adamantly. I was confused—until I saw a paper tied to the bird's leg.

The finch hopped onto my white dresser as I threw open the window. It chirped repeatedly, keeping its black eyes locked on mine as I reached for the note.

Laurelin,

Aaron is hurt. He needs elixir ASAP.

Up, around, over, and under—he said you would know what that meant.

Come now.

—Owen

The bird hopped out the window and took off into the night. I froze for a moment. From the desk, Aaron's unopened letter seemed to hurl accusations at me. Would he be mad I hadn't responded? Did it matter if he was hurt? All I knew was that I had to go.

I pulled on a pair of jeans, grabbed my backpack and bow, and said a hurried goodbye to Mom and Dad. I took a vial of elixir from the cabinet as I told them Aaron needed my help. They probably would have asked more questions if they hadn't been so happy to see me wearing jeans instead of pajama pants and leaving the house.

Once outside, I searched the skies for a pygsmy. A couple

miles out, I came across Sun Petal. I almost grabbed onto her, but I couldn't bring myself to face the mystic. Since the competition, I had searched a couple of times, wondering if Sun Petal would be close by. She was never as close as she used to be. I couldn't blame her for being angry, though I did wonder why she was still in Lingua at all.

With a sigh, I grabbed hold of a different pygsmy.

Up, around, over, and under was a reference to a black market trading post known as the Pit. It was located on the outskirts of Sedona and just south of Meadow. I told the pygsmy how to get me there.

Weightlessly flying through the starlit sky almost helped me forget the tragedy at home. I closed my eyes as the wind brushed my face, feeling something close to peace. That made the sting of my wrist more startling. Confused, I lifted my arm, wondering what Eva was trying to teach me now.

You should apologize.

Apologize? Did Eva mean I should apologize to this pygsmy? In my rush, I hadn't exactly treated her with respect like I'd been taught...

My wrist burned again.

That too, but I was talking about Sun Petal.

The words changed.

Remember to listen.

I didn't know if I was ready to face Sun Petal. Her shredded tendrils would be an awful reminder of what I put her through.

With a surge of guilt, I ignored Eva's instructions and pushed the new pygsmy forward. She dropped me near a boulder that concealed the entrance to the trading post. As the mystic fluttered off into the night, I regretted not taking the time to ask her name.

I shoved the thoughts away. It was time to focus on Aaron.

Twenty years ago, the Pit had been an amphitheater for some edgier performances that weren't tolerated in public squares. After waves of criminal activity began to accompany the underground performances, the authorities shut it down. So now, the Pit still hosted criminal activity, but it was less artistic.

The boulder butted up against a slate rock overhang. On one side, Sedona was visible. The other side was the beginning of Lingua's southern forest. Beneath the overhang, the ground had been hollowed out and concealed. I squeezed through the crack between the boulder and the overhang and jogged down the stone steps to the abandoned amphitheater. Worn, graffitied benches made of wood were spread out across the space. Half of them were broken. The stage was mostly rock with plywood planks evening out some low places.

Aaron sat on the ground in front of the stage, leaning against it for support. He wore no shirt, allowing me to see the gaping wounds that dotted his chest and abdomen. Owen kneeled next to him with a spool of gauze in his hand, working to bandage the sores.

"Oh, my. What happened to you, Aaron?" I asked. I ran to his side, kneeling opposite Owen.

"Nice to see you too, El." He grimaced as Owen dabbed at a wound with a piece of gauze. The smell of alcohol burned my nose.

"We were attacked by a pack of scrawl in the forest. Owen protected himself with a cougar. I wasn't so lucky."

"What were you doing in the forest? And why are you together?" I asked.

Aaron's eyes shifted to Owen. "Uh, we'll get to that later."

"Some elixir would be nice, Laurelin," Owen said as he worked.

"Right. Sorry." My fingers trembled as I searched around my jean pocket for the vial. "This won't taste good, but I don't think you can afford to be picky right now."

"I don't care what it tastes like, El," Aaron said as he snatched the vial from my hand. He pulled the stopper out and tipped it back. His face puckered like he'd swallowed a shot of whiskey.

Immediately, his wounds glowed with golden light. His flesh stretched, pushing out bubbles of new muscle and skin, filling the holes that covered him. Aaron's face began to relax. The new skin was pink at first, then faded to a normal color. Now, the only sign of his injuries was the blood smeared across his body.

"Amazing," Owen breathed.

"Have you never seen elixir at work?" I asked.

"Once or twice." He shrugged. "Never to heal anything like this, though." Owen wiped a bloody hand across his forehead and leaned against the stage. "I'm sure glad you got my message."

"Me too," Aaron said. "I didn't know if you'd come even if you got the note. You ignored my letter." He sniffed and looked away, then touched his shredded shirt and created a new one for himself.

I blushed and stared at my hands. "Yeah, I'm sorry about what I said the day I lost. You both saved my life. I just wish I'd been strong enough to finish. That's all."

Owen looked at Aaron. "Should we tell her?"

"That was the plan, wasn't it?" Aaron replied.

"Tell me what?"

Aaron rose from the ground and grabbed a camo-print backpack from the stage. He shuffled a few things around, then pulled out a cream file folder. "Owen and I were traveling through the forest because we were trying not to get caught. We found something important, and we were bringing it to you." He passed the folder to me. "El, you weren't just sick or weak the day of Lingua's competition. Someone tried to kill you."

Alarmed, I opened the cover and scanned the page inside. It was a report of the lab results from my examination at the hospital. Under the section titled *Foreign Substances Detected,* there was one word.

"Pygruim?" I read. "They found traces of pygsmy poison in my blood?"

"If you read the whole report, you'll see that it says 'minute' traces of pygruim. Before the competition started, how were you feeling?" Aaron asked.

"I was dizzy, nauseous, and my vision was blurry."

"Look down at the section about symptoms of pygruim poisoning."

I scoured the page. "It lists the same symptoms."

"Exactly. Someone gave you a very low dose of pygruim. The amount of pygruim in a pygsmy sting almost instantly kills. But a low dose will cause sickness before it kills. According to the doctor's notes, the amount of pygruim found in your blood would take approximately sixteen hours before it would result in your death, and it was administered through food or drink," Aaron explained.

"Well, sixteen hours before competition would have been during the social. I didn't eat anything there, and I only had one soda."

I looked at Owen, who stood with his lips pressed together.

"A soda that Owen brought to me."

Chapter Twenty-Two

In all my life, I never expected to stand face-to-face with someone who tried to murder me. Was this entire encounter nothing but an elaborate ruse to lure me here and finish the job?

"Winning was that important to you? So important you'd be willing to kill the competition?" I glared at him, hating the way he kept his eyes on the ground, as if he was ashamed of his crime.

"Hold on a minute, El." Aaron placed his hand on my shoulder.

I swatted at him. "You're going to defend him? I almost died! It's his fault I'm not on my way to the Matrons right now, about to have my wish granted!" My vision turned red as I filled with anger. Pippin would die because Owen couldn't stand to lose. I launched myself at him, my fingers curled into claws.

Aaron caught me around the waist. "El, wait a minute. You need to hear the rest of the story. Think about it. Without Owen, I never would have made it to you in time to give you elixir. He saved you. How would that make sense if he tried to kill you?"

I stopped struggling against Aaron's hold and tried to think clearly.

"Okay, somebody better start talking. Now," I growled.

Aaron kept his hand on my waist as he spoke. I wasn't sure if he was still trying to restrain me, or if he was just grateful to be close, like me.

"After you ... were eliminated," Aaron began, "I knew you were mad at me. I sent the letter, but I didn't want to force myself into your life again. So I went back to the only thing I know. Trading. Three days ago, I found myself in Creo preparing for a meeting with one of the biggest hawks on the market, Jorge Mendoza. He deals in meat, primarily. Imagine my surprise when I showed up for my meeting and found myself staring at Owen Mendez, the Rook who was eliminated from the Pentax in a surprise twist just a day before. It turns out Jorge Mendoza is an alias. He is really Lord Julio Mendez, one of the highest-ranking aristocrats in Ausland, and Owen's father. In the trade business, it's all about your suppliers, and Julio has the best around—his son, Owen, who can create wildlife. That gives him an unlimited supply of livestock, and with Creo's vegetarian ways, there's a high demand for meat on the black market."

Shocked, I looked at Owen, who pushed a pebble around with his toe. "That is very fascinating, but I don't see how it excuses Owen for what he did to me."

"Just hang in there. Owen, would you like to take it from here?"

Owen sighed. "You're right to be angry with me, Laurelin, but it's not exactly what you think. The truth is, my family squandered our money generations ago. When my dad came to me with the idea of using my gift on the black market, it just made sense to go for it. I wanted to help my family, and life got so much better for us when we had the funds to back our title. But it all came back to bite me during the Pentax. On our third night there, I found a letter waiting for me on my pillow. It was blackmail." Owen stopped, returning his eyes to the stone on the ground.

"Keep going. Laurelin deserves to know the truth," Aaron nudged.

Owen exhaled and squared his shoulders. "Whoever wrote the letter said they would reveal my family's secret if I didn't agree to help them. At the time, they didn't say what I'd have to do. The letter said they'd be in touch. If my secret got out, I knew I'd be disqualified from the Pentax, not to mention ruin my family's good name."

"If you think that's enough for me to excuse attempted murder, you're insane," I said.

Owen put his hands up. "Hang on a minute. The next day, right before the social in Lingua, I found a new note in my room. It said I was to go to the bar and ask the bartender for a 'stalewater soda,' then get the drink to you. The letter promised it wouldn't cause you any serious harm. But when I finished the competition and saw you collapse on the temple steps, I knew I'd made a big mistake. That's why I offered to give Aaron a ride to save you. It's also why I bombed the third round of competition. I knew I didn't deserve the crown, and I didn't want to hang around the Pentax, waiting to be manipulated again. Or worse, become king with a blackmailer on my back. When my dad mentioned a meeting with Aaron, I knew I had to take it so I could explain what I'd done." Owen's brown eyes locked on mine. "I'm sorry, Laurelin. I feel terrible that it all turned out so badly."

In some twisted way, I understood Owen's perspective. He was trying to protect his family, just like I was. Still, I couldn't quite find the words to forgive him. The fact remained Pippin could have been saved if he hadn't spiked my drink.

Aaron broke the silence. "After Owen told me what happened, we decided we needed to break into the hospital and find out what was in that drink. The document was marked as reported to your family, but that obviously isn't true. We knew someone with connections would have to sweep that under the rug, so that's why we weren't using the rail system to get to you. We were worried we might be followed."

"One Rook dead from a pygsmy sting, another slowly poisoned by pygruim. That can't be a coincidence," I said.

"Yeah, whoever wanted to kill you almost certainly killed Tobias, too. The only question is—why?" Aaron said.

"Do the words 'Stone Seekers' mean anything to either of you?" Owen asked.

My stomach dropped, remembering Eva's journal. "Umm, yes. Why?"

"The day Tobias was murdered, a couple of officers were talking outside my bedroom. It was when I was supposed to be training, so I don't think they knew I was there. I heard them say that Tobias had written the words 'Stone Seekers' on the dirt floor of his room."

I gasped. "Eva Evermore wrote about Stone Seekers in her journal. She said they were thieves who tried to steal the Matron's crystals so they could have Ausland's magic for their own. She did say the Matrons were especially vulnerable during the Pentax." I paused. "Do you think someone is after the crystals?"

Aaron nodded slowly. "It's possible, but I don't see what that has to do with Tobias's death. And why would they be after you?"

"Well, if someone is seeking the stones, it means they know the old ways. Eva said whisperers used to be protectors of the stones. They worked alongside pygsmies to guard the meadows. Maybe they think I'm a threat?" I shrugged. "I wish I still had that journal. Maybe she wrote more about it."

"Did you say this was Eva Evermore's journal? As in, the last whisperer before you?" Owen asked.

"Yes. Do you know something about it?" I asked.

Owen squirmed. "Was it a leather book with a pygsmy etched on the front?"

I gasped. "Have you seen it? Do you know where it is?"

"I've seen it all right. It was in Amelia's room on our last night in Creo. Come to think of it, she acted suspicious when I asked her about it. She said it was just an old sketchbook and then she hid it in one of her drawers."

"El, I saw Amelia outside your room that night, remember? When she tried to kiss me? She probably snuck in right after we left."

Owen ran his hands through his hair. "Amelia is one of the only people who knows about my family's black market trade. Her dad's a big business guru in Amare, so we've done a few roundabout deals with them. I never thought she'd use it against me."

"Well, I think it's safe to assume Amelia has the journal. And Tobias writing about Stone Seekers is too much of a coincidence to dismiss. Amelia probably took the journal for information about how to get them. I wish I'd taken time to read the whole thing before I lost it."

My heart was torn. On one hand, I wanted to ignore this problem and focus on getting across the meadows for Pippin. On the other, if Amelia or someone else was after the stones, Ausland's magic could disappear any moment, and then I'd be left with no way to help Pippin.

My wrist burned, showing what I already knew.

Whisperers are protectors.

I squared my shoulders. "We need to find Amelia and that journal. You boys up for a trip to Amare?"

I sent a pygsmy with a note for Mom and Dad. Traveling for an undetermined amount of time to confront the woman who most likely tried to kill me was the kind of message that should have been delivered in person, but I didn't want to give them the chance to stop me. I also left out the murderer bit. There was no need to have them wringing their hands back home.

We dropped by Aaron's hideout to grab supplies for our trip. Aaron loaded us up with rusty cans, shattered lamps, broken pencils—a mess of random material so he could create anything we'd need while we were gone.

With heavy packs on our backs, we hopped on a railcar and headed east toward Amare. The railcar was full of street performers and other late-night travelers, but as we got farther and farther from Meadow, it began to empty out. We transferred rail lines in Dade, the easternmost town in Lingua. After that, there was a long stretch of empty forest that separated Lingua and Amare. Outside the window, an endless sheet of tall pines and elderberry brush flew past us.

In the far corner of the car, Owen had fallen asleep, using the wall to support his head. Aaron and I sat on the same plastic bench, but we'd kept a careful distance between us. Maybe my hurtful accusations after he saved my life had driven us too far apart. All I knew was that it was painful to sit here in strained silence when we'd been perfectly in sync a week ago. As I twisted the lifestone on my finger, I stared at it to avoid his eyes.

"Do you think he knows he snores and drools when he sleeps?" Aaron jabbed his thumb in Owen's direction, breaking the silence. "We should probably tell him. It would be good for his ego."

I snickered. This felt familiar. It was the Aaron I knew. "Nah, he'd probably take it as a compliment that we analyzed him in his sleep."

"Good point. Especially if it came from you."

"He does seem to love all things female. I wonder if he honestly never suspected Amelia before tonight. Do you really think we can trust him?"

Aaron watched Owen carefully. "I think we'd be smart to keep our eyes and minds open. But he did save your life, and he didn't have to say anything about the blackmail. That has to count for something."

I nodded. "Maybe, but I think you're right about needing to

watch our backs."

"So how is Pippin? How are your parents?" Aaron's eyes tightened as he asked the question. What I'd said when I lost in Lingua must have really affected him.

I reached out and touched his arm. "Pippin's condition is not your fault. I know I said it was, but I was just angry. I said something stupid that I didn't mean, and I'm sorry for it."

Aaron gave a half smile. "Thanks. But I am still sorry that things turned out the way they did. You deserved to win."

I cleared my throat, which was thick with emotion. "To answer your question, Pippin is having a hard time seeing a point in continuing to fight. And Mom and Dad are ready to give up too." I kept my eyes on the lifestone as I spoke, clinging to the fact that there was still some red in the corner.

"Is there ... reason to hope he might get better?" He raised one eyebrow.

I sighed. "Well, what's the alternative? Throw my hands into the air and say 'oh well, I tried?' We're talking about my little brother's life here. There's no other option but to keep fighting. Once we stop Amelia, I'm going to cross the meadows and demand a wish from the Matrons. They will heal Pippin."

"El, the Matrons don't just hand out wishes like a prize for reaching Everark. And crossing the meadows is a death sentence. Don't you think it's time—"

"Don't say it." My voice cracked like a whip. "Do not tell me it's time I accept that Pippin is going to die. I'm his sister. I've kept him alive for four years, and I'm not about to quit. I will fix this, with or without your support."

"I'm just trying to say that it might be time to start thinking about your own future."

The shred of progress we'd made in returning to normal went up in flames. I couldn't sit here and discuss my brother's life as if we were mulling the weather forecast for tomorrow. "There is no future without Pippin. Or at least not one I want to live through."

Chapter Twenty-Three

"El, wake up." Aaron's voice pulled me from my dreams. "We're almost there."

At some point in the long night ride, the hum of the car against the rails must have lulled me to sleep. With a foggy head, I sat up. The morning sun was bright, like it had been up for a few hours. Outside my window, I saw Amare for the first time. The buildings were so enormous, they made Silas's mansion look like a matchbox. They were made up of strange, mismatched shapes and colors, with blocky, gray buildings turning into colorful curves, which faded into crisp, clean lines. It was as if original structures had been added onto for centuries, each with a different architect. If I could pinpoint any common theme amid the jumble, it would be color, with red hues the most frequent.

"What are the buildings used for? They can't be homes, can they?" I asked.

Aaron chuckled. "They're a little bigger than what you'd see in Lingua, aren't they?"

"Well yeah, but it's for a reason," Owen chimed in. "They live in families in Amare. Like big families. Grandparents, aunts, uncles, cousins, and it's been going on for generations. They grow when someone gets married or has a baby, and each new branch matches the tone of the family that occupies it."

The railcar stopped at a red brick station. A handful of people shuffled in, giving us suspicious stares. They probably thought we were runaways, carrying around big packs and looking very much like we'd slept in the car. Owen joined Aaron and I on our bench to make room for the newcomers.

"How does a family know where to live?" I asked. "If I got married, would my husband come live with my family or would I go to his?" I worked hard to keep my eyes from flashing to Aaron.

"They follow maternal lines, so the husband always goes to live with his wife's family, and he takes on her last name," Owen explained.

"Dinner with the in-laws every night. Yikes," Aaron mumbled.

The railcar pulled into a station with a sign that read *Hillsborough.*

"This is it—Amelia's neighborhood," Owen said as he rose from his seat. His family had been invited to one of their parties a few years ago.

The platform was full of men and women dressed in business attire, headed to work for the day. As we hopped out, I nearly knocked over a man in a blue suit and chukka boots. "Sorry!" I called, narrowly missing him with my pack.

Angrily, he mumbled something that I missed, then boarded the car with a huff.

"Might be the province of the heart, but that language was not nice," Aaron muttered as we walked up a cobblestone street to enter the gated neighborhood.

We were stopped short at the black gate with a silver padlock.

"Now what?" Owen grumbled. "They didn't have this the last time I was here."

"Let's not panic. It's only a gate," I said.

A few people looked back at us from the platform, whispering to each other.

"We're making people suspicious. Follow me. We can get in at a less public spot," I said.

We walked west along the fence line until we were out of sight from the platform. I ducked down and touched the iron fence. "Move," I commanded. The metal bent under my touch, creating a hole wide enough for Aaron's broad shoulders to squeeze through.

"Cool," Owen said as he climbed through. "I guess Lingua's powers aren't all lame."

Aaron elbowed him in the ribs.

"Thanks," I said.

Once inside, we rushed down the streets as quickly as we could without drawing too much attention to ourselves. Each sprawling home had a family name written above the gate. The properties were so large, it took more than five minutes before we'd reach the next one. My stomach growled, and my back ached from the heavy pack.

After three more houses, we finally found a gate that said *Allred* above it.

Aaron whistled. "Home sweet home. Can you imagine living in that thing? I don't think I'd be able to find the bathroom, let alone the way in or out."

A colossal mansion sprawled across acres of land, and it had the most cohesive look to it of the many we had passed. The manor was mainly shades of red, gold, or white. A flower-lined brick path led from the gate to the opulent, heart-shaped front doors where golden pillars lined the porch. On the front lawn, white geese wandered around, pecking at the ground as they went.

"How are we supposed to find Amelia's room in all of that?" Owen asked.

"We don't. We let a pygsmy do it for us."

I bent the bars of the fence and we slipped through. The

flower gardens provided nice cover as we skulked from bush to bush, making our way around the side of the mansion. We stopped in a thick patch of garden, behind two boxwood bushes and a couple of low-hanging fruit trees.

I closed my eyes and searched the skies, looking for a pygsmy. I was shocked when I felt Sun Petal's familiar prickle nearby. I hesitated. Did this mean Sun Petal wasn't mad at me? I didn't need Eva's words to remind me that I should apologize.

I braced myself and called to Sun Petal. Before she was in sight, I heard her.

Took you long enough. I hope this means you're ready to say you're sorry, she said as she zoomed toward me.

I am so, so sorry, Sun Petal. I didn't mean to hurt you. I should have released you as soon as I saw the scrawl.

The tiny mystic appeared in front of my face. I gasped as I counted—six tendrils, fully intact. No cuts or scars or any sign she had been hurt.

What are you talking about? Sun Petal asked.

How are you okay? The scrawl shredded right through you! I said.

Elixir, of course. I may be out of spare elixir, but I still have the elixir I need for myself. It healed me in minutes.

I paused. *So you're not mad at me for hurting you?*

No, but I am mad at you for forcing me away. I thought we were past that "commanding" stuff. Just because you can whisper, doesn't mean you should force me. I could have stayed and helped. I was already healing when you sent me away. Sun Petal knocked my cheek with her wing, which I'm sure was intended to hurt, but it was like being brushed with a feather. *And then you go and fly with some other pygsmy. I thought I meant more than that to you.* Sun Petal crossed her front tendrils and turned her back on me.

I breathed deeply, trying to process what Sun Petal had said. *I'm sorry I forced you. I won't do it again. And last night, I wanted so badly to call out to you, but I was scared. I thought you were mad at me, and I didn't want to see you hurt. Can you forgive me?*

Sun Petal turned slightly, her eyes meeting mine. *So I'm still your favorite pygsmy?*

I smiled. *You are absolutely the best.* I reached out and stroked her back.

Mmmm that feels nice, Sun Petal said.

Owen gasped. "Are you sure you should be getting that close? What if it stings?"

"Sun Petal won't sting, will you?" Aaron said. He reached toward Sun Petal.

My name sounds so silly in your language, Sun Petal said as she flew over and brushed Aaron's neck with her tendrils.

Aaron squirmed. "Hey, stop that, Sun Petal. You know I'm ticklish."

Never gets old, she said as she flew back to me.

"Okay, it's time to get moving. We don't have time to waste. You two, go hide behind that bush or something." I gestured to the next flowerbed.

Obediently, Aaron and Owen moved. They huddled together behind a four-by-four bush, looking ridiculous as they struggled to conceal their large bodies.

"Can you give me a little more space?" Owen asked.

"And where am I supposed to go? Behind that stick-of-a tree? Yeah, that'll work," Aaron hissed. "I'm bigger than you. You move."

I forced myself to focus on Sun Petal. *All I need you to do is find a room for me. I know human spaces make you uncomfortable, but I'll keep you safe.*

Sun Petal shrugged. *I'm not worried,* she said, but I could feel a nervous edge to her thoughts. She became a faint glimmer in the sunny sky as she darted toward an open window on the ground floor.

Concentrating very hard, I blocked out external sounds, cutting off my own senses so I could use Sun Petal's. A vision of a red hallway brimming with art, marble statues, and vases of flowers filled my mind. As Sun Petal darted down the hall, I noticed first names were written on most doorways. When there were hundreds of rooms in a house, there had to be some way to keep them all straight.

Sun Petal made it to the end of the long hall, where a cherry wood staircase extended to the next level. I directed her to go up and search the new hall. On what had to be the fiftieth door, I saw the name *Amelia* written in loopy cursive. My heart leapt with excitement.

That's the room. Slip under the crack. I want to see what's inside.

The balmy scent of Amelia's perfume was overwhelming. I wasn't sure if it only smelled so strong because I used Sun Petal's nose or if it would be this potent in person. The carpet was a light beige, and the sofa that sat in front of a mocha coffee table was cream with red throw pillows. Fresh roses were displayed on a brown writing desk pushed against the opposite wall from the oversized red bed.

Grab one of those roses and leave it on the windowsill, then come back for me. I want to check out the room for myself, I said.

Sun Petal snatched one of the flowers. *Oooo, I love roses. Especially red ones,* she said as she left the rose at the window.

When I opened my eyes, I found Owen and Aaron wrestling behind the bush.

"What are you doing?" I snapped.

They froze. Owen had Aaron in a headlock, but Aaron had Owen's legs pinned to the ground.

"He doesn't know how to respect personal space," Owen growled.

"And he's too used to getting whatever he wants. Just because you tell me to move doesn't mean I'm going to," Aaron said.

"It might interest you to know I found Amelia's bedroom. Or maybe you're too busy acting like five-year-olds to care."

Aaron and Owen released each other and scrambled to their feet, looking embarrassed.

I scanned the second-story windows, searching for Amelia's rose. A tiny green leaf caught my eye. "Gotcha," I whispered.

Will you take me to the window? I asked Sun Petal. *You don't have to go inside this time.*

Sun Petal tried to hide her relief as she picked me up.

"I'll be back soon. Please try not to kill each other while I'm gone."

"Wait, you're going in? Alone?" Aaron asked.

"We're less likely to get caught with only one of us inside. I just want to dig around a few places to find the journal. I'll be fast, I promise."

"El, stop! Let me go with you!" Aaron called, but I was already in the sky.

We soared to Amelia's window, and I touched the pane. "Open." The window slid to the side. Sun Petal zoomed in and quickly released me.

I'll let you know when I'm done, I said as Sun Petal fluttered back out the window.

Be careful, she said.

Wasting no time, I pulled open every drawer in Amelia's dresser and shuffled through the contents. I found nothing. I checked under her bed, in the couch cushions, her writing desk drawers, and her closet. All I uncovered was further proof that Amelia had very expensive taste.

With a sigh, I placed my hands on my hips and looked around, searching for any obvious spot I had missed. My eyes zeroed in on a silver box that sat on top of Amelia's white vanity. I rushed over to it, but the box was locked. I covered the keyhole with my pointer finger. "Open," I commanded. The lock popped, and the lid released, but the only thing inside was a bunch of jewelry.

Dang it. Where could that journal be? Maybe she kept it with her at all times.

I caught sight of my reflection in the vanity mirror. Yesterday's mascara was smeared beneath my eyes, and my clothes were wrinkled from sleeping on the railcar. But more importantly, I saw a gap along the mirror's edge. I dug my fingernails into the space and pulled. The glass gave a satisfying pop as it swung away from the wall, revealing a small metal box set into the space behind it.

"Open." The metal door swung forward, revealing a red notebook.

Red. Not brown with a pygsmy on the cover. The journal wasn't here.

Hoping I might still find some valuable information about Amelia, I flipped it open and scanned the more recent entries. A list of familiar names caught my eye.

- *Saundra Garcia. Royal spokeswoman from Creo. Intensely jealous of her sister, Queen Isadora. Always wanted the crown on her head.*
- *Arthur Thomas. Judge from Fortis. Recently lost his wife to a stroke. Heart isn't in the competition.*
- *Owen Mendez. Rook from Creo. Not attached to any specific person, just wants to prove himself in general.*
- *Aaron Gray. Trainer from Lingua. In love with Laurelin.*

In love with Laurelin? Was this based on Amelia's ability to read relationships? Or was it just some of her flighty gossip? My head spun at the silly word, *love*. I was getting carried away. It was probably just gossip.

- *Laurelin Moore. Rook from Lingua. Cares most about brother at home, not the crown.*
- *Faye Bennett. Rook from Scentia. Desperately wants her dad to love her.*
- *Silas Evermore. Duke of Lingua. Secret daughter is Faye Bennett.*

Whoa. Faye was Silas's daughter? Neither of them ever acted like they knew each other, let alone like they were family.

Underneath the notebook was a tiny vial. The swirling liquid inside was milky white with golden flecks. Pygruim.

"Will you get my riding boots ready? I'd like to leave as soon as possible." Amelia's voice came from down the hall.

I froze.

The doorknob twisted, and my heart stopped. There was nowhere to hide.

Chapter Twenty-Four

"What are you doing here?" Amelia demanded.

"I think the better question is," I held up the notebook and vial, "why did you try to kill me?"

Amelia's eyes narrowed. "You're so full of yourself, Laurelin. Not everything is about you." She kicked off the black heels she wore with a practical, black pant suit and walked toward me.

I raised my hands, ready to defend myself. With her eyes fixed on mine, she reached for the hairbrush on the vanity behind me and began combing her hair.

I exhaled. "Is now really the time for personal grooming? I want an answer to my question. Why did you try to kill me?"

"The vial isn't mine. I stole it as insurance."

"Do you really think I'm going to buy that lame excuse? Owen already admitted someone blackmailed him into spiking my drink the night before I was disqualified. You have a notebook full of information about people from the Pentax. And Owen saw you with Eva's journal, which you stole from my room. Do you deny any of that?"

Amelia walked to the cream sofa and sat down. She crossed her legs, completely unfazed by my accusations.

"No, it seems you are in possession of all the facts."

"So who does the vial belong to if it isn't yours?"

"Faye Bennett, of course. Our new queen. She's the one who tried to kill you."

Aaron and I sat in the two red armchairs across from Amelia and Owen on the couch. She had agreed to explain to us what she knew, but only after I mentioned Owen was outside waiting to find out if she was a murderer.

"Okay, Amelia. We want answers. Tell us what you know from beginning to end," I said.

Amelia glanced at Owen, who gave her an encouraging nod. She exhaled sharply. "This all began the night of the social in Creo. Silas and Faye were sitting at a table together, along with Arthur. That's when I got the read on their relationship. Silas hasn't been a part of Faye's life in any way. There was a lot of shame and embarrassment coming from Faye, especially. I don't know the full story, but it's not hard to do the math. Faye's mother has been married to Lord Bennett for twenty-one years. Faye is sixteen."

A memory clicked in my head. "You know, Faye talked to me for a minute that night. She said something about wanting to get away from her family."

"Exactly. Some relationships are so new or insignificant that I have to see the two people interact to get a read, but the deeper relationships are obvious even when the other person isn't there. From the moment I met Faye, she seemed desperate to be something to somebody. Her mother sees her as a nuisance—a sticky reminder of her scandalous affair, which Lord Bennett holds over her head relentlessly. And Lord Bennett only tolerates Faye to protect his family's wealth. They receive all their money from Faye's maternal grandparents, so that's why he stays. As Faye sat with Silas, hope emanated from her. She wants to make a parent proud for once, though it'll be hard wearing those ridiculous pantsuits and glasses." Amelia snorted.

"You're wearing a pantsuit," I pointed out.

Amelia sneered. "I have to dress like this when I attend business meetings with Daddy."

"Can we get back to the story? I don't see how this connects to the journal or Laurelin," Aaron said.

Amelia raised her chin in defiance. "Well, when I realized Silas was Faye's father, I decided to use it to my advantage. I confronted Silas and told him I'd tell what I knew if he didn't pad my scores."

"So *you* were the original blackmailer," I said.

Amelia shrugged. "It didn't matter in the end. Faye slipped me a note later that night. She knew something about my daddy's business deals. She said she'd expose him if I ever told anyone about Silas."

"How does Faye know so many secrets about everyone?" I shifted in my seat. "She knew about my brother's illness, she knew about Owen's black market business, and now you're saying she had dirt on your family too?"

Amelia's eyes sparkled. "I wondered that too, so I sent a letter to Daddy and asked him to do some digging. Turns out Faye lied about her gift. She doesn't remember everything she reads, she's just smart. Her real gift is that she knows people's weaknesses. Whatever secret you're keeping buried in your head —the one you don't want anyone to figure out—she'll pick it out of your brain the second she meets you."

"That's just creepy." Owen squirmed.

"Agreed. That's why I knew I had to stop her. After the first round, I found another note on my pillow. It was a threat. I was told to steal a journal from Laurelin or I'd end up like Tobias. The note wasn't signed, but I knew who it was from. I took the journal and left it where I was instructed. Later, when we were in Amare for competition, I snuck into Faye's room. I found the pygruim and told her the blackmail better stop or I'd expose her as a murderer. I haven't received any communication from her since then."

I sat back in my chair. "Well, assuming you're telling the truth, that clearly identifies our killer. Does she think the journal will help her steal the stones and that will impress Silas? Eva wrote that Julian—the last Stone Seeker—talked to a seer named Baltazar for instructions."

Aaron sucked in a sharp breath.

"What is it?" I asked.

Aaron looked like he'd seen a ghost. "Eva wrote that Baltazar gave Julian instructions? You're sure?"

I nodded. "I'm sure. Why does that matter? It was a hundred years ago."

Aaron ran his hands through his hair. "It matters because Baltazar is still alive."

I balked. "He's still alive? How is that possible?"

Aaron shrugged. "Something about his visions slows his aging. He's one of the most sought-after sources on the black market. A visit with him will cost you the equivalent of eight vials of elixir. Or any random object Baltazar picks. He likes to choose things that mean a lot to people, because he's cruel, and he likes to see how badly they want his knowledge."

Owen whistled. "Eight vials of elixir? That's worth a lot of meat. Why do people want to see him so badly? Aren't seers a dime a dozen in Scentia?"

"Yes, but Baltazar is special. The future isn't a set course. It varies as people change their minds. Baltazar is able to see multiple ways the future could go. He can tell you what might happen if x, y, or z were decided. Other seers see pieces of the future, but Baltazar can see the whole picture."

"How do you know all of this?" I asked.

Aaron avoided my eyes. "It's my job to know the black market."

I knew that wasn't the whole story, but I wouldn't push here.

Owen spoke up. "If Faye has the journal, she either knows

how to steal the crystals already because Eva recorded that somewhere, or she knows Baltazar is the key to figuring it out."

"And she won the Pentax, which means she has the diadem to protect her as she crosses the meadows. She'll be able to go straight to the Matrons without any pygsmies to stop her," I said.

Owen nodded. "It won't even be questioned. She'll be going to Everark for the coronation anyway."

"When does she leave for that?" I asked.

"Tomorrow morning," Owen answered.

I grabbed Aaron's arm. "We need to find Baltazar and get those instructions as fast as possible. We have to know how to stop Faye."

"But if Baltazar is as popular as Aaron says, he's not going to take a meeting with us last minute," Owen said.

"I can get eight vials of elixir if that's what it takes," I said.

"No, Owen is right. Elixir won't be enough on short notice. But I can get what we need for a visit with Baltazar," Aaron said, though he looked as if he'd rather confront the devil himself.

Chapter Twenty-Five

The sun was beginning to set as the railcar slowed. We had reached the outskirts of Amare.

"Are you sure we can't come? We could help," Owen said as he held Amelia's hand.

I was annoyed to have Amelia with us at all, but Owen had insisted she be allowed to come or he'd go home. His talents were too valuable to give up when we faced so many unknowns.

"Sorry, Owen. You know the code of the black market. Gotta keep my hideouts a secret." Aaron stood, pulling me up with him. "El and I will go grab what we need, and we'll be back in an hour. Then we'll leave for Scentia together. Just hang here for a bit. I'm sure you two lovebirds will find something to do." Aaron wiggled his eyebrows.

Owen's face turned red.

We hurried out of the railcar and were quickly lost in the trees of Amare's eastern forest. Twigs and rocks crunched beneath our feet as we pushed forward.

"How many of these hideouts do you have stashed across the kingdom anyway?" I asked as we jogged.

"Twenty-seven, but only three in Amare. I don't trade here often."

We reached an old, abandoned building made of cinderblock. The few windows along the top were boarded up. I was surprised when Aaron twisted the doorknob and the door swung open with no lock.

"Aren't you afraid of people stealing your stuff?" I asked as I followed him inside.

Aaron grabbed something I couldn't see, then changed it into a glowing lantern. We were surrounded by shelves stuffed with trash. There was only a small, five-by-five square of empty space to stand in the middle.

"Not really. Nothing here is worth taking." He held up a crushed aluminum can as an example.

I cocked my head to the side. "Fair point. But what do you see when you look at that can?"

"What, this thing? The possibilities are endless. I could create a new frying pan, a fancy picture frame, a chair, or a bicycle. This old can would easily become five darics in my pocket."

"That's one thing I like about you. Where someone sees a dirty sneaker, you see a new armchair. You're an optimist, and I haven't been around much that gives me hope lately."

Aaron paused and looked at me. The light from the lantern flickered across his face. "I wasn't an optimist on our way to Amare, and I'm sorry. If you want to keep fighting for Pippin, I'll go with you. I'll cross the meadows. We can demand a wish from the Matrons at knife-point if we have to."

"Oh, yeah. I can see that ending well. Confronting five goddesses with a four-inch blade and some attitude." I laughed.

"Seriously though, I can see you doing that. If you believed there was an infinitesimal chance they might say yes, you wouldn't think twice."

I didn't know if it was a good or bad thing that he was right.

I put my hands on my hips. "So Baltazar won't accept elixir, but he wants something from this stash of treasures?" I held up a teddy bear that was missing its eyes and had stuffing coming out of its stomach.

Aaron snatched the bear and shoved it back on a shelf. "There is one thing. One very specific thing ..." Aaron dug around a set of shelves until he found an old wooden jewelry box. He pulled open the bottom drawer and quickly slid the object into his pocket.

"Do I get to know what it is?" I asked, my curiosity burning.

Aaron gave a sad smile. "Not today. But I imagine you'll know soon enough."

I wanted to press for answers, but the look on his face made me stop. "You're a man of mystery, Mr. Gray." With a sigh, I turned to leave.

Aaron reached out and grabbed my hand. "El, stop."

I turned.

He stood with his eyes squeezed shut. "I want you to know I'm not hiding anything serious from you—nothing I've done wrong." He opened his eyes. "I'm just not ready to talk about it, okay?"

"That's all right. I can wait until you're ready."

Unexpectedly, Aaron moved his hand up my arm, leaving a trail of goosebumps where he touched.

My breathing stopped. This was sudden, but I was pretty sure it was what I wanted.

"It's important to me that you can trust me. Before the whole debacle at the end of the second round, I was rather hoping I might add the role of boyfriend to your bill." He gave a half smile.

My heart was flying at his words, but I worked to keep it from showing on my face. "That's a paid position now, is it?"

"Well, depending on your answer, I'd take the role at a heavy discount."

I pulled myself closer to him. "Oh, how generous of you." I paused. "That sounds like an offer I can't refuse."

Aaron smiled. "Really?"

I nodded.

His breath was hot on my face as he moved closer. He squeezed my hip, sending my heart into overdrive. I threw my arms around his neck and pulled him into me.

Kissing Aaron twisted my stomach in foreign ways. Somehow, finding his lips only made me want more. His hands gripped the small of my back as he pulled my body against his.

Then, as quickly as it had begun, Aaron pulled away. He rested his forehead against mine. "We should probably go," he whispered.

I shuddered as he ran his hand down my arm. I hated that he was right.

"One more kiss?" I asked, reaching up on my tippy-toes.

Aaron chuckled. "You drive a hard bargain, but I'll give in."

Our lips touched again, and I knew I'd never get tired of how it felt to be so close. Then he took my hand, and we ran back into the forest.

It was a five hour ride from Amare to Scentia, and the last three hours were through a barren desert where the rail lines were in poor condition. I worried about Sun Petal, who flew above us. I tried to convince her to come inside, but she didn't trust Owen or Amelia yet.

I wished for solid sleep, but I couldn't through all the bumps. Everyone else seemed unfazed by them. Amelia rested her head on Owen's shoulder, and Aaron was spread out along the bench on the other side of the car, snoring.

Aaron's body must have been so used to traveling between provinces that his subconscious kept track of the distance. He began to stir one minute before we pulled into the transfer station.

"Did you get any sleep?" he asked as he slipped on his jacket and gathered his pack.

I rubbed my eyes and stretched as I stood. "Maybe an hour's worth in ten-minute chunks." The straps from my bag were beginning to leave raw marks on my shoulders. I cringed as I put it on.

"Here, let me take that for a while," Aaron said, and slung it over his shoulder.

The cement platform was covered in sand and dry brush with gaping holes in the concrete surface. The only visible feature across the dark landscape was the spiny branches of a cacti army.

When Amelia exited the railcar, it flew in reverse toward Amare.

"Great," I said, looking at the empty track that ended ten feet beyond the platform. "What do we do now?"

Aaron walked over to a metal column at the head of the cement slab. He placed his hand on it and it glowed a vibrant blue. "I just called for a car. It will be here soon," he said.

Amelia crossed her arms over her chest and bounced on her toes.

"Are you cold?" Owen asked.

She nodded.

"Here, let me warm you up." Eagerly, he grabbed her in an embrace.

"You're sure a car is coming?" I asked. "I don't see how. There's no more track. I thought Creo was the only province that didn't use the rail system."

"Technically they are, but Scentia's rail system hardly resembles our own. They only share the most basic technology with other provinces. Their system is more advanced—"

Aaron was cut off by a high-pitched whirling in the sky. A giant metal ball was hurtling toward us.

"Ahh! Get out of the way!" I screamed and ran from its path.

Owen and Amelia followed, but Aaron stayed on the platform, grinning at us. The metal ball was covered in blue and silver paneling, and it landed in a C-shaped cradle on the opposite side of the platform from the rails. With a pop and a whoosh of air, a door opened up on its side, revealing a circle of tan leather seats.

Aaron chuckled. "You'll probably want to grab Sun Petal. She won't be able to keep up with this thing," he said. Then he walked up three steps and entered the sphere.

I took a few deep breaths to calm my racing heart. "I guess this is our ride."

I searched for Sun Petal and found her just above us in the air. *Aaron says you won't be able to stay with us if you fly. Do you want to come with me? I'll keep you safe.*

I find it offensive he thinks I'm so slow, Sun Petal huffed.

If the ball moved as quickly as it had come to us, I was sure Aaron was right. Sun Petal wouldn't like that, though. *I'd be more comfortable with you close. I don't think I'm going to like these railcars very much,* I said.

Sun Petal eyed Owen and Amelia as they entered the sphere. She sighed. *Fine, I'll come with you.*

The pygsmy fluttered down to my shoulder and nestled into my neck. I sensed relief in her thoughts. It had been a long flight.

I climbed the few steps into the sphere. Once inside, the door slowly lowered, then clasped shut with a hiss.

"That incoming was terrifying," Amelia said.

"It gets worse," Aaron responded with a gleeful smile.

A metal rod with a wheel-shaped handle on top rose from the ground in the middle of our seats. There was a screen in the center of it, which glowed when Aaron tapped it, bringing up a map of Scentia. He zoomed into the northeast corner and scanned the streets, squinting at each blue dot that appeared every so often.

"Got it," Aaron said as he tapped one of the locations. "You'll want to hold onto something," he said. With one hand, he grabbed the handle in the center of the car.

Sun Petal wrapped a tendril around my neck just in time. We were tossed violently into the air. I threw out my hands, grasping for the handle as my stomach entered my throat. The car was filled with Amelia's shrill scream. I probably would have joined her if I'd been capable of making any noise. Owen stayed silent as he clung to the handle with two hands, his eyes wide open.

Whoo! Sun Petal thought. *This is almost as good as flying!*

With a jarring clunk, our wild flight came to an abrupt halt. The car's roof attached to something in the sky. We swayed in the breeze for a moment. Then the car released and we entered a free fall.

"Make it stop!" Amelia shrieked as we jerked to the right.

My body slammed into Aaron's with such force I couldn't pull myself upright. We changed direction again, gradually descending until the car came to a stop. Not fooled, I kept a tight hold on the handle and braced for another toss. Amelia and Owen did the same.

Aaron laughed. "You can let go. We made it," he said.

Aww. I want to go again, Sun Petal said.

"That was insane," I said through heavy breaths.

"Insane, yes. But very effective. We just crossed a quarter of the province in less than two minutes," Aaron said.

The flying ball's door opened, and we filed out onto another platform. I thought Sun Petal would take off the moment we were free, but she stayed with me, still resting.

"How does it work?" I asked.

"Powerful magnets," Aaron answered. "Each car has a specific charge, and each platform can emit a magnetic field that attracts that particular car." He pointed to a massive, circular hub suspended in the air. "When I selected our stop, the nearest docking station pulled our car up from the desert. Then the magnetic field on the base station engages, pulling the car down from suspension. Pretty cool, huh?"

"If you don't mind feeling like a scrambled egg," Amelia complained.

To the east, light was beginning to peak over the horizon. Its vibrant orange was reflected off of Skara's many glass buildings. If I tried to be objective, I could see how the city might be pretty, but it was so different from Lingua. The edges of every structure were cut at austere angels, and any part that wasn't glass was either black, gray, or white.

"We need to get moving. The market opens with the sun. Our best chance to see Baltazar is to get to him early," Aaron said. He marched down the metal steps of the platform, and we followed.

We wound our way through Scentia's streets, which were designed to be a perfect grid. As more people filled the street, I noticed a pattern. The men wore sharp suits, short hair, and shaved faces. The women wore sensible shoes, simple hairstyles, and minimal makeup. Faye was beginning to make more sense to me.

"Why is everyone watching us?" I whispered to Aaron as a woman gasped and pointed at me. "Do they recognize us from the Pentax?"

"You've got a pygsmy on your shoulder, El. It's unusual."

I looked down at Sun Petal, whose color was perfectly solid instead of the translucent shimmer it would be in the air. I suppose it would be shocking for most people.

Do you mind flying? I don't like the way everyone is staring at you, I said.

Sure, I'm rested enough, and I could use some food. I can smell lyre berries a few miles out. Call for me when you need me, she said as she flew off.

We continued down the street, and the nutty aroma of coffee grew stronger. Aaron stopped in front of a black shop where the smell originated. "Owen, Amelia, you wait in here. It's going to be hard enough for me to get El inside the market. There's no way I can talk Esmerelda into accepting three newbies. We'll probably be gone a while, but stay close. We will come back."

Owen's face fell, but Amelia tipped her head back and said,

"Thank the Matrons. I'm dying for a cappuccino." She marched to the door of the shop without looking back.

Aaron unzipped the front pouch of his pack and slipped something in his pocket, then handed both of our bags to Owen. "Keep this with you until we get back. If Ezzy sees our packs, she'll want everything we have."

Chapter Twenty-Six

With a quick glance over his shoulder, Aaron ducked into a gap between two shops. I followed him down the narrow alley. A rat ran past Aaron and toward me. I squealed and threw myself against the side of the brick building.

"Points for poise under pressure," Aaron said with a smirk.

"Hey, I'm not used to them. I don't live under rail tracks."

On the side of the brick building, Aaron slid a panel to the side, revealing a small touch screen beneath. The panel was well-disguised to blend in with the white bricks around it. He punched in a very long string of numbers that I would not have been able to memorize. Then he waited.

"Who's there?" a female voice growled from a small speaker at the side of the screen.

"You know who, Esmerelda. I used my code." Aaron rolled his eyes.

"What are you doing at my front door? You know I don't like attention drawn to it."

I glanced around the abandoned alley. This was a front door?

"I need an appointment with Baltazar. Stat," Aaron whispered into the speaker.

"Too bad," Esmerelda snapped. "He's not seeing anyone today."

Aaron placed his palm against the side of the building and pinched the bridge of his nose. He paused for a long moment. "I have what he wants," he mumbled.

The only sound that could be heard was a slight hum from the speaker and the squeak of a rat. My skin crawled.

Finally, Esmerelda said, "Come in."

Beneath the speaker, the four-by-eight block of bricks dropped out of sight, revealing a cement staircase that descended into darkness.

"Are you ready to tell me what you have that Baltazar wants?" I asked Aaron as I followed him down the drafty steps.

He was quiet for a beat. "My mom's necklace and a ring," he said.

I gasped. "Aaron, no. You can't give up the necklace. It's the only thing you have left of her."

We stopped in front of a wooden door with green, peeling paint. Aaron knocked and waited.

"That's exactly why Baltazar wants it. He knows it's the most important thing to me."

"Why would he know that?" I asked.

Aaron didn't answer my question. "One thing my line of work has taught me is that stuff is just stuff, El. What good is this necklace if the crystals are taken? I don't want to live in a kingdom without magic. My gift—that's the real piece of my mom I want to hold onto. She was a Linguan. My father wasn't. My magic comes through her." He gave a sad half-smile.

The green door whipped open. A plump woman with wild black hair and a floor-length purple dress stared at me, the corners of her mouth turned down. "No strangers," she said as she grabbed Aaron's shirt and pulled him inside.

Aaron wrapped his fingers around the side of the door, preventing her from shutting it. "Whoa, Ezzy. Hold on there. Laurelin comes with me. That's part of the deal."

"Laurelin Moore? The whisperer?" Esmerelda opened the door again and studied my face, this time with a spark of interest.

"Her gifts are not for sale, Ezzy."

She looked at Aaron with narrowed eyes. "Then it's Esmerelda to you." Abruptly, she turned and marched down a dimly lit hall.

Aaron grabbed my hand. "That's about as good a welcome as you're gonna get from Ez," he said. "I don't think she actually hates me, but it's hard to tell."

The hallway was plastered with dark purple wallpaper that had begun to bubble. Every so often, a painting hung on the wall, each with a bizarre theme. After a graphic depiction of a woman's heart being eaten by a nighthowler, I decided to keep my eyes on my shoes instead.

Esmerelda stopped at a wood door and rapped the metal knocker.

"Ahhh, Aaron Gray," said a high male voice on the other side. "Come in."

Esmerelda opened the door just wide enough for us to squeeze inside. As it snapped shut, I was instantly claustrophobic. I breathed deeply, trying to shake the feeling.

A man with long, blonde hair sat cross-legged in the center of the room with his eyes closed. He wore a shiny blue vest with no shirt, revealing smooth skin on his bare chest. I was surprised. Aaron said Baltazar's visions slowed his aging, but considering this was the seer in Eva's journal, I'd expected an old, shriveled man.

Orbs of blue light floated around the space. In them, scenes from a hundred different lives were playing out. A low hum buzzed in my ears as the people in the orbs conversed in muffled voices. I ducked out of the way as one of the orbs floated by my head.

Baltazar opened his eyes. They had no pupils and glowed a haunting blue that sent a chill down my spine.

"Time really is a thief, Aaron Gray. You're bigger and stronger than you seem in the visions I have about you. I've been expecting you, though, admittedly, I forgot you were coming today. On the other hand, there were a thousand reasons that would keep you from coming, too. But I should have known. The girl would win out in the end." He turned his frightening eyes on me. "She makes all the difference, doesn't she?"

Aaron didn't answer as he sat down in front of Baltazar. Cautiously, I joined Aaron on the floor, kneeling so I could make a quick getaway if needed.

"You could have been queen," Baltazar said. He held out his palm, drawing an orb into it. As it floated over his hand, the image inside grew larger. I saw myself kneeling in a crystal palace as Mira placed a crown on my head. Baltazar closed his fist and the orb dissipated, falling in streams of blue mist between his fingers.

"Though the same could have been said about any of the others. You, however," he shook one finger at me, "I did see you most often. And oh, the joy! Pippin, your mother, and your father. Their pride. The reunion. It was going to be glorious."

My heart squeezed painfully in my chest, thinking of what could have been.

"Enough." Aaron's fists were clenched. "Stop taunting her. She's already hurting, though I wouldn't expect you to care. You revel in it."

Baltazar slowly turned to look back at Aaron. His movements were strange—long and drawn out. His eyes shined brighter. "I know you don't believe me, but I cared very much about your mother's pain, Aaron. It's not my fault she wouldn't listen."

"Listen to what?" Aaron spat. "You, spinning a hundred different futures in front of her, each ending the same way? You're the reason she got hooked in the first place, and you're the reason she thought she'd never be free of her addiction. But I know the truth. You never wanted to show her the other paths because then she might slip away from you. It was always about maintaining control, and now she's dead."

Baltazar's cool mint eyes burned a fiery red. "You don't know half of the story, son. I loved Adriana very much."

Son? Did he mean that literally? I examined Aaron's face. There was nothing but hatred in his eyes.

"Here." Aaron yanked his mother's necklace from his throat and flicked it at Baltazar, along with the ring. "It's what you've always wanted—her necklace and wedding ring. Now tell us what we need to know. How do we protect the crystals from Stone Seekers? And do it quickly. I'm eager to leave."

Baltazar's chest heaved for several long seconds. Slowly, his red eyes faded to orange, then yellow, then back to blue. He picked up the necklace from his lap and dangled the jewel in front of his face. He slipped the ring over his finger and stroked the giant ruby. "My Adriana," he cooed.

"Can we get on with this?" Aaron asked through gritted teeth.

"Interesting you should ask. There have been others asking these questions lately. Well, others who want to know how to take the stones, at least."

"Who?" I asked.

Baltazar's eyes flickered. "I can't say. It would ruin my reputation if I blabbed about every customer who sought my knowledge. But you can rest easy. I haven't made the mistake of telling that secret. Not since Julian. You see, I live a comfortable life." Baltazar's chuckle raised the hair on my arms. "Near immortality suits me. If the stones were taken, I would lose my power. I have turned every Seeker away."

"We aren't Seekers, we want to protect the crystals. We have good reason to believe Faye Bennett is after them, and we need to know how to stop her," I said.

"Yes, I have seen you fight." Baltazar's eyes snapped shut, and the orbs began to swirl in a clockwise motion. As they picked up speed, wind blew my hair around my face.

Baltazar's eyes opened. "There are many scenarios that could play out. With nearly every choice, I see you fail—sometimes with more drastic consequences than others."

Nine orbs descended from the storm and came to rest between the three of us. In each one, we stood in a crystal room. Around us, the Matrons were frozen on five pedestals. Some of the visions showed Faye with a glowing crystal around her neck, her eyes victorious. One showed Aaron dying with an arrow in his chest. Another showed me lying in a pool of blood. Owen and Amelia, lying unconscious on the crystal floor. With each orb, my heart sank in my chest. Were we on a pointless quest? Was there any possibility of success? Overwhelmed, I began to close my eyes, shutting out the flashing images and hopelessness that filled me.

Baltazar spoke slowly, and his voice was now distinctly female.

Five stones, their colors bright.
Magic given for man's delight.
Powers protected in crystal form.
From it, Ausland's provinces born.
Through the meadows one must go
Matrons waiting kept in stone
Seize the magic but beware
Mystics must be used with care
Only one will leave with power
Unite the stones atop the tower

The orb in the middle of the group lifted above the others, ballooning in size as it glowed brighter. Then the orb exploded, shattering all of the others, and filled the room with a yellow blaze. The pieces of vision prickled my face and arms as they fell past me, leaving me covered in tiny slivers of glass. But I hardly noticed the commotion around me. I was too stunned.

"Silas," I whispered. "He's behind this."

"El, are you okay?" Aaron asked as he dusted me off.

I grabbed Aaron's arms. "Eva's journal, the poem written in pygsmish, the second round of competition. It was all Silas."

Aaron's eyebrows drew together. "Slow down, El. What are you saying?"

"I have heard Baltazar's prophecy before but in two halves." I shook my head in disbelief. "Oh, Silas is good. He's really good." I'd believed I was safe with him—that he was trying to help me.

"Where have you heard it? And what does it have to do with Silas?"

"It all makes sense. Eva wrote the prophecy Baltazar just gave us in the back of her journal, but she wrote it in pygsmish. Silas needed a whisperer to translate the words, and when I put myself forward for the Pentax, he saw the perfect opportunity. That's why he chose me as Rook. He never wanted me to have the journal, but he was bound by the blood contract. He said his mark started to hurt him. He must have known he couldn't put it off any longer. But it was way too risky to give the journal to me with all the information about Stone Seekers *and* the instructions written in the back. So he separated the info. He tore most of the poem out of the journal and disguised it in the riddle round of the Pentax. I was told to write the translation down, and I never got my bag back from that round. Then he tried to kill me. I wasn't supposed to make it out of the competition alive. I knew too much. And now Silas has the full poem, which means he has the instructions to steal the stones."

Aaron squinted his eyes. "I'm mostly following you. But how does that explain Faye blackmailing Amelia to steal the journal?"

I thought for a moment. "It's the blood contract again. Silas must have shown Faye the journal. I bet she's marked too. They didn't want me to have it with all that information, but they also couldn't take it back from me themselves because the contract would kill them. So they had to have someone unmarked steal it from me."

"Why would Silas include Faye in this plan at all? Amelia said they had no relationship before the Pentax."

"Eva said the Matrons were most vulnerable during the Pentax, but she wouldn't explain why. He must need her for something."

Baltazar laughed. "You are putting the pieces together very nicely, young whisperer. But yes—you are missing a part of the riddle."

Aaron's eyes were flat. "Let me guess. You know the answer."

"Of course. I was the one who told Julian he would have to force a Pentax in order to get to the stones."

"So? What's your asking price this time?" Aaron grumbled.

"I'll take an IOU from the whisperer. Sixteen vials of elixir delivered by the end of the month." Baltazar's eyes glimmered.

"Sixteen? That's not fair! That's double your asking price," Aaron said.

"Done. Tell me what we need to know," I said. We had no time to waste.

Baltazar swirled his hands together, creating a wide, rippling blue pool between us.

"The Matrons are not all they have led us humans to believe. We worship them for their kindness in sharing their powers, but it's as much for their good as it is our own."

In the pool of blue, the forms of the five goddesses appeared. I recognized them—Mira, Amiah, Ember, Everly, and Seersha. But there was a sixth woman with the same long nose as the others.

"Who is she?" I asked, pointing to the woman in gold.

"Gianna, Matron of Health," Baltazar answered.

Strange. I had never heard of her.

The six women stood around a floating crystal. I watched as they began to fight. First, it was silly—hair pulling, shoving. Then it became aggressive. Their magic swirled around the room in bursts of light and smoke.

A scream from one of the Matrons pierced the room.

When the smoke cleared, Gianna lay on the floor, unmoving. I shivered.

"Power as great as the Matrons' has a way of corrupting the soul. Gianna became greedy. She wanted all of the power for herself, and her sisters could hardly blame her. They'd been feeling the same compulsion. They knew if they wanted to avoid another tragedy like Gianna's death, they had to share the burden of their magic.

"The Matrons decided to hold a competition to discover which of the human kingdoms was most worthy. Darius, King of Ausland, was the winner. The Great Crystal was broken into six pieces. Now, each Matron wears her crystal around her neck. When she enters immortal sleep, her powers leave her and project onto the people of her province. One Matron remains awake at all times to guard the crystals. When she wakes, her magic returns to her. This is why you temporarily lose your powers from time to time."

I nodded. "So we lose our magic when Mira is awake and acting as guard."

"Yes, and I lose mine when Seersha wakes, but there is one exception," Baltazar continued. "When Darius accepted the Matrons' gift of magic, it was under the condition that Ausland be allowed to hold a similar competition to choose their next ruler. He believed this was the right way to find a successor, so the Pentax was born. The Matrons agreed to enter immortal sleep during the course of the competition so all five provinces could compete, but they knew this was dangerous. There would be no one to protect the crystals. Using Gianna's portion of the crystal, they created pygsmies to act as guardians while they slept. The diadem that is passed from ruler to ruler allows one to cross the meadows without danger. Once inside Everark, the person who places the diadem on their head and makes a wish will wake the Matrons."

I looked at Aaron. "That's why he needed Faye—to cross the

meadows while the Matrons are still sleeping. We better hurry. No one will be protecting those stones."

Aaron jumped to his feet and pulled me up.

"Remember, Laurelin. *Mystics must be used with care.*" Baltazar dipped his head.

"Er, right," I said. "We'll be leaving now."

Just before the door shut behind us, Baltazar called, "Wait!"

Aaron closed his eyes and took a deep breath. "What is it now?"

Through the cracked door, Baltazar tossed Adriana's necklace back to Aaron. "I'll keep the ring, but consider this appointment done on the family discount. I'll see you again, son."

"I wouldn't count on it," Aaron said. He shoved the necklace into his jean pocket, then slammed the door. "Let's go before he comes after us with those freaky eyes."

Aaron grabbed my hand and pulled me down the dark hall while I worked through everything I had just learned.

"Well you're off in a hurry," Esmerelda said, emerging from another door.

"Stuff to do. See ya, Ezzy," Aaron mumbled.

I tripped up the steps as Aaron dragged me along. "Aaron, let go. I'll be faster without the tow rope."

"Sorry." He released me.

My eyes watered as they adjusted to the bright light and white buildings above. Aaron placed his hands on his hips as his breaths came in short gasps.

"Are you okay?" I asked.

He leaned against the brick wall and closed his eyes. "I will be. I just need a minute."

Witnessing the encounter between Aaron and Baltazar made me feel I'd walked in on a stranger naked—I was an intruder in a private moment. I examined the white walls of the smelly alley as if they were a great work of art.

"We better find Amelia and Owen. They're probably panicking by now," Aaron said.

It hadn't occurred to me that the sun was much higher in the sky than I expected. "How long were we in there?" I asked as I followed him down the alley.

"I don't know. There's something about Baltazar's visions. Time melts away with him, along with everything good or valuable."

"Do you want to talk about him?" I bit my lip.

"Not really. Do you?" he grumbled.

"Well, I would like to know. It seems important."

"Important how?"

Aaron kept a careful step ahead of me, making it impossible to read his face. I didn't know if he was sad or angry or annoyed.

I pushed on with my question. "So Baltazar is your father?" I cringed, waiting for backlash.

Aaron's shoulders tensed. "Strictly on a biological level, yes, he is."

"But you don't speak to him?"

"I don't know, El. I used to love him. What kid doesn't idolize his father? Then I got to know him. I saw what he really is. He's a man who loves power and money and his near-immortality, and he lords it over anyone who gets close. He was constantly holed up in some room receiving visions. He left when I was seven. When Mom was particularly weak—either when she was using or going through withdrawals again—she'd run back to him until they'd fight and one of them would leave. And when she was dead, he never bothered to check on his son."

"I'm sorry, Aaron. I wish I knew what to say."

Aaron shrugged. "Most of the time, he's easy to forget. The important thing is that we got the info we need. Now we have to find the others and get through the meadows before it's too late."

Chapter Twenty-Seven

T
he meadows were located in the center of Ausland,
which meant we had to travel through Scentia's desert
to get there.

Even through my jeans, the hot sand burned my skin as I sat
on the ground, staring at a handful of fried cacti leaves that
Aaron had proudly prepared for us. We had packed plenty of
granola bars and dried fruit, but Aaron believed on a quest like
this, we needed to truly experience the survivalist lifestyle.

"Cacti have tremendous health benefits," he said as he
shoveled in a fork full.

If I weren't still feeling sorry for Aaron, I would have refused
to put the prickly leaves in my mouth. As it was, I forced myself
to pick up the charred lump and take a bite. My eyes watered as
I fought the urge to gag.

"Why can't you create, like, a salad out of this, or some other,
normal green vegetable? Wouldn't that be an easy shift for your
abilities?" Amelia complained, eying her leaves with disgust.

"Sorry. My gift doesn't extend to living things. I can only
change inanimate objects."

I knew he was lying. I'd seen him shift plant-based objects
before.

Amelia sniffed the cacti leaf and almost put it in her mouth. Then she tossed her paper plate on the ground and said, "No thanks. I'll have another granola bar."

I couldn't blame her.

Owen picked up Amelia's plate and put it on top of his own empty one. "It's not much different from the usual Creo diet, in my opinion," he said, eying the leaves hungrily.

I shuddered as I took another bite, washing it down with a swig of water from my bottle. When Aaron was busy readjusting his pack, I slipped Owen my second leaf.

"So, does anyone have any tips on how to control four pygsmies in flight? Because last time I tried two at once, Aaron smashed a ten-foot-tall structure in his fall."

Amelia's eyebrows reached her hairline. "Well, that sounds promising. I guess I better say goodbye to my powers now."

"Stop it. El can totally do this. That was on her first day of training, and she's gotten way better at connecting with pygsmies since then. Right, El?"

"Yes. Definitely."

Well, I was better at connecting with Sun Petal. Other pygsmies, not so much.

Sorry I can't fly all of you at once, Sun Petal said. *My tendrils just won't stretch that far.*

It's okay. I can do this. I put the thought into words, hoping that hearing them might convince me too.

I closed my eyes and breathed while I pictured Pippin. Seeing him always gave me courage to do things I couldn't face on my own. This night was the most important of them all. If Silas succeeded, I couldn't save Pippin, and Ausland would never be the same. Somehow, I had to be strong enough to get all of us across the meadows.

When I thought I had good control over my emotions, I opened my mind to the pygsmies. For a long stretch of blackness, there was nothing, but when I reached the borders of the meadows there were hundreds of specks of light. I sifted through them, searching for sparks that felt courageous. Four mystics stood out to me. I latched onto them and chanted, *Lyrun rach min baum. Help me serve and protect.*

When the pygsmies appeared, Amelia squealed. "Oh, they're so cute!"

One of the pygsmy's thoughts were happy. She enjoyed being complimented, just like Amelia. At least I knew which one would fit her best.

What's your name? I asked.

I'm Simper, she responded as she did a little twirl in the air.

Nice to meet you, Simper. And what about you two?

The largest of the pygsmies shot forward. *My name's Forest Moon.*

And I'm Rexil, the last one said.

You're all very brave to show yourself in front of humans. Thank you. I have a very important job for you tonight. I know it's been a while since the meadows faced any Stone Seekers—longer than any of us have been alive. But someone is after the Matron's crystals, and it's up to us to stop them. Are you with me?

If it's for the Matrons, of course, Forest Moon said.

Same for me, Simper said.

Rexil nodded.

Do any of you have any experience flying with humans? I asked.

The pygsmies looked at each other.

Umm, no, we don't, Forest Moon said.

Well, I have loads of it now, Sun Petal said. *It's really easy. You just have to follow Lur-a-laun.*

Right. Just follow me. I hoped they wouldn't notice the sweat on my forehead.

I turned back to my group. "Okay, I've got us some pygsmies, and they're ready to help. Let's start small. I'm going to try flying with just Aaron and me first."

Aaron stepped forward. If he was afraid after his last experience, his face didn't show it. If only I believed in myself as much as he did.

I chose Sun Petal for myself and Forest Moon for Aaron.

Aaron laughed as Forest Moon wrapped his tendrils beneath his armpits. "Sorry. I've always been ticklish," he said between giggles.

Are you sure I have to fly with him? Forest Moon asked me, but there was an endearing undercurrent in his mind. It was hard not to like Aaron.

With Sun Petal holding me securely, we lifted off the ground. This part was second nature to me. But as I expanded my mind to control Forest Moon, I found myself slipping toward the ground. It was like trying to solve a calculus problem while writing an essay on the properties of water ranunculus.

I refocused on Sun Petal, correcting our course. Then I stretched my mind and latched onto Aaron's pygsmy, trying to keep both mystics under my control. But one kept coming into focus, shoving the other pygsmy out of the way.

Aaron grunted as Forest Moon dipped with my lack of concentration. His leg snagged a tall cactus, putting a hole in his jeans and a cut on his calf.

"Sorry!" I yelled.

Then I hit the sand.

I'd lost control of Sun Petal as I focused on Aaron. This was hopeless. I couldn't manage two pygsmies, let alone four of them.

You can put your human down, Forest Moon. I need to think, I said.

Forest Moon gently put Aaron on the ground. A couple hundred feet separated us from Amelia and Owen now, though I could see them watching us with wary expressions.

I pulled myself up and shook sand out of my hair.

"That wasn't so bad, El! I felt like you had better control than last time." He touched his jeans, making them whole again.

"This isn't a training session. 'Not bad' isn't good enough. I needed to be able to fly four people across the meadows, like, five minutes ago. We don't have time to waste."

"Let me ask you a question. Why do you want to stop Silas?" Aaron asked.

I rolled my eyes. "You know why I want to stop him. I need to save Pippin."

"Okay, now just go with me for a second. Imagine Pippin's not part of the problem. He's a totally healthy and happy kid. If you knew Silas was going to steal Ausland's magic tonight, would you still fight to stop him?"

I didn't hesitate. "Yes, I would."

"Why?"

I pictured Lingua with boring buildings trapped by the laws of physics. I thought of Creo with trees, vines, and flowers that stood still and didn't glow. Amare, with a million regular sized homes dotting the landscape. Scentia without giant magnets in the sky. All of these scenes made my heart ache for a kingdom that sparkled with magic.

But the real image that dominated my mind was one of me, connected to Sun Petal. The feeling of freedom as we soared through the air. The pygsmy's gentle touch, and the trust that formed in her mind when we connected. And best of all, the satisfaction that came when I used elixir to heal. For a year, I'd almost exclusively used it for Pippin, but before that, I'd been able to share it with others. Like Crede. The look of relief on his face when he realized his parents wouldn't have to grapple with losing two sons in forty-eight hours.

"I want to stop Silas because I'm a whisperer. For too long, I've been afraid to embrace my power because I haven't wanted to accept responsibility for what that means. But it's who I am. I'm the girl who can talk to pygsmies. It's been a gift for my family, and I know it can be for others too. I'm a protector."

Aaron smiled. "That's my girl. Now you know what to do."

I was surprised to find he was right—I did know what to do. It didn't feel easy, but it felt possible. It was as if acknowledging my gift had unlocked its full potential. I shut my eyes and focused, plucking the four pygsmies out of the sky. They hadn't wandered far.

I started with Owen and Amelia, since they were farthest away.

Amelia dodged Simper as the pygsmy tried to pick her up. "Laurelin, what is it doing?" she yelled.

"Just trust her!" I called back.

Amelia flinched as Simper wrapped her tendrils around her.

"Whoa! This is not normal!" Amelia screamed as she was lifted into the air.

Owen was the opposite. He was used to flying. "Hey, little buddy," he said as Rexil pulled him in.

Does he know I can't understand him? Rexil asked me.

I laughed. *He was just saying hello.*

Oh, well, you can greet him for me, I suppose.

"Rexil says hi back!" I yelled to Owen.

The pair soared over to us. Instead of feeling like I was trying to control two disconnected parts of my body, it was like patting my head and rubbing my tummy at the same time—tricky to coordinate, but possible.

"If you let me fall, Laurelin, I will kill you!" Amelia roared as she flew over us.

"Do you think she realizes how tempting that is to me?" I mumbled to Aaron as I pictured Amelia crashing into the sand.

Aaron smiled, his eyes soft. "You're doing it, El."

"Now I just have to add in two more balls to the juggling act." I exhaled. "You ready?"

"Always have been. I believe in you." Aaron winked.

Directing the other two pygsmies was challenging. At different times, I allowed both Owen and Amelia to slip as I worked on getting Aaron and myself in flight. But their shouts of fear were enough to snap my mind back before they really fell.

Somehow, I managed to get all of us in the air. We flew through the sky as the sun began to set behind the sandy plains of the desert.

At times, the pygsmies' minds were like a cohesive unit that I could direct in unison. Other times, my concentration slipped and I had to bounce between their four brains, checking in to make sure no one had gone too far off track. As the miles passed beneath us, it became easier. More often, we flew in unison rather than four creatures acting on their own.

The landscape began to shift. The dry desert floor turned to marshy dunes as we reached the end of a stream. We flew along the riverbed as the water gained strength. Patches of grass, water lilies, and duckweed grew along the banks. Ahead was a mound of lush grass and wildflowers.

We made it to the edge of the meadows.

Aaron looked at me. "Are you ready?"

I gave him a stiff nod. "We can do this."

Chapter Twenty-Eight

E verark, the majestic home of the Matrons, loomed over the grassy plains, more like a mountain than a castle. The creeks ran toward it, the wildflowers faced it, the peaks of the rolling hills bowed to it, even the blades of grass angled in its direction. The sharp columns of crystal that pointed to the sky were both awe-inspiring and foreboding.

Beneath us, we saw a variety of creatures I'd only read about in books. We flew over pairs of unicorns, a pack of gnomes, several sphinxes, and a herd of centaurs. I nearly had a heart attack when a griffin soared past us in the air. It watched us with wide brown eyes but made no move toward us. None of the creatures did. Pygsmies really must be sacred in the meadows. All of them noticed us, but they only looked for a moment before returning to their business. When I saw a manticore stalking a deer through the tall grass, my heart stopped, but the beast barely lifted its eyes to acknowledge us. I hoped the moment's distraction was enough to let the deer get away.

"El, look up ahead."

Aaron pointed to a caravan parked about a mile outside Everark. There was a blue box-shaped carriage, several horses, and guards wearing royal uniforms. I watched for a moment, noting they weren't moving.

"Do you think Silas and Faye are with them? Why are they stopped?" I asked.

"Usually, the royal entourage escorts the victor all the way to Everark, where they're crowned king or queen. But we know that's not what Faye has in mind. My guess is that she ordered them to stay back. If the guards figure out what she and Silas are trying to do, they'd probably stop them. No one wants to lose their magic," Aaron explained.

"Well, that's one bit of good news. At least we won't have to fight the guards too," I said.

Let's take the circular route to Everark, I told the pygsmies. *We want to avoid the guards.*

The meadows were vast, but with the pygsmies flying at full speed, it didn't take long to cross the distance.

Drop us right there, in the thicket of trees, I said.

When the pygsmies lowered us to the ground, I rubbed each of their backs. *Thank you. You were fantastic. Now go find some lyre berries. I'm sure you're hungry and thirsty after that flight.*

Simper, Forest Moon, and Rexil fluttered away, each of them exhausted.

I'm staying with you, Sun Petal said.

I hesitated. I didn't know what we were about to face, and I didn't want to put Sun Petal in danger again. But I hadn't forgotten my promise. *You can come if you're sure.*

I'm absolutely positive, Sun Petal said.

Aaron was already busy. From his pack, he unloaded a pile of garbage. He changed broken pencils into sets of bows and arrows and several old leather shoes into quivers. Then he shifted bent forks and spoons into lethal knives with long blades. He tore strips of brown leather from a large sheet and changed them into belts that would give us a place to store our knives and clip the bow.

"Let's review what we know," Aaron said as we strapped on

our gear. "Faye will be able to find your weakness, and that will make her tough to fight. El, tell us about Silas's gift."

"Well, Silas's magic is common in Lingua. He's a high-level orator. That means he can control inanimate objects, like me, but he has an advantage. He doesn't have to have physical contact with an object to control it, so that makes him a bigger threat. Keep your backs to walls or other solid objects as much as possible so you can see what's coming at you. We can do this. We've made it this far. Now all we have to do is get inside."

It was as if my words were a jinx. A burst of orange light erupted from the tip of Everark's highest crystal. It shot twenty feet in the air, then fell in a spherical, shimmering circle around the palace, enshrouding it with a protective dome.

"Well that doesn't fit Faye or Silas's powers," Owen pointed out.

"It's orange magic," Aaron said.

"Which means someone from Fortis is nearby," Owen finished for him.

"Wait a minute. We've seen that power before. Remember that night at the social in Creo? Arthur separated Owen and Tobias with a shield," I said.

"Yeah, but powers repeat among people all the time. Just think about how many storytellers there in are Lingua. It could be one of the guards. Maybe they were instructed to protect the castle once Faye was inside," Amelia said.

"I doubt it. Most gifts have a tight radius for their use. The guards are at least a mile out. Whoever is projecting that shield is inside Everark," I said.

"Know-it-all," Amelia muttered.

Another eruption sounded from the castle as blue, green, orange, and purple light emanated from within the orange shield.

"We need to get inside, now," I said. "They might have just taken the crystals."

Our time to create a plan was long gone. I ran from the cover of the trees, with the others following at my heels, but we were stopped short at the shield. Though it appeared as thin as a soapy bubble, it was strong as a rock. No amount of shoving, kicking, or slamming against it made any difference. Even the tip of an arrow snapped as I shot at it.

"You know, I doubt the shield extends below the earth," Owen said, a confident smile on his face.

"You're brilliant, Owen," I cheered. "How fast can you dig a tunnel inside?"

"Wait and see," Owen said.

Suddenly, a hole opened up in the earth beneath him. He fell into it and I gasped.

"Are you okay?" I called into the darkness.

Owen's only reply was a chuckle. "Get down here already!"

"Ladies first," Aaron said, looking at the hole with apprehension.

I moved to the edge, but Amelia pushed me out of the way.

"I'm next," she said.

"Be my guest."

Her manicured nails dug into the grass as she lowered herself into the hole. With a deep exhale, she released her hold and dropped out of sight.

"I was joking, you know," Aaron said. "I'll go first if you'd like me to."

"No, help me down," I said.

Are you sure you want to go with me? I asked Sun Petal.

I already said yes.

Then you'd better hold on tight.

She perched on my shoulder and wrapped a tendril around me.

Aaron grabbed my hands and lowered me. "Ready?" he asked.

"Let go!" I called.

For a few seconds, I sailed through open air before my legs collided with rocky earth.

"Was it really necessary to dig so deep?" I asked as I dusted myself off.

"What's a quest without a little adventure, eh?" Owen nudged me.

I moved out of the way just in time. Aaron landed with a thud. He tossed a flashlight to Owen and kept one for himself.

Watching the earth split in front of Owen was fascinating. Dirt, rocks, and roots filled the walls on either side of us, but we forged ahead at a steady pace.

After a minute, we began to walk uphill.

"Are we getting close?" I asked.

"You sound like a child. 'Are we there yet?'" Amelia mocked.

"Excuse me for being a smidge anxious about saving the world's magic."

"I think you have a hero complex."

"Better than a mean girl one," I shot back.

"Ladies, stop," Owen said.

"Why should I?" Amelia whined. "I'm tired of—"

"Shhhhh," Owen cut her off. "I think we're there."

Amelia crossed her arms over her chest with a huff.

"I'm going to make a small hole and peek through it," Owen whispered. He dug upward and climbed three distinct steps he created in the dirt. "Everly," he cursed. "They're right above us!"

"Can you see what the room is like? Get us to the side of it," I hissed.

Owen created a shallow tunnel near the surface. We had to crawl through it on our hands and knees.

We'd gone about thirty feet when Owen stopped again. He created another peephole to the surface.

"This is it," he said as he widened the space.

The crystal floor of the palace was about six inches deep. With Owen's powers, it crumbled to dust, creating a hole just large enough for Aaron to get his shoulders through. One by one, we took our turn hoisting ourselves through the narrow opening.

The main floor of Everark was a rotunda with a circular hallway surrounding. Five daunting, eight-foot granite panels separated the hall from the center space. Owen had created our entrance behind one of those panels. We huddled behind it, trying to get a grip on our surroundings. A low hum filled the air, as if we'd entered a hive of bees.

"We need to get eyes on them," I whispered.

"Yeah, preferably without being seen," Owen answered.

"I've been waiting three years for a scenario like this," Aaron whispered, digging around the small backpack he'd brought with him. "I got this drone in a sweet trade in Scentia." In his palm, there was a controller and a small, black circle that was no bigger than a refrigerator magnet.

"Does it have a camera?" I asked hopefully.

"As long as it still works," Aaron whispered. "I haven't used it in six months."

The little drone lifted into the air, its noise covered by the hum that vibrated through Everark. On the controller, a screen lit up with footage from the camera.

I grabbed Aaron's arm. "It's perfect!" I squeaked. "Now get it up above their heads."

Aaron cranked the joystick upward, and the rotunda came into view.

"Well, we know where the shield came from," Aaron said.

I couldn't believe it. Silas and Faye weren't working alone. Four people stood in the center of the floor with their backs to each other. Arthur was one of them, and Saundra was the fourth. Her betrayal felt personal. All my life, she'd been the warm face of the palace—someone I could trust.

"It makes sense Silas would have needed help from others inside the Pentax," I whispered. "It would be the only way to make sure I made it through the first round so I could translate the poem, and then make sure Faye won overall. If he was giving wildly high scores to Faye and me on his own, he would have been too suspicious."

Aaron nodded. "Yeah, but is it worth the trade-off? Anyone

willing to steal power from an entire kingdom doesn't seem like the type who would want to share."

"True. I wonder what his endgame is."

In front of the five black slates of rock, the Matrons stood on low pedestals. Their bodies were covered in a thin layer of clear crystal, frozen in immortal sleep. Their pallid skin tones, open eyes, and eerie stillness were reminiscent of dead bodies. My heart chilled as I watched them. Around each of their necks, a crystal hung from a black band. Four of the five crystals glowed vividly. A stream of light extended from them to the palms of the four thieves in the middle. The only crystal not lit up was Amiah's, Matron of Heart.

The drone shifted and now I had a better view of Mira. I studied the face of the woman I'd worshiped all my life. Her red hair was pulled into a thick, elegant braid that cascaded down her back. Loose, curly strands framed her heart-shaped face. Her green eyes were larger than a human's would be. She wore a simple lavender dress that gathered flatteringly at her waist. Looking at her made me wonder why she had chosen to share her powers with me. Why burden me with such a gift?

Aaron slowly circled the drone around the rotunda so we could see each of the Matrons. In their slumber, I wondered if they were aware of what was happening but unable to act, or if they were oblivious to the threat in front of them.

"Why isn't it working?" I heard Faye ask through gritted teeth.

"Just focus," Silas snapped. "It takes time."

"Do you think he's in denial?" Owen scoffed. "Isn't it obvious what's missing?"

I'd been so distracted by the Matrons that I hadn't thought much about what they were actually doing, but Owen was right. It was obvious. "They're missing someone from Amare," I said.

"Which is great news. Buys us some time," Aaron said. "Have you felt anything, El?"

"What do you mean?" I asked.

"You know, like when you search for pygsmies in your mind. Can you feel the Matrons? Can you speak with them? Try to wake them up before it's too late?"

My stomach was tight with nerves. The thought of talking to the most powerful beings in the universe was terrifying. Still, I closed my eyes and searched. I felt a hundred prickles from the consciousness of pygsmies—the meadows were full of them— but there was nothing else. I pushed the black edges of my mind, searching.

"No, I don't feel anything," I said.

There was a strange, green flicker across the controller's screen. Then the image went black.

Chapter Twenty-Nine

A green vine whipped around the black stone and wrapped around my middle, then flung me high into the rotunda. Sun Petal was launched off my shoulder with the force. I clung to the vine as I screamed, trying to make sense of my whirling surroundings. Amelia, Owen, and Aaron were each wrapped up in their own vine, bobbing up and down in the air.

"You're proving to be an irritant that wouldn't go away, Laurelin," Silas sneered from below. "When you survived the poisoning in Lingua but got eliminated, I figured I could leave you alone. I should have known better. I should have killed you myself before we ever left the province." He lunged for a bow and quiver propped against Everly's pedestal, and I panicked, trying to break through the vines.

"No!" Aaron shouted, wriggling furiously.

My arms were pinned against my sides, but I fumbled for the knife on my hip with my fingers.

Sun Petal? Where are you? I could use some help, I said.

As a backup, I sent out a general call, *Lyrun rach min baum,* but the pygsmies outside couldn't get through Arthur's shield.

Silas pulled back the string of his bow and closed one eye, focusing the tip of his arrow at my chest.

Relief flooded me when I finally found the knife. I slashed the bottom band of vine, slicing my own wrist in the process, but it gave me just enough wiggle room to reach my arm across my body and cut the vines that held me there. Silas released the arrow at the same moment that I fell.

Catch me! I called out, hoping Sun Petal could hear me.

When I was an inch away from the crystal floor, I felt elastic tendrils wrap around me, pulling me up into the air.

Oh, thank you, Sun Petal.

Sorry, I hit my head when I got thrown. Still a little dizzy.

Are you going to be all right? I asked, but Sun Petal had no time to answer. Another arrow whooshed past my ear as Sun Petal jerked to the right.

Close one, I said. *Get me to Aaron. We need to cut the others free.*

Owen created four lions below as I sliced the vine that held Aaron. He grabbed onto the vine and swung down to the ground to safety.

The four lions had focused on Silas and Saundra and prepared to pounce, but orange defensive shields shot out in front of them. In the same instant, thick vine wrapped around the beasts, restraining them.

Sun Petal lifted me up to free Amelia and Owen. Amelia ran behind one of the black slabs of rock and hid.

Aaron focused his attention on Silas and sent a relentless string of arrows at him.

"Miss, fall, reverse," Silas said, and the arrows changed course or dropped out of the air.

Owen took on Saundra and Arthur at the same time, opening hole after hole in the floor underneath them, and he sent a steady string of beasts to attack them. But Arthur produced protective shields to shelter him, while Saundra quickly conjured up vines that would snatch her up before she could really fall, then used them to trap the animals.

"I suppose I get the honor of eliminating the great Laurelin Moore," Faye taunted. She held a knife in one hand and one of her blue disc inventions—a paxum—in the other.

I drew my bow as I hovered above her. "I don't want to kill you, Faye, and this won't be a fair fight. I've seen you in combat, and you've seen me. We both know how this will end. Just drop the knife and surrender. The game is up."

"Oh, Laurelin. Always so confident. You see, I know the truth about your weakness. Pippin has been holding you back in more ways than you realize."

A wave of anger crashed over me. "Don't talk about my brother. It's your fault he's not healed right now. And you can stop acting like your knowledge about my secrets somehow makes you superior. I know about your gift."

Faye smirked. "Ah yes. My gift has been incredibly useful in our little plan. It's how I knew about Amelia and her family's shady business deals. And then there was Arthur's hatred for you. His wife just died from a stroke, and he knows a gift like yours would have saved her. But you're too selfish to share elixir. When Silas approached him, he practically begged to join our little team so he could have power for himself. Then he wouldn't have to rely on little brats like you."

"What about Tobias? Why did you kill him?"

Faye's eye twitched. "His death was an unfortunate necessity for our plan to move forward."

At this point, I shouldn't have been surprised by anything, but it made me sick to hear her discuss murder so casually.

"Tobias overheard Silas ask Arthur to give you favorable scores. That's why he confronted you about cheating. Arthur miscalculated when he gave Tobias an explanation. He thought Tobias would agree to help. His gift would have been useful when we faced the Matrons. At the time, we didn't know they would be sleeping, only that the Pentax was our best time to try for the crystals. But Tobias planned to turn us in. We had to get rid of him."

"You're sick, and this has to end." I released my bow, aiming for Faye's thigh.

She pushed a button on the paxum, and the arrow was incinerated, dropping to a pile of ash on the ground.

Let's fly, I said to Sun Petal. *We've got to be faster than her.*

The pygsmy buzzed around Faye in a rapid, zigzagging pattern, and I shot arrow after arrow. Every time, Faye stopped me with the paxum. She threw her knife, which grazed my shoulder and sliced one of Sun Petal's tendrils.

Ahhh, Sun Petal gasped.

Are you okay?

I'll be fine. I'll heal soon, Sun Petal said.

Faye pushed another button on the outer ring of the paxum. The clear jelly in the center of the disc vibrated. Victory was plain in her eyes. "Pipler seeds. Ever heard of them?"

Dread filled my chest. In small amounts, exposure to piplon would put a pygsmy to sleep. Too much exposure would kill one.

"Ah yes, so you know. Pygsmies are very sensitive to pipler seeds. Of course, most pipler plants were removed from the kingdom a century ago. Most. But not all. I was able to find one and extract piplon from it. And this handy dandy paxum will project it through the whole room."

Sun Petal, how do you feel? Are you okay?

Mmmm, Sun Petal said, her mind already cloudy.

I wished I had never promised that I wouldn't force Sun Petal. I couldn't lose her. Not now. And the little pygsmy was trapped. She couldn't even fly away with Arthur's shield over us.

Sun Petal lost her ability to fly, but our fall wasn't far. I landed on my feet and sprinted the few yards to the hole Owen had dug to get us inside Everark. I shoved Sun Petal down it and hoped that would be enough coverage.

Faye was right on my tail. She swung her knife, but I whirled in time to catch her first and throw her back. She stumbled, then placed the paxum on the ground. "Let's have ourselves a fair fight, shall we?" She touched a button and the entire floor was transformed from crystal to steel, eliminating one of Owen's powers.

"I wouldn't call it fair when your side gets to keep all their magic, and we only have half of ours. But that's okay. We can beat you without our gifts." I let my arrow fly, aiming again for her thigh.

Faye dove to the left, then lunged for me, knife in hand. I trapped her arm between the shaft and string of my bow and twisted, bringing her arm behind her back at an awkward angle. She swung her right foot backward into my stomach. I bent forward in pain, forced to release the hold I had on her arm.

Her knife slashed at my throat. I threw my head back and thrust my elbow into her rib cage. Her cough morphed into a roar of rage. She charged at me with fiery eyes.

I caught her right wrist, her knife's tip inches from my chest. I managed to get my fingertips on the handle of the blade and said, "Melt!"

The knife dissolved into a puddle of steel.

Faye's left fist slammed into my cheek. Blood filled my mouth as my teeth sliced the flesh on the inside. I spun away from her and threw my elbow into her face. Her glasses shattered, and blood poured from her nose.

From the chaos on the other side of the room, I heard a groan of pain mixed with a shout of victory. My heart sank. Aaron tumbled backward, an arrow protruding from his chest, only an inch from his heart. Fifteen feet away, Silas looked at him in triumph, then immediately swiveled to Owen and took aim. Owen was already struggling to keep up with Saundra and Arthur with only half his abilities at his disposal, and Amelia was nowhere to be found.

Fierce anger rose inside of me. As Faye lunged again, I pulled an arrow out of the quiver and allowed her to tackle me. Her hands wrapped around my neck, choking me. Her brown eyes were wild with hate.

With the arrow gripped tightly in my hand, I thrust it into her back.

She let out a scream of pain, but I didn't have time to see how badly I'd hurt her. I rose to my feet and drew my bow, turning my sights on Silas.

"Stop!" a female voice broke through the clamor.

It took me a second to figure out who was speaking.

"Laurelin, drop your bow or I'll kill him."

Amelia knelt on the ground, Aaron's head in her lap. She held her knife at his throat. Already, Aaron looked minutes from death. Blood pooled around his body from the wound in his chest, and his eyes struggled to stay open.

"Amelia, what are you doing?" I asked.

She turned to Silas now. "To steal the crystals, you need one gifted person from each province. You need someone from Amare. I can help."

"No, Amelia. You don't want to do that," Owen said. His face was full of disappointment, as if he truly believed Amelia had been a good person beneath her snobby bravado.

"Shut up, Owen. And drop your bow, Laurelin, or he's dead." Amelia yanked Aaron's hair. His head jerked back. She pressed her blade into his neck, drawing a drop of blood.

Unsure of any other choice, I dropped my bow and put up my hands in surrender.

Silas's eyes glistened with understanding as the missing puzzle piece snapped into place. He needed one person from each province. "Yes, of course. You are welcome among us, Amelia. Come. You can be all-powerful, too."

My body was full of panic as I watched the last bit of life drip out of Aaron, but I put on a false calm. "There's one problem with your plan," I said quietly.

Silas whirled around. "And what might that be?"

I stepped to the side, revealing Faye behind me. Like Aaron, she lay in a pool of blood. "Faye won't be able to help you." I yanked the arrow out of her back and rolled her over. Her eyes fluttered feebly. "You're still missing one province."

Silas's face contorted in rage. He drew his bow and pointed it at my heart. "Kill," he whispered.

I kept my composure. "I can solve your problem," I said.

The tip of the bow dropped a centimeter.

"Let's make a deal. I will command a pygsmy to heal Faye if you allow me to heal Aaron first."

Silas paused before he spoke. "You heal Faye first, and then you can heal Aaron."

"No deal," I said. "I don't trust you to keep your promise."

"I could say the same about you." Silas peered at me around his still-drawn bow.

"I am the one with the healing ability. I call the shots. It's my only offer."

Silas dropped the bow and paced.

"Your daughter will be too far gone any second now. It's time to choose, Silas."

Just let me save Aaron! I screamed in my head.

"Fine, you have a deal," he growled.

I snatched the blue disc from Faye's belt and stomped on it. Then I ran to Aaron's side as I said, "I need Arthur to drop his shield. I can't get a pygsmy through it."

"Arthur, drop it, but you're only allowed to bring in one pygsmy, Laurelin. If you try to sneak in any others, the deal is off and Aaron dies," Silas said.

I nodded my agreement.

"Get out of the way." I shoved Amelia to the side.

She scoffed but rose to her feet. Silas and Amelia kept their bows drawn and pointed at me.

Aaron's closed eyes twitched as I grabbed his hand.

I called for a pygsmy, and one floated down from the high windows. I'd never been happier to see one in my life.

Please, heal him, I begged.

I ripped Aaron's shirt open to allow the mystic to make

contact with his skin. The gentle creature cooed as he wrapped his green tendrils around Aaron's chest. He rested on Aaron's collarbone, glowing a vibrant gold as he began to heal.

Aaron's grisly wound started to pull together. I let out a breath I didn't know I'd been holding. The hole faded to white, then disappeared.

"What is taking so long?" Silas asked through clenched teeth.

"Your arrow went very deep. It takes time to heal the internal injuries," I said.

The pygsmy stayed put for another few seconds. Aaron's face returned to its normal color. His breathing grew stronger. He was going to be all right.

Silas let out an exasperated growl. "Enough already. It's time to heal Faye."

I turned and glared at him. I had no long-term plan. As soon as I healed Faye, we were all dead, thanks to lovely Amelia's betrayal.

"Do it now!" Silas yelled. He pulled his bow tighter.

Saluoir, I said. I had to force myself to say the word as much as I had to force the pygsmy to carry out my command.

The mystic flew to Faye's neck, beginning to heal her.

Silas turned to Saundra and Arthur. "Tie them up somewhere out of the way but within sight. We'll deal with them after we have the crystals. And make sure you keep your bow on her until Faye is healed," he said to Amelia.

Chapter Thirty

With rough hands, Arthur shoved me to the ground between Owen and Aaron. Our backs were turned to each other as Saundra bound us with vines. The plants snaked around our wrists and ankles, cutting off my circulation with their tight hold.

When the pygsmy finished healing Faye, I let him go. As I watched the gentle creature flutter away, part of Eva's poem filled my mind. *Mystics must be used with care.*

But the phrase had been connected to the line before that. *Seize the magic but beware, mystics must be used with care.*

"Elixir," I whispered to myself. "I need elixir."

"What, El?" Aaron asked.

"Stop talking!" Amelia shouted. She kept her bow on us as the other four joined her in the center of the floor.

Arthur put his shield back in place, then joined Silas, Faye, and Saundra in a circle as before. They kept their backs to each other and turned their palms out. When their thumbs touched, the crystals around the Matron's necks glowed vibrantly, filling the rotunda with a rainbow of color once more. The only crystal left unlit was Amiah's.

Carefully, Amelia placed her bow on the ground, then linked

with the others. When she connected her hand with Arthur's and Faye's, Amiah's crystal cast red light across the room. In unison, the crystals slowly lifted off of the Matrons. The heads of the five thieves were thrust upward as their eyes clouded over. In a trance, they stared at the ceiling as the crystals floated toward them.

I used the moment to act. "Open, lift, come, dump," I whispered to the vial that rested on my chest.

Obediently, it rose and the stopper flipped open. It floated to my lips and released the six drops of elixir into my mouth. It tasted acidic. I resisted the urge to spit it out, making a bowl shape with my tongue to hold the liquid in place.

The crystals slipped over the heads of the Seekers. As they did, a wave of fatigue washed over me, draining life out of me as it went. My breathing changed, becoming shallow and rapid. Sweat gathered on my forehead. I was sure I was going to vomit.

"Are you okay, El?" Aaron gasped, though it was obvious he was struggling too.

"I'm not," Owen panted. "I find out my girlfriend's psychotic and I can feel my magic leaving. It's like I was just run over by a railcar."

I panicked. We just lost our powers? To check, I closed my eyes and searched for a pygsmy. The familiar call, *Lyrun rach min baum,* echoed in my head, but it was clumsy and forced. There was no space within my mind to search. It was nothing but a pitch-black wall—no door, no opening to the pygsmies. I looked at Mira. Perhaps I was projecting my own feelings onto her, but her eyes seemed empty and mournful.

"How does it feel to be powerless?" Silas asked, his eyes taunting.

With the elixir still in my mouth, I was unable to answer him, though I wanted so badly to tell him where he could go.

Saundra and Arthur admired the glowing crystals around their necks with satisfied smiles. Amelia turned the red stone over in the palm of her hand. Her eyes flickered to mine for a moment. In them, I saw confusion.

She turned to Silas. "I don't feel any different."

Saundra looked up. "Honestly, neither do I," she said.

Silas didn't answer. He looked at his four partners for a moment. His hand twitched at his side.

Then, unexpectedly, Amelia wrenched the crystal from her neck. She tossed it at Silas and ran toward the front doors of Everark.

"What—" But Saundra's question was cut off when Silas plunged a dagger into her back. Before I had time to react, he whirled around and stabbed Arthur, too.

Amelia's gift must have warned her about what was going to happen next.

Only one will leave with power. Unite the stones atop the tower.

Silas hadn't shared the full poem with his cohorts. They didn't know only one of them would leave with the magic.

Faye's eyes were suddenly full of fear. She clutched her glowing blue crystal and slowly backed away from Silas.

Blood dripped from the tip of his long dagger as he walked toward Faye. "I don't want to hurt you, sweetheart."

"Then put the knife down," she said, her eyes wide.

"I will, just as soon as you hand me your crystal." He held his palm out. Like the rest of him, it was spattered with blood.

"This?" Faye looked at the vibrant blue stone in disbelief. "Everything you've said over the last month—every apology you gave for being an absent father, every promise to be better, every 'I love you'—it was all about this?" She held up the crystal, her hand shaking.

"No, Faye. Of course not," Silas said. But he inched closer, his eyes full of greed.

"Prove it then. Let me keep the crystal," Faye said.

"I can't do that. Just give me the stone, sweetie. You will still be queen of Ausland. Isn't that enough? You'll have enormous power, it will just be a different kind."

Faye stared, open-mouthed. She looked crushed as she tossed the stone. "You can have the stupid necklace. I should have known better than to believe a word you said." She turned to me and ripped the diadem off her head. "Here, have it." She flicked the crown at my feet. With one last hateful look at Silas, she followed Amelia's path out the door.

Silas plucked the crystal out of the air, his face triumphant. He gathered the other province's stones and snapped them together in a star formation that was larger than the palm of my hand. His greedy eyes pored over the illuminated crystal. He lifted the band over his neck, wearing the star proudly in the center of his chest.

"Now, one final loose end to wrap up," Silas said, fixing his eyes on me.

I hoped my assumption about the poem's meaning was right as Silas drew back the dagger he had already used on two people tonight.

"No! Stop! You can kill me instead! Please!" Aaron yelled.

Before Silas could respond, I spewed the elixir from my mouth onto his star-shaped crystal.

Seize the magic but beware, mystics must be used with care. Immediately, the crystal began to react. Wherever the elixir touched, the light went out and the crystal turned black. Cracks began to form in the stones, crossing the surface in hectic, jagged lines. Pieces of crystal fell to the floor.

"No," Silas cried. He held his hands underneath the crumbling star, catching chunks and dust in desperation. "NO!"

The last of the star broke from its leather band. It lay in scattered pieces, charred and utterly colorless.

"You." Silas jabbed his finger at me. "You are going to pay for this." He raised his hand and plunged the dagger into my chest.

"Aghhh!" I screamed, feeling the searing blade dig deep to my heart.

"No! Laurelin, no!" Aaron cried as he wriggled against the vines that held him tight.

Blood soaked my shirt, and I worried about Owen and Aaron. Surely, they would be next. But Silas's body fell to the ground with a thud.

"No, it can't end like this," Silas said.

The red, irritated veins from the mark on his wrist formed a snake that slithered up his arm, just beneath the surface of his skin. Horrified, I watched as the serpent crawled up his neck and wrapped around it, choking him. He thrashed around, tearing at the snake as his face turned red, then purple.

I looked away, unable to watch. My head was beginning to cloud over from loss of blood, but the tight hold from the vine loosened. I was glad, except that I knew it meant Saundra had really died. The vines dried up, turning to brown, setting me, Owen, and Aaron free.

"No, El," Aaron said as he pulled me into his lap.

Behind him, the sounds of Silas's struggle weakened and then stopped.

"He's dead?" I whispered.

Though I wasn't asking her, Eva responded with a message on my arm.

He kept part of the journal from you. When he acted to end your life, his decision became final.

Aaron pulled my chest against his. He buried his face in my hair. "I can't lose you, El. Please don't go."

I was losing feeling in my arms and legs. "Aaron, look at me."

He pulled away. One of his tears splashed down on my cheek. His blue eyes searched mine and he smiled. "I love you. I have for a long time," he said.

I smiled weakly. In any other situation, his words would have made my head spin with excitement. Here, they only made my heart ache for what might have been.

"I love you too, Aaron," I said.

My vision slipped away, fading to black. I was barely conscious, but I could feel Aaron's arms around me as sobs wracked his chest.

I wished I could say something to comfort him, but my mouth forgot how to make words.

Everything was fading. A low hum filled my ears.

A new sensation pulled me back from the brink of emptiness. A warmth around my neck that spread down to my chest. It grew stronger, burning like a flame.

I gasped as my eyes opened. Aaron hovered over me, his hands covering his mouth. His eyes were hopeful.

"El? You're okay?"

I threw my arms around his neck and laughed. "Yes. Somehow, I'm okay. What happened?"

Aaron's face fell. He reached around me and picked up something from the floor.

In his hand was a lifeless pygsmy.

"No." I sucked in a sharp breath. "No, no, no. Not Sun Petal. Why would she do that?"

My favorite, loyal little pygsmy healed me without any elixir to spare. She gave me the elixir she needed to live, and now she was gone. Tears filled my eyes.

"I don't know. I guess Sun Petal really loved you," Aaron said.

I cradled Sun Petal against my chest. "You deserved so much more out of life. I'm so sorry," I said.

Owen's hand touched my shoulder. "I'm sorry about Sun Petal, but I'm really glad you're okay."

My arm burned with a new message. I didn't want to read it. Eva would probably scold me for allowing a pygsmy to sacrifice herself for me. The words grew hotter until I couldn't ignore them anymore. I flipped over my arm and read:

Don't let Sun Petal's sacrifice go to waste. Save the magic.

"Save the magic," I repeated. "But how?"

The words changed.

Use the diadem. Make a wish.

A few feet away, next to Silas's still body, the diadem sparkled. Gently, I placed Sun Petal on the ground, then walked over to the diadem and picked it up. I turned the crystal crown in my hand, admiring its glowing stones that matched the provinces.

"El? What are you doing?" Aaron asked.

I held up a finger. "Shhh. I need to think."

Could I make a wish? I hadn't won the Pentax, but it couldn't hurt to try.

Every inch of me longed to wish for the one thing that had filled my mind for years. I could see Pippin, healthy again, running, laughing, his green eyes full of life. Didn't he deserve that? Didn't *I* deserve that?

But Ausland's magic. I looked around the room at the dust from the ruined crystals, the blood, the bodies, the withered vines—all of the destruction. Silas hadn't been successful this time, but what would stop Faye from trying again? Or Amelia? Or anyone they decided to tell about the ways of the Stone Seekers? My wish could do more than just restore the crystals. I could find a way to protect the stones for good. No one else would be able to steal them, and no more lives would be lost in that pursuit.

Pygsmies are protectors, which means whisperers are too.

I closed my eyes and breathed, hoping I could be as brave and selfless as Sun Petal.

I placed the diadem on my head. "Matrons of Ausland, I wish for the crystals to be restored and then divided into thousands. Let them be carried by the pygsmies—protectors of this land. And if any should try to take a stone, even a whisperer, let the pygsmies stop them with a sting."

"El, are you sure about that?" Aaron asked. "What about Pippin?"

"It's not the wish I wanted to make, but it was the right wish," I said. "Now Ausland's magic will be safe."

A breeze blew through the rotunda, sending shattered pieces of crystal across the floor. Then the breeze intensified, becoming a true gust of wind. My hair covered my face, obscuring my vision as my skin was pelted with little bits of crystal that flew through the air. An ear-splitting screech echoed around the steel rotunda. Startled, I brushed my hair back from my face just as the crystal surrounding the Matron of Courage cleaved in two, then fell to the floor with a deafening shatter.

Ember focused her sharp, brown eyes on me as she stepped down from her pedestal. Immediately, Aaron, Owen, and I dropped to our knees.

Her voice was like windchimes as she spoke. "Laurelin Moore, thank you."

I was surprised to feel her touch on my shoulder. She picked me up from the ground and pulled me in for a hug.

"You have saved Ausland. I speak for all of the Matrons when I say that we are very grateful."

Pride filled me, but it wasn't enough to take away the sadness. I'd failed Pippin once again.

Ember released me, then looked down at Owen and Aaron. "You can stand."

They quickly rose to their feet but kept their heads bowed in respect.

Ember looked back at me. "Your wish has been granted, Laurelin. The crystals are re-formed, and we will do as you've asked. It's a brilliant idea to divide them. Each Matron will keep one piece, but the pygsmies will guard the others. It would be impossible for any Seeker to gather that many stones. Well done."

"Thank you." I gave a smile that faltered. I couldn't stop thinking about Pippin.

"Come with me, dear." Ember took my hand and pulled me over to her granite pedestal. It was strange to sit next to someone so powerful she could incinerate me with a glance. I tried not to think about it.

"What's on your mind, Laurelin? I can see that you are very unhappy," Ember said. She took my hand. Her rich skin was beautiful next to my pale color.

I bit my lip. "I know this is going to sound horribly selfish. I already got a wish. But I was wondering if it might be possible to have another?"

Ember stroked my hair and gave a small laugh. "I'm afraid not. We are bound by our law, and it clearly states that only one wish is to be given."

Fear choked me. "I was afraid you were going to say that."

"How about you tell me what you want? Maybe I can help you find a way to get it without a wish."

I looked at Pippin's lifestone. The red corner was weaker than ever. It flickered back and forth between black and red. "There is no other way. My brother is sick with cancer. I was going to ask you to heal him."

Ember grabbed my ring and examined the stone. "Indeed, it looks like his time has nearly passed. I am so very sorry, Laurelin. In some small way, it may comfort you to know that I wouldn't have been able to grant that wish even if you asked. The Matrons are very powerful, but even we cannot change the course of life. The timing of when a soul enters or leaves the human world is out of our control."

"You can't heal Pippin?" I asked, shocked. I had always believed the Matrons' magic would be enough.

"No, I'm sorry. Throughout history, there have been a few who have tried to alter this natural process. In fact, you've met the result of such a wish. Nearly three hundred years ago, a boy named Gabriel Hague won the Pentax and asked us to heal his sick father. When we told him we could not fulfill his wish, he changed it. He asked that his father be allowed to live a long life. He was searching for a loophole, and he found one. Gabriel's father is Baltazar Hague, the seer you met in Scentia. Baltazar does not age when he is in a vision. It was the only way we could think to grant Gabriel's wish.

"Since that time, Baltazar found healing for his illness through dark magic. You've seen what he has become. He is so consumed with living forever that he'd rather spend all his life in his visions than with people he should love and care about."

Ember's eyes flashed to Aaron, who was listening to us from across the room.

"One of the great challenges of being human is learning to appreciate life—to protect it furiously—but also to know when it's time to let go. Your role as a whisperer will help you understand this more than most."

Ember may as well have run me through with a sword. I was speechless. All the hope that had pulled me through the last few years was gone in an instant.

"You will want to get home to your family, Laurelin. It seems Pippin is nearing the end. But there is one more thing you should know. As the Rook who presented herself with the diadem and received a wish from the Matrons, you accepted the title of Queen. I'm aware it's not a role you want, but the law is binding." She held out her hand. In it, a star appeared. Each of the five legs was a different color, representing the provinces of Ausland. "This amulet marks you as the person the Matrons have accepted as queen. When you are ready, show it to the provincial leaders. They will know what it means. And Laurelin, don't take too long. Your kingdom needs you."

I took the amulet and shoved it in my pocket, fully intending to leave it there until the day I died. All I cared about was getting back to Pippin.

Ember touched my shoulder. "I have one bit of good news for you. While I am not able to save a human life, I can save a pygsmy one." She swept her hand over Sun Petal, who rose from the ground with vibrant, gold markings.

Sun Petal sped over to me. *Laur-all-in! You're okay!*

I stroked Sun Petal's nose. *I'm so glad to see you again. Thank you for saving my life. You're incredible.*

But even the joy of seeing Sun Petal couldn't eclipse the ache in my chest.

I looked at Ember and wiped the tears from my cheeks. "Please send me home," I whispered.

Chapter Thirty-One

For one moment, I paused outside the back door of my house, remembering a time when Pippin ran in and out of this door, cackling as he tracked mud through the kitchen and Mom chased him with a spoon.

Our home wouldn't be the same without Pippin. It would be nothing more than a building—a roof and four walls that kept Sedona's frequent rain off our heads. Pippin brought the spark, the joy, the purpose to our family. What were we without him?

For a moment, I wished I had said yes when Aaron asked if he could come with me. I thought I could handle this on my own, but I couldn't seem to move forward. My hand remained on the scuffed doorknob, refusing my brain's command to twist. Instead, I watched the rain as it dripped down the red paint in front of me until the door suddenly swung open.

"Whoa," I said, as I was pulled along with the motion.

"Laurelin," Mom breathed. She wrapped me into a hug that chilled rather than comforted. I felt surrender in her arms as she gripped me.

"He's been asking for you. He only has minutes left." Mom's green eyes were haunted, her face gaunt. I wondered how long it had been since she last ate a decent meal.

I was at a loss for words. I pushed past her and walked through the kitchen to the stairs. My feet moved without my permission, dragging me up step-by-step.

Pippin's bedroom door was wide open. Dad sat in a wooden chair next to the bed. I could count on one hand the number of times I'd ever seen Dad upstairs. It was a tremendous feat to drag himself up all fourteen steps using only his arms.

In the bed, Pippin's body was barely visible beneath the covers. Dad held Pippin's hand in both of his and kept it pressed to his lips. He turned at the sound of Mom's approach. She appeared next to me, just outside Pippin's door.

"You ought to go in and say goodbye. You won't get another chance. It's time." Gently, she nudged me forward.

I knelt beside Pippin's bed and buried my face in his side, breathing in his scent. The rise and fall of his chest was barely palpable.

"Laura." Pippin's voice was a faint, cracked whisper.

I lifted my head. His green eyes peeked open.

"Read this," he said. He passed a crumpled paper he kept in his right fist.

I took the wrinkled paper and smoothed it out.

Laurelin,

I decided not to fight. I won't drink any more elixir. I know you're disappointed in me. You're a fighter, and I tried to be, too, for a long time.

You're going to blame yourself for this and that's stupid. Probably no one else will have the guts to tell you to suck it up and move on, so I guess that's my job. Sure, you can be sad for a while. But don't let me hold you back anymore. Chase a dream of your own for once.

Give the elixir to someone who can be healed. You've been scared to share your gift, and I know it's complicated. But bottom line? The world is full of situations just like ours. I know you're afraid to choose who to help, but you'll know. Trust yourself.

I'll always be grateful for the time you bought me. It allowed me to be with you, Mom, and Dad when I wasn't ready to go. Now, it's my time to move on. I hope you'll let me.

I love you, Laura. Be strong, like you always are.

XO—Pippin

I twisted my fingers through Pippin's curls and rested my palm on his cheek. "Are you sure, Pip? This is what you want?"

His lungs rattled as he breathed in. "I'm ready. I love you." His eyes locked with mine for a moment, then shifted to Mom and Dad.

"I love you, too. I'll never forget you," I whispered.

Epilogue

S eeing Pippin's name written in stone brought such finality to his death. It had been two months since he passed, but it didn't sink in that he was really, truly gone until I saw the headstone with my own eyes. Because it was only placed today, there was a gap between the marker and the grass around it. I hated to think about the day when the earth would try to climb over the headstone and reclaim its ground. It would mean Pippin had been gone for too many years.

I didn't know how long I'd been here. Mom and Dad had left a while ago. Now, my only company was Sun Petal and two other pygsmies—Tria and Prix. Ever since I fully embraced my gift, I seemed to attract pygsmies whenever I was alone. At first, it was a lot to get used to. I never seemed to have a private moment. Now, their natural tranquility was restful and sometimes helped to quiet the vicious thoughts that tore at me.

Sun Petal nestled into my shoulder. *Is there something I can do to help?*

I reached up and stroked her nose. *Not this time. People say grief gets easier with time. I'll believe it when I feel it.*

Sun Petal cooed. *I'm sorry.*

"Hey, stranger."

I whirled at the sound of Aaron's voice. Tria and Prix scattered into the sky. None of the pygsmies ever stuck around when other humans were with me, except Sun Petal. She was used to Aaron and my parents, but she lifted off my shoulder this time, hovering far above us in the air.

Aaron's jaw was speckled with brown scruff, as it so often was after a black market excursion. His blue eyes crinkled as I ran toward him. He dropped the massive pack from his shoulder and held his arms wide. I leapt into them and kissed him.

He ran his hand through my hair. "I'm sorry I was late. I hoped to be here when they set the headstone."

"You're here now, and that's what matters."

Aaron set me on the ground and rested his forehead against mine. "I missed you very much."

"Get anything good in your trades?" I asked.

"Of course. I never walk away from a deal with the short end of the stick. But I must say, it's getting a lot harder to be away from you when I leave." He tucked my hair behind my ear and cupped the side of my face in his rough palm.

"I have a solution. Don't leave ever again."

Aaron laughed. "It's that simple, huh?"

"Or you could take me with you next time."

"Now that's an idea I could get behind." He kissed me again, but we were quickly interrupted.

"Your Majesty?"

I turned to find Chelsea, my personal assistant, at the top of the hill.

"Your mother sent me to collect you. She said you're fifteen minutes late for a meeting with Lord Salsbury."

I groaned. Some things about being queen were tolerable—maybe even fun, in a few rare cases. But diplomatic meetings were at the bottom of the list.

"Remind me again why you accepted the crown?" Aaron asked as we held hands and walked toward Chelsea.

"The Matrons didn't leave me much choice, but believe me, I

ask myself that question every day. Sometimes, I feel like it would've been much easier to leave the amulet in my pocket as I planned."

We reached the top of the hill, which gave a good view of Sedona. I looked over the quiet neighborhood and saw the new school under construction, and the rail line that had been extended to reach the poorest district of the town. The Swenson home was nearing completion and would include an elevator for their toddler in a wheelchair. And there were hundreds of similar projects either planned or in the works across the kingdom.

I gestured out to the city. "But that's my answer. I've been given a chance to make a difference for people. I hope I can. It's what Pippin wanted for me."

Aaron kissed the top of my head. "You're doing a great job, El."

"Eighteen minutes late," Chelsea said as she bounced on her toes.

I chuckled. "We're on our way, Chelsea. It'll all work out."

My childhood home was no longer recognizable as its transformation to the palace of Ausland was almost complete. The best orators in Lingua were working on changing it, and in some ways, I was glad. Our home was a painful reminder of Pippin. Every room held memories with him that were difficult to relive. On the other hand, it felt like another piece of him had been taken away. I didn't care for the fanciness of palace life, but I was happy to give Mom a chance to live in lavish circumstances for once. Plus, the elevator was great for Dad.

Inside the front door was a grand, double-wide staircase. We took it to the second floor, where my family's "sitting room" was located. That term was so formal.

A fire burned beneath a white stone mantle. In front of it, Mom sat in a red, wing-back chair with her reading glasses on and a book in her lap. Dad was next to her in his wheelchair, whittling a horse for a carousel he'd been making.

When we entered the room, Mom looked up. "Hi,

sweetheart. You've missed Lord Salsbury. He left a few minutes ago in a huff, mumbling about how disrespectful your tardiness was. He said he should expect no different from a commoner queen." Over her glasses, she gave me a stern glance. Apparently, I got no time off. Not even on a day like today.

I sighed. "Sorry, Mom. I'll reach out to him in the morning and make amends."

"Thank you. And remember you have a dress fitting with Tess before breakfast tomorrow. You also have a new batch of letters to sort through from Isabel." She gestured to a large stack of new envelopes added to the ones that already covered the coffee table.

"Better get to work," I said, taking a seat on the blue, velvet rolled sofa in the center of the room. On the table, four bins sat with a zillion letters inside. "Tell me if you come across something I should read?" I asked Aaron as I handed him a stack.

"You got it, babe."

"Her name is Laurelin," Dad said without looking up from his knife.

Aaron grimaced and I snorted.

I sifted through letter after letter, each with their own story that pulled at my heart. For one reason or another, different ones stood out among the crowd, and I had no choice but to trust my gut and hope I wasn't choosing wrong. Sometimes, I liked to imagine Pippin was guiding me, helping me know who really needed the elixir. Occasionally, Aaron would hand me a letter from his stack to review.

The sun began to set as Mom left the room. Shortly after, Dad rolled by in his chair, too. Dutifully, Aaron stayed by my side as we made a small dent in the never-ending requests.

My eyes began to blur so much I couldn't read the writing. I set down my letter and yawned, leaning into Aaron. He wrapped his arm around me and we watched the fire for a moment.

"I have a surprise for you." His low voice rumbled in his chest as I leaned against him.

"I know what you're trying to do. You want to distract me from thinking about Pippin."

Aaron laughed. "I've been working on this for a few weeks and planned to give it to you today. The fact that it will also distract you from your sadness is just an added bonus. The surprise is outside, so grab a jacket and come on."

Aaron pulled me up from the couch. We slipped on our coats and then Aaron led the way to the only part of the renovation I enjoyed: the rooftop garden.

"You *have* been planning this," I said, seeing the firepit aglow next to my favorite collection of planters. They were filled with purple daylilies, and the gardener sprinkled in fresh branches of lyre trees at my request. When I was alone, it was swarmed with pygsmies.

We sat on the black iron bench next to the fire pit. Aaron reached beneath it and pulled out a box that had been cased in black leather. As he undid the metal clasp on the front, he said, "There's something you don't know about me. I've always been interested in carpentry, like your dad. As a kid, I used to try it when Mom would drag me all over the kingdom on her trades. Obviously, your dad is amazing at it, so I asked him to give me some lessons." Aaron's face went red. "Okay, and he gave me a lot of help on the project. But anyway, I made this for you."

I opened the box, which folded out into a chessboard. Along the edge was a golden inscription that read, *In memory of Pippin Alexander Moore, the greatest chess player we ever knew.* Two cherrywood boxes were tucked into each end of the board. Inside, I found the chess pieces, carved by hand and carefully painted.

I ran my finger over the inscription, then reached up and gave Aaron a soft kiss. "It's the perfect gift. Thank you."

He smiled. "You're welcome. Neither of us were good enough

to beat Pippin, but whaddaya say we find out who's best between us?"

I laughed. "You're on. But you should know I am well trained by the master."

Aaron put up his hands. "Now hang on a minute. I'll have you know that I survived thirty-four whole moves against Pippin."

"What? You did not. You're just trying to psych me out."

Aaron wiggled his eyebrows. "There's only one way to find out."

We lined up our pieces and Aaron gave me the first move.

I didn't know what to expect from the future, but I intended to remember the one thing Pippin taught me best: life is precious and fleeting.

I was determined to make the most of mine.

Acknowledgments

I owe many thanks to so many people, but my husband, Ryan, is at the top of the list. Thank you for allowing me to take all the time needed to dive into this project. You have supported my writing ambitions from the beginning, and it means more than I can say. Thanks for the countless times you stepped up and did more than your fair share of laundry, dishes, being with our kiddo, and so many other things. You made this possible.

Thanks to my parents, Kirk and Annalisa, who believe in me endlessly. Your confidence and enthusiasm about my writing pulls me through the hard parts.

More thanks to Spencer, Kiranne, Jessalyn, Bill, Kathy, and other family and friends who are always excited to hear about what I'm working on. Your support means so much to me. And a big thanks to Spencer and Michael for time spent helping me with cover design ideas.

I'm so thankful to my editors, Jodi Keller, Erin Howard, and Kaci Banks who helped me shape this story into something worth reading.

Tamara Grantham has been an incredible mentor to me through the Storymentors program. Thanks for all your advice, insight, and your encouragement on the path to publication. It has been so helpful to have an experienced author by my side through all the ups and downs.

I am forever grateful to Linda Fulkerson. Thank you for believing in my story. Thank you for all the hard work you put into the production of this book. Your many talents are incredible.

About Janilise Lloyd

Janilise Lloyd lives in Northern Utah with her husband and their son. She likes to be outdoors and balances her love for running with a love for all things dessert. Her little family likes to be on the go, so you'll probably find them at the zoo, on a hike, or skipping rocks by the river. There are usually crumbs on the kitchen counters, dishes in the sink, and toys on the floor while she and her family are out playing.

Growing up, Janilise never intended to be a writer but always had a love for books. She's grateful life took a different turn and brought her into the writing world. Now, she can't imagine doing anything else. Janilise is the coordinator for the ScrivKids community for student writers, and she's a member of the Storymakers Guild.

More than anything, Janilise loves her family and is grateful for the encouragement and support they've given her in her many (MANY!) wild ideas.

If you'd like to connect with Janilise, find her on social media @janiliselloyd or visit her at www.janiliselloyd.com.

Interested in reading how Laurelin and
Aaron first met?

Sign-up for Janilise Lloyd's newsletter at
https://janiliselloyd.com/ and receive the ebook for
free.

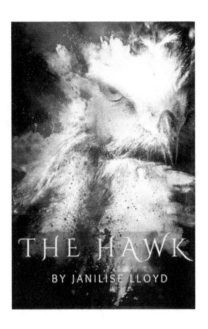

As Pippin's health condition gets worse, Laurelin turns to
the black market to sell elixir in order to ease her family's
financial burdens. But her trusted contact on the market
turns out to be a kidnapper intent on exploiting her
abilities. When a strange boy turns up and unintentionally
saves her, Laurelin isn't sure if she's any better off—after
all, he's a black market hawk too. Laurelin must get
herself out of this mess before it's too late. And what of
the boy? Can she trust him? Or will he double-cross her
like the hawk before?

You May Also Like ...

Woodencloak by Dawn Ford

The Band of Unlikely Heroes - Book One

Thirteen-year-old troll princess Horra Fyd's life changes forever after an unexpected visit from the fairy queen and her two daughters. Tales of fairies gave Horra nightmares as a young troll. Before evening falls, however, a real nightmare unfolds. Horra's father, King Fyd, goes missing. Her woodgoblin instructor is poisoned and uses his magic to revert to a seed. And a mysterious, gaunt man wearing a cape and playing a panflute joins the fairies in trying to capture her.

Horra flees but is instantly lost in a world she's never had to travel alone. A letter hidden in her knapsack from her late instructor informs her that a power hungry Erlking seeks revenge against her kingdom and their allies for a two-generation old war. She is tasked with getting his seed to the Weald, a magical forest. There it can regenerate into a druid, the only creature with the power to hold the balance between good and evil, and who is able to defeat the Erlking.

However, the Erlking is always one step behind her. Horra must fight to protect herself, but she has no magic. She accepts a gift from a dead druid spirit of a charmed woodencloak to disguise her. But magic failed her mother, how can she possibly trust it?

Can Horra have faith and courage enough to trust a power she can't see, and become a warrior heroine her foremothers can be proud of? Or will she allow fear to rule over her and lose everything that matters—including her life?

Get your copy here:

https://scrivenings.link/woodencloak

Beyond the Gates by Erin R. Howard
Gates of Deceit - Book One

If playing by the rules means it keeps you alive, then seventeen-year-old Renna James should know better. She is, after all, the one who broadcasts these rules to the Outpost. What lies beyond the gates had always lured her, but her venture outside wasn't supposed to leave her locked out. Now, Renna's one chance to survive the next seventy-two hours just ran into the forest she's forbidden to enter.

Get your copy here:

https://scrivenings.link/beyondthegates

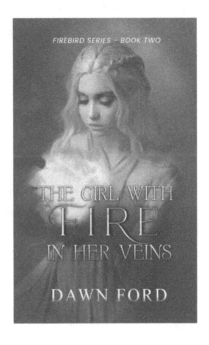

The Girl with Fire in Her Veins by Dawn Ford

Firebird Series - Book Two

Available April 25, 2023

Former servant girl Tambrynn struggles with her new firebird abilities, especially the internal fire she cannot control. So, she, along with her

Watcher Lucas, and her grandfather Bennett journey to a hidden mountain keep to find the answers she seeks before she sets the kingdom aflame.

But there's a new dragon who's targeting Tambrynn, a mergirl who wishes to manipulate her, and the froggen king, Siltworth, who hasn't forgotten that Tambrynn destroyed his watery reign. When her father, the evil mage Thoron, attacks someone she loves, Tambrynn's group is separated and she has to face another powerful foe alone.

Is she strong enough to withstand the deluge? Or will she drown in the fire and the flood?

Get your copy here:

https://scrivenings.link/thegirlwithfireinherveins

ExpanseBooks.pub (an imprint of Scrivenings Press LLC)

Stay up-to-date on your favorite books and authors with our free e-newsletter. Sign up here:

https://scriveningspress.com/newsletter-signup/